THE ENCOUNTER

KC SAVAGE

Copyright © 2022 KC Savage

All rights reserved. This book or any portion thereof may not be reproduced or used in any manner whatsoever without the express written permission of the publisher except for the use of brief quotations in a book review.

Any references to historical events, real people, or real places are used fictitiously. Names, characters, and places are products of the author's imagination.

Edited by Writing Evolution
Cover designer Carter Cover Designs

Printed by Amazon Inc., in the United States of America.
First printing, 2022

Lyla D Creations LLC
24445 Painter Drive
Land O Lakes, FL 34639
www.lyladcreations.com

DISCLAIMER

This book contains adultery, lying,
sexually explicit scenes,
and strong language.
Please read at your own risk.

Table of Contents

THE ENCOUNTER 1
CHAPTER 1 8
CHAPTER 2 15
CHAPTER 3 20
CHAPTER 4 29
CHAPTER 5 34
CHAPTER 6 38
CHAPTER 7 42
CHAPTER 8 47
CHAPTER 9 58
CHAPTER 10 65
CHAPTER 11 69
CHAPTER 12 76
CHAPTER 13 81
CHAPTER 14 94
CHAPTER 15 99
CHAPTER 16 109
CHAPTER 17 114
CHAPTER 18 121
CHAPTER 19 130
CHAPTER 20 137
CHAPTER 21 141
CHAPTER 22 146
CHAPTER 23 153
CHAPTER 24 158

CHAPTER 25	164
CHAPTER 26	169
CHAPTER 27	174
CHAPTER 28	180
CHAPTER 29	184
CHAPTER 30	189
CHAPTER 31	197
CHAPTER 32	202
CHAPTER 33	212
CHAPTER 34	218
CHAPTER 35	222
CHAPTER 36	225
CHAPTER 37	228
CHAPTER 38	235
CHAPTER 39	239
CHAPTER 40	243
CHAPTER 41	246
EPILOGUE	251
THE CHOICE	253
THANK YOU…	256
ABOUT KC SAVAGE	257
BOOKS BY KC SAVAGE	258

For Kelly and Amanda

The forbidden will always be desirable.

- Unknown –

CHAPTER 1

"Where the fuck are you?" Emma said, staring at her wristwatch with folded arms.

"I'm right here."

She spun toward the stranger's velvety voice. Her heart drummed as her eyes traveled up his body to his smooth, square jaw, pausing on his full lips. She caught her breath when she fell into the young man's soft blue eyes. *Holy God, he is beautiful.*

Emma swayed a bit but steadied herself before needing anyone's help. She couldn't look away from his gorgeous blue globes. They pulled her in, spoke to her soul.

She blinked as she checked out the tall, exquisite young man standing beside her again, taking in all she could. He dressed in a sport coat and slacks.

Her stare tumbled down on the opening where a tie should've been, instead his crisp, white shirt lay open. Her tongue wet her lips as she silently moaned, *mmm, yummy.*

Her fingers wiggled at her side as she smiled inside. She hoped his chest hair was as soft as it appeared laying nicely across his toned pecs.

"Oh, hello," Emma voiced softly. Her cheeks blushing, her body warming. She blinked rapidly as she realized her eyes were glued to his crotch. Clearing her throat, she tilted her head up again to meet his gaze before she continued. "Um...who are you?"

The corners of his mouth slowly curved as he extended his hand to Emma. "I'm Dr. Jack Bryant and who do I have the pleasure of meeting?"

Heat rose within her body when his sexy as fuck voice rolled over her sending a spark of desire to her core. Still, she hesitated a beat before placing her hand into his. "Nice to meet you, Dr. Bryant, I'm Emma Taylor."

Jack's hand engulfed hers as he held Emma's elbow, giving her a soft flirty squeeze. He gently shook her hand, his eyes never leaving hers and holding her grip longer than she expected.

She sensed an air of danger about him, yet somehow knew he would be exciting and fun. Her heart pounded against her chest. She took in several deep breaths trying to settle herself. *What the hell? Why am I feeling like this? I'm a married woman, happily married.* She shook her head to quiet the voices. *He's just being polite to an older woman.*

"Nice to meet you, Emma Taylor." Jack's hand slid down her arm when their handshake finally broke. Their fingers grazed. A shock of electricity went through her as his touch sent chills throughout her body. Their eyes met again as she quickly stuffed her hands into the pockets of her sweater to stop herself from reaching for him.

A polite grin appeared on Emma's face and Jack smiled back. "Will you join me for a drink while you wait for whoever it is you're meeting here?" Jack stepped closer to Emma and rested his hand on her shoulder.

"I really shouldn't. My husband should be here soon." Emma looked around the room for Matt.

He was supposed to meet her an hour ago. The party had begun, and he was, once again, running late. She bounced on her toes scanning the room hoping to find him, although she did enjoy the attention from a gorgeous younger man.

She glanced to her left, then her right, still no Matt. "I guess one drink wouldn't hurt." Emma shifted on her feet. Their bodies touched, and another shockwave traveled through her.

"Great. Come with me." Jack cocked his arm for her.

She hesitated for a moment. "I'll follow, you lead the way." She kept her hands in her pockets to avoid accidentally touching Jack again.

Weaving through the crowd of the huge ballroom, Emma noticed the chandeliers above, tables with floral centerpieces situated neatly around a dance floor and stage. A band played music as she followed Jack to the bar.

"Hi, babe. Who do you have accompanying you?" The female bartender winked at Jack.

"Jenna meet Emma. She's waiting for her husband. He's tardy and she looked anxious, so I asked her to join me for a drink. You don't mind, do you, sweetheart?" Leaning over the bar, he kissed the attractive leggy blonde.

"Not at all." She threw Emma a kind smile.

Emma looked away instead of returning a smile to Jenna and pretended to look for Matt.

Jenna's voice drew Emma's attention back when she addressed her properly, "Hi, Emma, it's nice to meet you. Don't mind my husband's advances. He's very friendly with everyone." Jenna patted Jack's hand resting on the bar. "What can I get you to drink?" She turned back to Emma.

Relief filled Emma and she smiled, "Whiskey, please." She leaned against the bar watching Jenna pour her tumbler half full of the amber liquid. She noticed how fit Jenna was and very tall for a female. She guessed Jenna stood at least five foot ten, with long blonde hair and green eyes. They made a very handsome couple. Jack had to be close to six foot five. She sensed they had a good relationship. Jenna knew her husband flirted and didn't mind.

Emma was sure his flirting with her was innocent; her mind made it more than it was. She welcomed the attention since her husband was so damn late to his own boss's retirement party.

"I'll have one too," Jack added.

"Coming right up." Jenna turned away from them.

Jack moved a step closer to Emma while Jenna made his drink and placed his hand on her lower back.

Her body tensed as she tilted her head up to see Jack's reaction.

His face beamed as he winked at her.

"Here you go, babe. I need to tend to some other guests. Try to behave Jackson." Jenna leaned across the bar, Jack met her, and they kissed quickly.

"I will dear." Jack squeezed Jenna's arm before she walked to the end of the bar to a group of young men. He turned back to Emma. "Cheers to a fun night." He held his glass up.

"Cheers Dr. Bryant." She clanked his glass and sipped her drink. The warmth of the whiskey traveled to her belly.

"Please, call me Jack." He touched her shoulder again.

She didn't back away, she remembered Jenna saying he liked to flirt. *He's harmless, just a flirt.* She patted his hand that rested on her shoulder. The warmth from the whiskey in her belly was now between her legs from his touch.

"Okay, Jack. Thanks for the drink, but I must find my husband. I'm going to go outside and call him. Maybe I'll see you later?" She placed her glass on the bar and smiled at Jack.

Emma jumped when she heard Matt's voice say, "Hey, Em, sorry I'm late." He kissed her cheek and turned to the bar. "Bartender, can I get a beer?"

"Bottle or draft, sir?" Jenna asked shifting her eyes from Jack to Emma, then to Matt.

"Bottle, thanks." Matt moved closer to Emma and slipped his arm around her. "Emma, are you okay?"

"Yeah, I'm great. I wish you would've called or sent me a text that you'd be late. You know I hate being treated like that." Emma held up her index finger to Jenna and she acknowledged her.

"I'm sorry. It won't happen again. Things are crazy at work. Some big jobs are coming in and with Joe retiring, well I'm going to be responsible. That is if Troy gives me that promotion." Matt took his beer from Jenna and nodded her way.

"You're lucky this time. This nice young man kept me company. Matt meet Dr. Jack Bryant and his wife, Jenna, the awesome bartender tonight." Emma's hand grazed Jack's arm as she waved in his and Jenna's direction. She blinked slowly as she noticed his grin. Jack nodded toward Matt.

Jenna brought Emma another whiskey, then turned to some other guests.

She watched Jack lean against the bar sipping his drink seeming to have lost interest in her since Matt arrived. A bit of reality hit her as she realized Dr. Jack Bryant was the flirt his wife said he was. She moved closer to Matt.

"C'mon, Emma. Let's go and enjoy the party." He slugged the rest of his beer and placed the bottle on the bar.

She smiled sweetly at Jack as she slipped her arm through Matt's.

He returned her smile with one of his own and gave her a wave.

She turned to Matt and walked into the sea of people before them.

Emma's mood softened as Matt took her into his arms and they danced to the slow music playing before the festivities began. After several songs, they made their way to the table assigned to them.

Everyone from Matt's office attended the party. The CEO of Marcus Construction took to the stage, approaching the microphone as the crowd grew silent.

"May I have everyone's attention, please? I'm Troy Burns just in case anyone was wondering." There was a rush of laughter throughout the ballroom. Once it began to wane, Troy called out, "Where's Joe Thomas?"

Emma squeezed Matt's arm and threw him a smile, her annoyance with him overshadowed by her anticipation. "Honey, it's going to happen, isn't it?"

"I don't know. Let's listen," he said as he embraced his wife.

An elderly man brushed by Emma and made his way to the stage. With some help, he stood beside his CEO.

"Everyone, this is Joe Thomas. He has been with us for as long as I can remember. Tonight, is his night. He's officially retiring to go spend his days with his wife, Sophia, and fish along Florida's beautiful Gulf Coast."

A round of applause filled the room as Joe took several bows and mouthed the words, "Thank you." When Troy handed him a box, he took it and smiled. He opened it, reached in, and held up a watch for all to see.

"What kind is it, Matt?" Emma's voice sounded gleeful as she strained her neck to get a better view.

"It's a Rolex," Matt whispered. "Troy went all out for Joe; he deserves that and more. The man worked his ass off for this company. Those are big shoes to fill."

"And you're the man who can fill them, I know it."

"Thanks, babe." He kissed Emma's cheek.

As Joe took the microphone, everyone clapped. Bowing his head, he waved his hands in the air to quiet them.

"Thank you, Troy, for this incredible retirement party and gift. I'm honestly going to miss seeing everyone. Maybe I should stay."

Joe winked at Sophia. "This company has been my life. I grew old here. All the jobs I managed, the clients, the complaining. I wouldn't change a thing. I've had a successful run. It's time to spend the rest of my life with my better half. I hope you're ready to be with me twenty-four-seven, my darling." Another wink. "Thank you to everyone. Let's party!"

The room erupted in applause. Everyone moved toward the stage to speak with Joe. After a few minutes, Matt and Emma finally reached him.

"You're going to be missed, old man," Matt teased as he shook Joe's hand and drew him in for a hug.

"Are you ready to take over, Matt?" Joe asked.

"You bet he is," Emma piped in before kissing Joe's cheek. "Congratulations on your retirement. Matt will miss you. I will too, especially at all the company events. We must keep in touch. Please come by the gallery. I have something for you and Sophia."

"Emma, you're the sweetest. Thank you," Joe said. "Matt will take the reins and make this position even stronger. I have faith in him. Let me speak with Sophia about coming by."

"Of course."

"Thanks, Joe, for all your mentoring. Your advice about work, life, and most of all thanks for your friendship. Like Emma said, please call us to have dinner or go out dancing. I'll miss you," he said, hugging Joe.

They left Joe and headed back to their table. Matt suddenly stopped, "There's Troy, come with me Em. You have a way of convincing people to do the right thing." He led her over to the company's CEO.

"Good evening, Matt, Emma. Nice to see you again. How's your gallery doing?" Troy asked.

"Hello, Mr. Burns. It's nice to see you too. My gallery is doing well." Emma shook Troy's hand, then stepped back for Matt to speak with him.

"About Joe's job, now that he is retired…" Matt led Troy.

"Yes, I know you're next in line Matt. You've given my company your loyalty and we all appreciate that. I'll be deciding about Joe's successor soon."

"Matt will do his best for you as he always has, Mr. Burns. You can count on him," Emma interjected, smiling brightly.

"I know he will, Emma. He's a lucky man to have you by his side. Matt, you're on my list of top contenders. Be smart and the job is yours." Troy grasped Matt's hand and shook it. "I need to go find my beautiful wife and get out of here. Emma, I hope you enjoyed the evening. Goodnight to you both." Troy spun to his left and scanned the room.

Emma squeezed Matt's bicep and kissed his cheek. "Sounds like the job is yours. Don't stress over it. It's probably a formality to be fair to everyone. You know, business shit." She slipped her hand into his and locked their fingers.

"I don't know, Em. Troy didn't sound so sure it was mine. He said he will decide. No one else has been with the company for as long as I have. I'll do whatever I need to get this promotion," Matt sighed heavily as he shook his head.

"You're overthinking it already, why do you do things like that?" Emma shrugged.

"I'm not overthinking, I'm preparing to work my ass off to get something I want, what I deserve. What's wrong with that?" Matt released his hand from hers and came to a dead stop.

"Please. Not here. I don't want to get into this right now. Let's go home and fall into bed." Emma nudged against him.

There was a bit of silence before he spoke. "Sure." Matt took a step ahead of Emma.

She grasped his hand, not letting him get away from her.

Right as she was about to step outside, her chest tightened. Her skin tingled as she felt someone watching her. Turning her head toward the bar, her eyes met Jack's.

He flashed a gorgeous smile at her.

Her insides melted as a slow grin formed and held Jack's gaze.

Tugging on her arm, Matt pulled her to the valet.

CHAPTER 2

"Yes. Matt. Oh my God," Emma gasped as she clutched at her husband, her slight frame quivering under his powerful thrusts.

A resounding crack emitted from below them. The bed fell to one side. Emma held onto Matt to avoid sliding off.

"Damn, we did it again." Matt grazed his lips across her damp neck.

"Yes, we've broken the bed again. Time for a new one, don't you think?" She teased as they rolled off the bed together. She landed hard on the wood floor, winced, and bit her lip.

"I can fix it," he stated.

Her eyes captured him as he rose, taking in the glorious view. Six foot tall with dirty-blond hair and big brown eyes, he was two hundred pounds of pure muscle. She licked her lips as her eyes roamed across his biceps. She loved that her small hands couldn't completely encircle them. And given she was only five-foot-two, he could easily lift her.

She wished he would lift her in more places than just the bed. Like the wall. Or the table, Or his desk at work.

Her body humming for him again, Emma moved to sit up, but knife-like pain pierced her left shoulder. As she collapsed back against the bed, biting her lip to stop from crying out too loud, Matt rushed to her side and turned on the light on the nightstand.

"What's wrong, babe?"

"I'm not sure, but it hurts like fuck right now. When we rolled off the bed, I must've knocked it. I'll be fine in a few hours; I'll take something for the pain," she said with a grimace.

His brow furrowed in concern. Gently slipping his arms around her waist, he lifted her.

She slid her uninjured arm across his broad shoulders, but just the jostle of that movement hurt her.

"I'm taking you to the hospital," he said, arms tightening around her.

She bit down on her lip as she shook her head. "No, it's okay. It's probably just bruised. You know I hate hospitals. It doesn't hurt that much."

When he shifted her in his arms, she took in a deep breath. Exhaling slowly, she kissed his warm bare chest. She felt safe in his arms, surrounded by his unconditional love. "You always take good care of me. I love you."

"I love you too."

Carrying her to the kitchen, he set her down at the breakfast table. Rummaging through the drawers and cupboards, he pulled out a packet of Tylenol and filled a glass of water. "You rest and I'll go fix the bed – again." He flashed her a boyish grin.

Smiling, Emma waited until he left, then grabbed some whiskey and shuffled into the living room. She laid on the sofa and waited for Matt to finish.

An hour later, he emerged from their bedroom, pumping his biceps.

Watching him, she chewed her cheek. The nightlight highlighted all the nice parts of his svelte body. Her eyes wandered across his dampened pecs, down to his abdomen, and for a man in his mid-fifties, he kept himself in top shape.

The corners of her mouth slowly curved into a sensual grin. Emma coaxed Matt over to her, curling her index finger, wetting her lips.

"How's your shoulder, honey?" Matt asked.

"It's fine. Now finish what you started," Emma said raising her arms to him. Pain shot through her shoulder, but she ignored it, her eyes fastened on his chest.

As he slid his muscular arms under her body, she embraced him. He lifted her, gently rolling her body into his warm pecs, holding her injured shoulder against him.

She nuzzled her nose into his shoulder, breathing in his masculine scent. Her body aching for him.

He strode toward their bedroom, but Emma grabbed the door jam. "Em, what the—" Matt looked at her.

"On the floor, Matt. Make love to me over there, on the floor." She breathed into his shoulder, hiding her pain.

"The floor is too hard, and besides, I fixed our bed. I want you there." He walked them back into their bedroom and laid her down. He found two more pillows and carefully raised Emma's upper body as he slid them under her.

She reached for him, caressing his scruffy jaw.

"I want you Em, but we have to be careful. Are you sure?" Matt's eyes shone worry as she held his gaze.

"I'm fine, I promise. Now please, baby, please make love to me." With her uninjured arm, she slipped her hand into his boxer briefs and smiled. "Mmm, that's what I want." She slowly stroked Matt's long hard cock.

"Damn, Em." Matt moved onto the bed and laid next to her.

In the darkness, she winced with pain.

Emma tugged on his boxer briefs until she removed them. She crawled onto Matt, her soft thighs on either side of him.

His shaft was at attention as she slid onto him. "Baby, you are so warm and slick. God damn." His hips shot upward as her body smacked down on his. They met with a fierce passion. He gripped her tiny waist and lifted her body while pumping his own into her.

"Matt, don't stop, oh Jesus, Matt." Emma's back arched, and she caught herself with her hands on his knees.

He rubbed her clit as their bodies pounded together. "Oh my God." Emma flung herself flat onto Matt's slick chest as her orgasm erupted. Matt's rod throbbed inside her as she sensed his cum flow into her.

His arms around her, caressing her soft skin. "I'm sorry about my attitude at the party. I love you, Emma. Forever," he whispered, his breath giving her chills.

"I know baby. It'll be fine. I love you too." She squeezed Matt causing the pain in her shoulder to return.

***

Morning greeted Emma with warm kisses on her neck. Her eyes blinked awake as she rolled over to receive those kisses on her lips. She snuck her tongue between Matt's full lips.

"Good morning," Matt said after their kiss broke. "How's your pain this morning?"

"Good morning. I rolled over and didn't scream, so I'm going to say it's okay, maybe." She shrugged with her hands in front of her.

"I'd love to stay in bed with you, but I have a busy day." Matt rolled out of bed and stood naked by the bedside.

"Then don't tease me like that Mr. Taylor." Emma frowned as she reached and ran her hand up Matt's thigh.

"I'll make it up to you later, promise." He leaned down and kissed her forehead, she cringed but didn't complain. He turned and went to the bathroom to shower.

Emma waited a while then tried to sit up. She let out a wail in agony as she fell back onto the bed.

Matt darted out of the bathroom. His towel fell from his waist midway to her. The sun sparkled on his half-wet body. Had she not been in such pain, he would've been extremely late for work.

"Your arm is still in pain," he said as he sat beside her.

"No, not at first, you saw me lay on it before you went to shower. Maybe it's stiff from sleep, or I placed too much weight on it trying to sit up, or I moved the wrong way. I don't know, but I'll take more Tylenol and keep track of it. Please don't worry, I'll be fine." Emma waved Matt off and carefully rose from their bed.

She didn't have time to be hurt or spend useless time at a hospital. She needed to get ready for the gallery's next exhibition. She'd been preparing for this for almost a year, and she wasn't going to let a bruised shoulder kill her hard work.

Painting was her life. She grew up in painting smocks, playing with paints as a toddler, using her fingers at first, then brushes. Her mom bought her paint by numbers when she could first read. The very first paint set hooked her for life when she saw what she'd created with her own hands. Emma enjoyed painting landscapes of beaches, mountains, city skylines, anything in nature. She'd also taken to painting family portraits in the past few months. She wanted to expand her portfolio with new and different settings. Her next step was to take Brandi, her best friend's photographs, and place them on canvas. They discussed selling them as a set. Pictures to Paintings, at BE Unique Gallery.

CHAPTER 3

Emma arrived at the small quaint coffee shop. It held its own against the larger chain down the street. As she entered, the aroma of freshly brewed coffee hit her nose. She breathed it in deep. She walked past a few tables with regular customers, nodding as she passed by. The small sitting area was empty as this morning it was quiet inside.

Emma found Brandi at their usual table, a coffee and a Diet Coke already ordered. Walking up behind her, Emma glanced at Brandi's open laptop. A search page of catering businesses filled the screen.

"Hey, sorry I'm late. Looks like you're ready to get this done."

"Did Matt make you late?" Brandi teased as she pressed on the refresh button.

"Um, no, actually, he left for the office early today. Funny story though," she said, sliding into a chair. "The bed broke again last night. I rolled off the edge and landed on my arm. It was killing me this morning, so I took one of Matt's hydrocodone pills. They always knock me out, and when I woke up, I realized I was going to be late."

"You crazy kids. You're going to break your hip next if you don't cool the sex," Brandi joked. Emma grinned at her.

It was her friend that had encouraged Emma to be braver with Matt in bed in the first place. "Add in some toys," she'd said. "Play with him," she'd said. "Spice it up," she'd said. Emma had taken Brandi's advice and now here she was with an injured shoulder.

She sipped on her lukewarm coffee as Brandi angled the laptop so they both had a clear view of the list on the screen.

"Oh, I almost forgot. I picked up a card from the catering company at Matt's office party." Digging through her purse, she placed a pink and white card on the table. "Maybe she can cater our next exhibition."

Brandi paused to read it, then did a quick Google search.

"Jenna's catering has 4.75 out of five stars. I wonder which ones brought her rank down from perfect?" Brandi pushed the page up to find the lower starred reviews. They both preferred to read the negative reviews. Anyone could post awesome things. It took a lot of guts to post bad reviews.

Emma gasped and covered her mouth to stop her belly laugh from escaping. She pointed to the only one-star review listed. "Look Brandi, this poster complained that the girls were too pretty. Oh my God, if that's the worst thing about them, I just don't know if we can hire them." Emma rolled her eyes and laughed out loud.

"Well, that's terrible. Do you really want pretty young women hanging around Matt?" Brandi teased.

"He won't notice, he's too busy worrying about being promoted at work since Joe retired." Emma shrugged and finished her coffee. She waived for Claire, the barista.

"Why is Matt worried? He's next in line, right?" Brandi sipped on her Diet Coke.

"He is, but Troy's being impossible as usual."

"Hi Mrs. Taylor, need a refill?" Claire asked reaching for Emma's mug.

"Yes, please." Emma handed her coffee mug to Claire. She turned back to Brandi, "I'm sure Matt will be promoted within the week. He's overreacting like always."

"Here you go, Mrs. Taylor." Claire handed Emma a nice hot coffee.

"Thanks so much, Claire. You're the best." Emma smiled as she took the mug in hand.

"I think we should call Jenna. Her reviews are outstanding, besides that one." Brandi tapped her cell phone and punched in the number. After a few rings, the call was answered.

"Hi." Brandi's smile bled through her voice. "This is Brandi Davis with BE Unique Gallery on Main Street."

After a few seconds of silence, Brandi nodded to Emma.

"Okay, great, Jenna. Could you come by the gallery for a meeting later?" Silence again, a thumbs up from Brandi. "Awesome, see you then." Brandi placed her phone back in her bag. She sipped her soda again then faced Emma. "Jenna can come by around six. You okay with staying later tonight?"

"Of course. We can go through our pieces and decide what to share with her. Give her a taste of our world." Emma finished her second coffee and rose from her seat. "Let's head back and get started. I'm excited about planning our event."

"Sounds like a plan." Brandi packed her laptop while Emma went to pay the tab.

On her way out of the coffee shop, Emma did a double-take. From the side, she noticed a handsome young man. She swore it was Jack from the party, but at second glance, this young man wasn't nearly as tall, nearly as gorgeous. He also greeted a young brunette and they walked to the counter.

Emma had driven to meet Brandi since she had been late, so they hopped into her black sedan and drove the short distance to their gallery.

"Emma!" Brandi shouted.

"Oh shit." Emma slammed on the brakes as the car in front of her came to a sudden stop.

"Where were you just then, girl?" Brandi teased and punched Emma's arm.

"Dreaming about Matt, of course," Emma fibbed. Her thoughts were with Jack as she wondered what he was doing. She thought maybe she'd ask Jenna about him later.

***

They arrived at BE Unique. Brandi found the keys and unlocked the back door. They each dropped their bags in their offices and met in the large main room in the front of the gallery.

The brick building sat perfectly angled on the corner of Main and South Streets in the suburb they lived in. The gallery consisted of three rooms for their pieces. One large and two smaller ones on either side. Brandi filled the room to the right with her photographs, while Emma took the room to the left for her paintings. The main room held combinations of their pieces.

The long windows had drapes from ceiling to floor in a cream color and multicolored beads hanging in the folds. Seating areas were scattered about with puffy colorful chairs, small brown sofas, and side tables.

For now, their gallery only showed their pieces hanging on the walls. They had talked about bringing in another local artist in the future but had yet to find one.

Emma walked to the front and switched the closed sign to open, then unlocked the door. She took a seat behind the small counter and pulled out her phone from her pocket.

Emma sprung from her chair when the bell clanged.

"Good morning." She glanced at her watch and smiled at the older couple before her. "Yes, it's still morning. Welcome to BE Unique. How may I help you?" She moved to the side to allow them to step further into the gallery.

"Good morning and thank you so much. We're here to speak with...oh shoot, I forgot the young woman's name. Brenda? I'm so sorry." She hung her head.

"You mean Brandi. Do you have an appointment with her today?" Emma asked and led them toward a group of chairs.

"No, we heard about her from friends. Is she here?"

"Oh yes, may I tell her who is here for her?"

"I'm Sarah Russell and this is my husband, Stanley."

"I'll go get her for you, Mr., and Mrs. Russell. Please wait here." Emma walked back to Brandi's office and knocked softly. "Hey, an elderly couple is asking for you."

"Okay, I'll be right there." Brandi pushed back from her desk and followed Emma.

"Brandi, this is Mr. and Mrs. Russell." Emma waved her hand toward them.

"Hi, it's nice to meet you. How may I help you?" Brandi extended her hand to them.

Emma interjected, "I'll leave you all to talk. Brandi, I'll be in my office."

"Okay." Brandi turned back to the Russell's and Emma walked down the hallway.

She straightened up her desk and made a list of supplies she needed.

"Hey, Em, want to order in for lunch today?" Brandi's voice carried to Emma in her office closet.

"Sounds good, get me something light and a coffee," she called out as she was knee-deep in blank canvases.

After lunch, a few customers were walking through their gallery. Only lookers which weren't too unusual early in the week.

The bell above the gallery door rang a bit after six. Turning from tidying up behind the desk, Emma saw the same woman from the party walking toward her. She glanced over the tall young blonde's shoulder, looking for a dark-haired man for just a second before focusing back on Jenna.

Stopping at the desk, the woman extended her hand. "Hi, I'm Jenna Bryant from Jenna's Catering. You're Emma, the lady Jack brought over to wait for her husband."

Emma wasn't sure how she felt about Jenna having such a great memory. She had to have seen and served over one hundred people at that party. Yet she remembered her, the woman her husband flirted with.

Emma cleared her throat as she took the woman's hand. "Hi, yes, you've got a great memory."

"Comes with the job." Jenna smiled.

Brandi joined them. "This is my business partner, Brandi Davis. Welcome to BE Unique."

Jenna smiled widely. "B and E? For Brandi and Emma. I love that." She glanced around the place. "And I love your work. Everything is quaint and beautiful here. You ladies are so talented." Her eyes lingered on a portrait of a couple very much in love, their chests naked and pressed together. "Maybe I can make an appointment for a photography session with me and my husband."

Emma scowled when she realized the photo Jenna stared at. Her imagination led her to a bedroom where a naked Jack laid across the bed, arms wide, inviting Emma to join him. She swayed in her chair while her daydream played on.

"Emma," Brandi's voice brought her back to reality. She glanced at Jenna, then felt her warm cheeks. Shaking her head slightly, she thought, she shouldn't ever daydream about another woman's husband. Only her own.

Brandi turned to Jenna, "I'm sure I can get you in for a photo shoot in the future," Brandi said, as she led them to the living room set, they'd put in for clients to see their paintings 'in situ.' "Now let's look at what we need from you and get your estimate," she said, sitting down on the brown sofa.

Setting into the armchair across from her, a dark wooden coffee table between them, Jenna placed her briefcase on the table. "I know you'll be happy with what I can offer you, ladies."

Brandi looked over the preliminary proposal, then handed it to Emma. After a quick scan through all of the different foods on offer, Emma nodded her approval.

"Well, Jenna, we'd love for you to cater our event," Brandi said. "We look forward to completing the menu in a couple of days. Does that work for you?"

"Absolutely. How does Friday sound? My husband always works late, so we can make it a dinner meeting."

"Perfect," Emma chimed in. *Just like Jack.*

The three women stood, shook hands, and walked to the gallery door.

"It was great meeting you. We'll see you on Friday at five. We can meet here and walk to our favorite restaurant," Brandi said as she held the door.

"It was nice meeting you and seeing you again, Emma. See you both then."

As the door shut behind her, Emma turned to her friend. "She seems nice. I'm confident she'll do a fabulous job catering for our event. I think we should invite her husband. He can get a look at your photography while Jenna works. Maybe choose his favorite scenes for their photoshoot." Emma held her hand's palm up, shrugging her shoulders.

"Jenna is nice. Sure Em, invite whomever you want. I'm heading home. Ben's waiting. Try not to break your bed tonight." Brandi winked and bumped Emma before leaving. She locked up and walked to her office to retrieve her purse.

***

Sitting at a red light on her way home, Emma glanced to the car beside her. She gasped when she noticed a young dark-haired man staring at her. She stared back. Her mind saw Jack, she smiled. The traffic light seemed to last forever. Her body heated up at the thought of it being Jack in the sedan beside her. Shaking her head, she dislodged that thought from her mind. The light turned green as she watched the car leave her behind. She drove on home to Matt.

"Hi, honey, how was work?" Emma asked Matt when she arrived home.

"Busy. How's your shoulder?" He edged his body against her right side to avoid her injury.

"It's fine. Go wash up while I whip us up a quick dinner. You can have dessert later," she teased.

"Okay, but please be telling me the truth. It's okay if you need to go to the doctor." He glided his hand across her round ass as he went to change.

Finishing the chef salad she threw together, she grabbed some plates, trying not to wince as the reaching movement troubled her shoulder. Walking to the table, she placed everything down, trying her best not to jostle her injury. When Matt came back, she sat next to him.

"Did Troy decide on Joe's successor?" Emma began their dinner conversation.

"Shit, no he hasn't. I don't know why he's waiting or even considering anyone else." Matt ran his hand through his dirty blond hair and rubbed his scruffy jaw.

"Who knows why Troy is taking his time. I know you'll be the one he chooses. Be patient baby." She leaned into him and kissed his lips.

"I hope you're right, Em." He poked his fork hard into his food, stabbing at the salad.

When dinner was over, he helped her clean up.

"What's for dessert, Emma?" Matt breathed against her neck, giving her chills.

"There's ice cream, pie, or me." Curving upward then licking her lips, she moved toward the bedroom.

He grabbed her in the doorway, his warm embrace causing hot moisture to trickle from her core and wet her panties. The edge of his mouth touched her ear, his tongue slithered down her neck.

She moaned and grasped the doorjamb.

Cradling her, he kept her steady.

"Take me here, baby," she said, resting her finger on his mouth, wrapping one leg around his. "Right here," she whispered, leaning against the wall.

"It's too risky. You could knock your shoulder. Let me make love to you in our bed."

Emma pouted as he scooped her up. She enjoyed sex with Matt in bed, but she was getting bored. She wanted them to be riskier. To have some excitement. She'd need to be more aggressive with Matt. Flirt with him in his home office, away from their bedroom.

As he laid her down on their bed, her fingers caressed his chest. Their eyes met, and she wanted to tell him about her desires, but she could see his concern for her in his eyes.

"Are you sure, Em?"

"I'm fine. It doesn't hurt anymore. Now please undress me, make love to me." Ignoring her disappointment, she raised her arms.

He lifted her top over her head and easily unhooked her lacy bra. His body pressed her down into the mattress, his weight gently resting on top of hers. His eyes gleaming, he nuzzled her ample breasts.

She giggled, loving how playful he was with her. Threading her fingers through his thick wavy hair as he sucked on her nipple, she brought his face to hers. She grazed her lips across his scruffy jawline, then nibbled on his earlobe. Their lips met lightly. "Please fuck me now," Emma begged. "I'm on fire for you."

Standing, Matt stripped the rest of his clothes off. Her eyes lit with delight; she licked her lips. Leaning down, he removed her slacks and panties.

Straddling her body, he teased her by dragging his hard shaft down her inner thigh. She moaned and pulled him onto her. She wanted him inside her. No more teasing. She needed him to fuck her.

Emma's legs fell open as Matt's body slid between them. He plunged deep inside her. Moaning louder, she arched her back when his body smacked into hers over and over.

"Damn Em, you feel so perfect." He raised her shapely leg and rested it on his shoulder, switching his angle as he penetrated her even deeper.

"Oh Matt, slow down baby, I want to feel you inside me for hours." She grasped his forearms, lowered her leg, and drew him back down onto her. "Slow baby, slow." Emma breathed into his ear.

Matt's rhythm slowed as he laid on her, careful to not crush her petite body, he lifted slightly onto his hands and kissed her glistening neck. His tongue traced her soft jaw, finding her soft lips.

She fisted his hair and opened her mouth inviting his tongue to come and play with hers. Kissing passionately as he pumped in and out of her hot wet core. She sensed his cock ready to explode.

"Emma, you're driving me wild; I can't hold on much longer. God baby, you're so damn incredible."

Gripping her waist, he sat up and pulled her petite body onto his lap.

She wrapped her arms around his neck and kissed him deeply, her tongue tasting every inch of his warm delicious mouth.

He pumped her faster and harder.

Their bodies became slick with sweat. Emma squeezed Matt tight as she reached her climax, feeling Matt's embrace, she knew he reached his bliss.

"I love how you taste." Arching her back, Matt licked drops of salty sweat sliding between her breasts.

"I love you so much. I don't know what I'd do without you," Emma whispered in his ear as she held him against her.

He breathed into her cheek. "I'll always love you, Em."

CHAPTER 4

Emma slept all night without pain. She hoped that meant her shoulder was not as bad as she'd feared. Gently rising to her feet, she sighed in relief. "Oh, thank God."

"What was that?" Matt came out of the bathroom shirtless.

Running her eyes down his sexy body, her lips slowly curved upwards. "My shoulder feels much better. I got up with no pain. I'm sure it was just a stinger the other night."

"I hope so, but if it flares up, please get it looked at."

"I will, I promise," Emma said as she slipped into her robe. "Coffee?"

"Not this morning. I have a deadline and need to get into the office."

"Okay. I almost forgot to tell you. Brandi and I hired a catering company. A young woman owns it – Jenna Bryant. I picked up her card from your work party. She seems perfect for our event in a couple of weeks. You'll be there, right?"

Matt pulled on a shirt and started to button it. "Of course, I will. It's on my calendar. I'll never miss one of your exhibitions, but I've got to run now. I love you, Emma." He kissed her on the cheek before heading for the garage.

"I love you too, Matt. Have a great day."

As the car's engine turned on outside, Emma dressed and gathered her canvases, sketch pad, pencils, and paints. Heading out, she walked to the nearby park, pulling her small wagon-type bag. The sun warmed up the ground and kissed her skin. There were wisps of clouds in the sky – the perfect shapes to paint. Studying the landscape, she decided on what the best angle would be to capture.

The palm trees were her favorite, but the large rocks behind them were so raw and powerful. She wanted an angle that captured them both, that contrasted the gentleness with the roughness.

She wondered briefly if Jack would be the roughness to Matt's gentleness. If he wouldn't mind taking her against the wall. Or on the floor. Or the desk, *her* desk.

Swallowing down those thoughts, she quickly opened her bag and started to set up. *He's married. I'm married...*

Forcing her mind to focus on the beauty around her, she quickly lost herself in her painting.

***

Her watch buzzed with a reminder to check with Matt about dinner. Emma sent him a text: **Dinner at home?** She went back to her painting,

After another couple of hours of sketching her landscapes, she sent Matt the same text. She waited for his response, folding her arms, plopping into the folding chair, and watched her watch screen.

She puffed a breath and stomped back to her easel. Emma hastily gathered her pencils and sketch pad. She'd brought her paints, but she decided to pack up and walk home without painting.

On her way, she sent a third text, the same message. By the time she reached her house, she expected Matt to answer. With nothing from him, she ordered herself dinner. She hated when Matt ignored her. He knew she hated it, yet he continued to do just that. She didn't care what he was engaged in, a simple text takes two seconds to send.

***

Emma finished cleaning up from her dinner. She relaxed in her recliner and thumbed through a magazine, waiting for Matt.

"Hey, babe." He leaned down to kiss her and she pulled away. "Okay, what did I do?"

"Where the hell have you been?" She drummed the cover of the magazine with her fingers.

"Sorry, Em. I told you this morning I had a deadline. I thought you understood I'd be late." Matt rubbed his chin.

She sat back and crossed her arms. "I texted several times. You could've sent one answer. You know how I hate being ignored. Especially by my husband."

He shook his head with an apologetic smile. "Okay, it won't happen again. Sorry. Is there any dinner?" he asked sheepishly.

"That's why I texted you. When you didn't respond, I ordered for myself. Figured you'd get something at the office."

"Well… I didn't think you worked today… so, I thought you'd make dinner… and keep it warm for me." Matt stammered through his words.

Emma's face grew hot. *Didn't work?* Anger coursing through her, she struggled not to scream at him.

"I sketched some today," she bit out. "Just like every day. My work isn't the same as yours, but it's just as important to me. I'm going to bed. Goodnight, Matt." Rising from her chair, she stormed past him and into their room. Why was he always like this? Her pulse pounded in her neck; she smashed her fist into her palm.

"Honey, wait. I'm sorry for being a dick. I know your work is just as important. I didn't mean it wasn't. I invested in you, remember? It's been a fucking horrible day. Please don't go to bed mad. I love you, baby."

Crawling into bed, Emma curled into a ball.

"Are you okay?" he asked as he sat on the edge of the bed.

"I'm fine, Matt. I get upset when you treat my work as though it's just for fun. You know it's not. Ever since Brandi and I bought the gallery and began our exhibitions and selling our pieces. It means a lot to me. I need your support."

"I'm sorry. I won't be an ass like that again."

"Please don't. I hate fighting with you," her voice softened. "So, tell me what was it that kept you from answering me?" She swung her legs off the bed, sat next to him, and placed her hand on his thigh.

"I don't know where to begin, Em. Since Joe retired the jobs are pouring in. It seems like everyone waited and now we have so much to do and a lot of it isn't local. I'm going to talk with Troy about hiring an assistant." Matt ran a hand through his hair, exhaling hard.

"I'm sure you'll find the perfect one to cover all that work that's not local; that way you can be here to run the local jobs and home with me." She turned and looked at Matt directly.

"Let me make it up to you." His hands disappeared behind her.

She grabbed his arm and stopped his advances. "You think fucking me will make this all better?" Emma put a small space between them.

"Oh please, Em. I'm so sorry. I won't ignore your texts ever again, promise baby. Please let me love you." He fell to his knees and placed his palms together.

She thought for a minute or two, making Matt nervous.

"Emma please," he begged some more. His hands slid up her thighs.

"Matt, dammit, I can't stay mad at you. Don't do that again. Ever." She held up her index finger as she scolded him.

A pouting grin formed on Matt's lips as he leaned into her, grazing her lips with his. She wanted more, but he moved too fast for her to recapture his lips. Slipping her bra from her arms, he smiled brightly at her perky breasts. He kissed each one, licking around her nipples. When they hardened in his mouth, he rubbed himself against her.

Sliding her hand down the front of his slacks, she wrapped her fingers around his hard cock. A light squeeze and she began stroking him. He moaned with his mouth full of her breasts.

"Slow down, baby. Let me pleasure you first."

"You are pleasuring me and driving me crazy. I'm so hot for you, so wet. Fuck me, Matt!" she demanded.

Taking off her shorts and panties, along with his clothes, he threw them on the floor.

Spreading her arms, Emma invited him into her hot private space – the one he loved to enter as often as she allowed him to.

His rigid manhood grazed her leg. Her body quivered. His tongue traveled between her breasts and up her neck. It plunged into her gaping mouth. Their kisses were deep and wet as they devoured one another. She felt his hard shaft graze her clit, waiting to penetrate her sopping wet tunnel. Lifting her hips, he plunged into her, their bodies smacking together, their passion erupted.

"Oh my God, Matt, yes, harder, faster, please, baby, please," Emma screamed. She dug her fingers into his shoulder blades and wrapped her legs around his body.

He pumped harder and faster as she wanted. Pulling out of her, he flipped her over onto her knees and entered her center from behind. His body smacked against hers over and over as she moaned and groaned with sheer ecstasy.

"Fuck, Emma!" Matt yelled, pounding against her sweet ass with such force, she collapsed onto the pillows.

Pushing in deep, he came inside her. His legs gave out, he laid on top of her. "My God, woman. I love you so damn much. You drive me insane." He kissed her back and slid his hand under her to caress her breasts.

"Oh, Matt, I'll always love you." She reached for his other hand, kissed it, and held him tight. All was forgiven as they fell into a deep sleep.

CHAPTER 5

Brandi and Emma waited for Jenna at the gallery Friday evening.

Jenna walked in just before five. "TGIF, ladies, are you ready?" she asked as she approached them.

"Hi Jenna, yes we are," Brandi said as they left the gallery and walked to KC's Clubhouse.

The hostess sat them in a quiet booth. Reaching into her briefcase, Jenna brought out her menu options. She had a vast list to choose from. Emma smiled at Brandi when she noticed how organized Jenna was.

"Wow," Emma said, scanning the extensive list, "I'm impressed with your ideas for the night." She looked at Brandi. "I think we should go with a wide selection of chicken, steak, and seafood, some vegetables, fruit platters, and a variety of petit fours for dessert."

"Yeah, sounds good," Brandi added.

"Well ladies, I'm positive we'll make your gallery event a tremendous success. I hope this is the beginning of a promising work relationship." Jenna slipped her brochures back into her briefcase. "Oh, we should do a tasting next week, so you know exactly what you're getting. How does Wednesday sound? That will give us time to prepare everything."

"Works for me, Emma?"

"Sure, that's fine with me. Hey Pete." Emma waved to their favorite bartender.

"Hi ladies, what can I get y'all for dinner?" Pete brought out his tablet and waited for each one to give him their order.

"Chicken salad and my usual, Pete. Thanks." Came from Emma as she woke her phone and thumbed through her email.

"I'll have a Cobb salad and a Diet Coke," Brandi said and handed Pete the menu.

"I'll have a steak, medium, baked potato, and a side salad with ranch," Jenna ordered.

"And to drink, Mrs. Bryant?" A sharp pang went through Emma when Pete addressed Jenna. Did she wish that were her being called Mrs. Bryant? *Maybe, no, definitely not*, she loved Matt. She shook her head from side to side to chase those thoughts from her imagination.

"Um, bring me a gin and tonic, thanks." Jenna smiled up at Pete and gave him her menu.

"I'll be right back with those drinks." Pete turned and left them for several minutes.

"Tell us, Jenna, how long has your business been open?" Brandi broke the short silence.

"I and my team opened up shop eighteen months ago. We've kept it to small birthday parties and graduations until recently when we felt ready to take on bigger projects."

"Here's your drinks," Pete interrupted.

"Thank you, sir." Emma smiled as she wrapped her hands around the tumbler of whiskey. Jenna and Brandi nodded their thanks.

"You bet. Your food should be here soon. I'll check back later."

Emma took a long slow sip as a vision of Jack appeared. Her lips sucked the edge of the glass as she enjoyed her mini dream of sucking on him.

"Emma." Brandi kicked her under the table.

"Oh sorry, I drifted off for a second. What?" Emma's face burned a bit from being caught fantasizing.

"Brandi asked what you thought of my company's performance at the party we catered for your husband's work," Jenna said.

"It was great. Everyone from the office raved about the food and the service. I know I enjoyed myself." Emma's smile turned sinful as her eyes danced, that vision of Jack returned, this time it was when she met him at Matt's office party and her first fall into his soft blue eyes.

"I apologize if my husband was too flirty with you," Jenna stated.

"Not at all. He was being friendly. I was frustrated Matt was late. Jack took my mind off my anger." Emma waved her hand in dismissal.

"Jack has a flirtatious nature. Always did, that's what attracted me to him. He knows I don't mind him flirting if that's all it is. Nothing more." Jenna laid down the boundaries of her marriage and Emma made a mental note of them.

"That's all it was that night, friendly flirting." Emma peered over the rim of her glass as she finished her drink.

"Good, because he tries to come to all my events, and I wouldn't want it to be awkward for any of us."

"Dinner, ladies," Pete announced.

Emma slowly released the breath she'd held. She knew Jack was more than flirting with her that evening when their eyes met as she left with Matt.

After dinner, they all ordered one last drink. Brandi asked Jenna, "How long have you and Jack been married?" Emma's heart tightened.

"We've been married for three years, together for eight. We waited until we finished college to get married."

"Any plans for children?" Brandi pushed on and again Emma's heart ached, and she glared at her best friend. Emma didn't want to hear all these personal details or what Jenna and Jack planned for their future.

"Yeah, maybe. I'd like to wait another year to try. I know Jack will be a fantastic father, he's the perfect husband," Jenna beamed. Emma wished she could crawl away from the conversation. She smiled weakly, nodded at the proper times as she pretended to be interested in what Jenna said. Her gut wrenched with each loving statement Jenna spoke.

It wasn't that she hated the woman, not at all. Jenna Bryant impressed Emma. Her work ethic, her poise, her talent with food. She didn't want to hear personal shit about her and Jack. Ever.

"I think I should head home, Brandi, are you ready?" Emma asked after much too much conversation about Jenna and Jack's happy marriage.

"Sure." Brandi waved for Pete. "I'll take the check."

"Hey, babe." Emma's insides rushed with heat when she heard his voice. Her cheeks flushed, her center became slick and hot. She smiled sinfully across the table as Jack kissed Jenna's cheek. His gaze met hers. The corner of his mouth tugged up into a mischievously inviting grin.

Emma shivered in her seat. She turned her gaze away, not wanting Brandi to notice, and reached down for her purse.

"Jackson." Jenna laughed as she greeted her husband with a kiss on his cheek.

Emma couldn't help but notice the friendly cheek kisses they exchanged. For being sort of newlyweds, she thought it odd that they didn't kiss full on. She knew she would kiss Jack full on his sensual lips if he were ever hers.

"It's nice to see you again, Emma." Jack held his hand for her to shake.

She met his gaze again, hesitated a beat, then stood as her hand melted into his. Remembering the softness of his palm, she gripped his hand tight.

"Nice to see you too, Jack. This is my friend and business partner, Brandi Davis. Brandi, this is Jack, Jenna's husband." Emma released Jack's hand and stepped aside for Brandi to greet Jack.

"It's good to meet you." Brandi's handshake was short and what Emma felt, very cold.

"Jack, we'd love for you to come to our exhibition. Jenna can take a break during the show," Emma said.

"Sure, I will. Unless I'm called to the hospital. I'd love to see your work, Emma. And yours too, Brandi," Jack added quickly and smiled.

"Fabulous, see you both next Friday," Emma beamed.

"Are you ready?" Brandi sounded annoyed as she tugged on Emma's arm.

"Yes. Bye Jack, Jenna." Emma threw him a sweet smile as she watched Jenna reach for her briefcase and didn't see their interactions. "See you soon."

CHAPTER 6

"Holy shit," Emma said as she entered Jenna's shop. Brandi followed behind her. The door buzzed. But all of Emma's attention was on how organized Jenna's place looked.

The large open room had three tables filled with samples. A table with assorted meats, one with vegetables and the last with desserts and drinks.

Impressed with the set-up, Emma realized what Jack saw in Jenna. Not only was she beautiful, but she also appeared talented in her chosen field. Jenna obviously could hold her own and tolerated Jack's flirty behavior with other women.

Hmm, maybe they had a marriage of convenience.

"Hi ladies. Please don't mind my mess. I've been a little busy with my team getting all this ready for you." She wiped her flour-covered cheek with her hand, spreading the flour into her hair. She wiped her hands on the stain-filled white apron covering her tan slacks and orange polo.

"Hi Jenna," Brandi said.

"Wow, Jenna, this is quite a lot to taste," Emma said, still marveling at the food.

"Thanks, Emma. I hope y'all like what we've made. Some of these samples are Jack's favorites. Now grab a plate and fill it up." She waved her arm over the tables filled with food and drink. "I'll leave you two to enjoy and be in the kitchen. Holler if you need me." Jenna turned and went through a double swinging door.

Emma cringed inside when Jenna mentioned Jack. *Why did she make Jack's favorites for us to taste?* She moved her thoughts of Jack from her mind and to Brandi as they each picked up a plate.

Placing a bit of chicken, roast beef, shrimp, and sausage on hers, she said, "Jesus, she's got so much. We need to keep her around for future shows."

"I agree, and look, she knows you already. There's whiskey," Brandi teased.

"I saw that. I think I may love her." Emma winked.

Brandi nearly dropped her plate of food when she burst out laughing.

After tasting the meat selections, Emma filled a plate of broccoli, cauliflower, asparagus, and roasted brussels sprouts. Enough for them to share.

Brandi brought over a plate with chocolate mousse, crème brûlée, several petit fours, and a simple fruit cup.

Emma had a couple of shots of whiskey, while Brandi stuck with her usual Diet Coke.

"Jenna," Emma called out when she and Brandi had finished tasting everything.

"I'm here." Jenna came back through the double doors in a clean white apron. "How did you ladies like the array?"

"We loved it. The whiskey sold me." Emma smiled at Jenna.

"So, you're a whiskey drinker. Jack enjoys that too as you know from the other party," Jenna mentioned.

Emma glanced at Brandi when Jenna brought up Jack for the second time. Her cheeks warmed when Jenna shared information about Jack and not their personal life together. Emma wanted to know all she could about him. Her curiosity about that beautiful man was insatiable. She had to be careful questioning Jenna; she didn't want to appear obsessed with her husband.

When she saw him again, she'd remember to buy him a whiskey, it gave her something to build on. Begin it all on a friendship and see where it went.

"Yes, I love my whiskey, but I don't need it. It's something I enjoy."

"Funny, that's what Jack says. A bit of whiskey takes the edge off after a long day at the office for him."

"He's got that right." Emma agreed. Thrilled to know she and Jack not only enjoyed whiskey, but he drank it to relax with, just as she did. She could hope to share a relaxing evening drinking whiskey with Jack, only Jack and her, in a hotel room, blinds closed, laying across the bed as he poured the whiskey between her breasts, catching it with his tongue before it soaked the sheets.

"Emma." She felt a tap on her arm and turned toward Brandi.

"What?" Emma blinked her salacious thoughts of Jack from her mind.

"Where'd you go just now?" Brandi asked.

"I don't remember, why?" Emma shrugged and looked for some water. "Jenna, can I get a glass of water?"

"Of course. Be right back. Brandi, can I get you water too?" Jenna asked before going back into the kitchen.

"No, I'm good thanks."

Jenna left them for a few seconds and returned with a glass of ice water. "Here you go, Emma."

"Thank you." Emma sipped a small amount. "Does Jack have a favorite whiskey?" She prodded for more information about him.

"No, he enjoys all kinds," Jenna answered as she began to clear the tables.

"I think we should get out of your way. Thanks for the preview of what we can expect on Friday." Brandi grabbed Emma's arm and held tight.

"Ah yeah. See you, your team, and Jack at the gallery." Emma smiled. Brandi tugged harder on Emma's arm as they headed to the door to leave.

"Looking forward to the exhibition and meeting your husband, Brandi." Jenna walked to the door with them. "See y'all Friday."

Brandi pulled Emma through the door of Jenna's Catering and to her car.

"What the fuck was all that about Jack, Em?" Brandi sat in the driver's seat but didn't turn on the car. Staring at Emma, waiting for an explanation.

"Nothing, why?" Emma asked innocently, pushing her hair behind her ears.

"You asked too many questions about Jack. We were there to sample her food, not her husband."

"I know and I did just that. So, I asked some questions. It's called conversation. Jenna brought Jack up first. You're making something out of nothing."

"Em, you were there when I nearly fucked it all up. Don't be stupid like I was. Matt loves you; you love him. Jack is flirty, Jenna admitted it. You aren't the only one he flirts with, I'm sure."

"Maybe he'll flirt with you on Friday." Emma grinned and buckled her seat belt.

"Doubtful, I'm clearly not his type." Brandi started the car and drove them home.

CHAPTER 7

"Damn, girl, tomorrow's going to be great," Brandi said as they stood back to admire their arrangements.

It was the night of 'Natural Beauties', the title of their exhibition.

They changed the drapery to a brown tone with sky blue ribbons hanging in the folds. Emma layered the brown tablecloths with the blue runners on top of each one. Small sparkling strings of lights connected each window all around the inside of the gallery.

In the main room, Emma and Brandi hung photos and paintings with similar themes. The landscape paintings matched the photos where the couples or families lived. The cityscapes, suburbs, and countrysides. There were a few beach high-rise paintings, with photos of well-known local celebrities.

Their favorites were the large families that lived well outside the city and its burbs. They made those as gifts if the family couldn't afford to pay. Giving back was what Emma and Brandi promised they would one day do. Their community gave them more support than they ever expected.

In Brandi's room, she chose her more seductive photos. She kept it clean, with her full nude couples holding each other in a close embrace. She'd been after Emma and Matt to sit for her for months now, but Matt always had an excuse. Emma couldn't wait to have nude photos of her and Matt. She'd work on convincing him, she told Brandi.

Emma's room featured all nature scenes. No buildings, no people, no vehicles, or train tracks. Just beautiful palm trees of all kinds, even some rolling hills from locations in central Florida. She spent days searching for those spots. Next on her list of scenes, she wanted to paint was a beach with rocks. Nothing too high where she had to use ropes to climb, but high enough to get the best vantage point for a spectacular sunrise and have the rocks in the foreground of another painting. Her vision was clear.

Hugging Brandi, Emma added, "Yes, it will. I'm so excited for it. Let's get some dinner. I'll call Matt and see if he can meet us. Oh, and thanks, Ben. Not sure what we'd do without you." Brandi's husband, Ben, had joined them.

"No problem, Emma. You know I'll do whatever you and Brandi need. Tell Matt to get his ass out of that fucking office and have some beers with us," Ben demanded.

"I will." Walking away for a bit of privacy, Emma pulled her phone out of her back pocket. Dialing her husband, she waited for him to answer.

"Hey, Em," Matt said quickly.

"I'm going out to dinner with Brandi and Ben. Ben said to get your fucking ass out of the office and join us for beers," Emma laughed.

"I'm about done. I'll meet you in half an hour."

"Okay, babe, we'll be at KC's."

***

Emma felt Matt's arms wrap around her tiny waist. She jumped, turned, and kissed her husband. "You made it," Emma said breathlessly after their kiss.

"Of course, I did. I wouldn't miss spending time with you and our best friends. Hey, guys." Matt fist-bumped Ben and kissed Brandi's cheek. "Where's my beer?"

Ben waved to get Terrell's attention. Pete, their normal server was off tonight. "Michelob Lite for my friend."

"Bring another round for the table too," Matt said to Terrell.

"So, ladies, are you ready for tomorrow's show?"

"Oh, are we," Brandi piped in first. "Wait until you see the spread Jenna has planned."

"We're ready. Jenna's the bartender from Joe's retirement party. Turns out she owns the catering company. If you remember, her husband was nice enough to keep me company until you got there, Matt. I invited him to attend the exhibit; Jenna can walk the gallery with Jack when she takes a break." Emma added glancing at Matt to catch his reaction to her inviting Jack to her show. He didn't appear to notice Emma's exuberance at Jack coming to her gallery. Relief filled her as she let out a breath.

"A tall pretty blonde, if I recall." Matt winked at Emma. "I'm happy for you gals. It's been a while since you've put together a big show like this. It's long overdue and the more the merrier. Here's to a successful night tomorrow." Matt raised his beer and the other three clanked their glasses to his bottle.

"Cheers," they all shouted at once.

Emma slid her hand across Matt's lap, he grasped it and squeezed. She slid as close to him as she could, placing her glass on the table, she brushed his cheek, licked her lips, and leaned into him.

"Hey, kids, save that for later," Ben teased. He signaled for more drinks, and they all ordered dinner.

Their night at KCs reminded Emma of when they hung out and Ben came home for leave. He'd enlisted with the Marines right from high school after he married Brandi. Matt went off to community college. Emma left the area for several years. She kept in touch with Brandi and Matt. She always knew Matt was her soul mate and they'd be together. Brandi and Emma already had their hearts set on one day owning a gallery and selling their works. It took a while for their dream to materialize, and now they were the proud owners of BE Unique.

Ben opened a small marketing firm that helped promote the gallery when they held exhibitions after finishing his time in the Marines. That was his way of investing in his wife's passion and Matt put up the cash for Emma. In a sense, the gallery belonged to all four friends.

Neither couple had any children. Life moved so fast and by the time Ben left the service, Brandi devoted all her free time to her photography and now the gallery.

"We should try and take a weekend away, like the Tennessee mountains," Brandi suggested.

"Yes, that sounds fun and so romantic." Emma leaned in on Matt again. He placed an arm around her and kissed her forehead. She hated being kissed there. It made her feel like a child. She knew

Jack would never kiss her there, he'd place his soft lips on hers, then all over her body. She shivered against Matt.

"Are you cold, Em?" He rubbed her arm swiftly.

"No, not at all."

"You just shivered."

"Oh, that was a pee chill. That's all." She covered for her wild thoughts of Jack's lips on her.

"Back to the weekend away. Matt you game? I can look for cabins for us," Ben offered.

"Man, I wish, but right now I have to stay close. Work is slammed. I can't get away. Maybe in a few months." He turned and saw Emma's pouting reaction. "Sorry honey." He kissed her forehead again.

She folded her arms and balled her fists. Her face heated as she counted in her head to calm herself. It was always work with Matt. She shot Brandi a look of despair and picked up her phone from the table.

Terrell showed up at the perfect moment saving the evening. "Anything more for y'all?"

"Yes, another one," Emma held up her glass.

"Anyone else?" Terrell asked the table.

"Sure, bring us all one more," Matt said and clasped his fingers with Emma's under the table. She tilted her head to him, squeezed his hand. He moved closer and kissed her mouth this time. "I'll make it up to you, I promise," he whispered to her.

"Yes, you will," she said without hesitancy.

***

Her eyes followed Matt as he got out of his car and came around to her driver's side.

"Join me." Emma batted her eyelashes as she patted the passenger seat next to her.

"Really, Em, in your car? Let's go inside."

"Yes, it's time to make it up to me, baby." She reminded Matt of the promise he made earlier.

"Em, I didn't mean right away. Besides, our bed is so comfortable—"

"Shut up Matt and get in my car," Emma demanded. Her eyes followed him as he walked to the passenger side and finally sat next to her.

"Baby—"

She placed her fingers across his mouth. Moved her head from side to side, blinking slowly as she walked her hand down his body.

"Relax and let's try someplace different, switch things up a little. I want my dessert now, please." Her hand rested on his bulging groin as she massaged his package. She unbuckled Matt's belt. She watched as his slacks grew tighter. She licked her lips; she was ready for dessert.

"Em, I'm not sure—"

She covered his mouth with hers. Her tongue dove inside, wrestling with his. Their kiss broke, his cock hard, she swiped his lips with hers.

"I am," she said and unzipped his slacks. She teased him with her fingers, tracing the waistband of his boxer briefs.

"Oh Emma," Matt moaned as her hand slipped into his briefs and found his rigid hot shaft waiting for her.

As she adjusted herself kneeling in front of him, she took Matt's cock into her mouth. Gliding her lips up and down slowly, listening to his moans, feeling his body writhe before her.

"Fuck Em! I'm going to come. Oh my God!" His hand slammed against the door; his body tensed.

Sucking on him faster, and massaging his sack, she felt his shaft throb. Pulling off him, she finished him with her hand, because that's what she always did.

He came on his stomach as he let out a sigh of relief. Reaching for a towel behind the driver's seat, she cleaned him.

"Holy shit. That was amazing." Matt kissed her and tucked himself back in before getting out of her car.

CHAPTER 8

Matt and Emma arrived before the exhibition officially opened.
Dressed in a mid-calf length body-hugging black dress, off one shoulder, with a slit on one side, wearing five-inch heels, Emma exited the car and smiled. She slipped her arm through Matt's; he wore a black suit with a silver tie. They walked toward Brandi who was in a mini camisole style navy blue dress and Ben had on a navy-blue sport coat, light blue shirt, and navy slacks.

"Are you ready, girl? This is it." Brandi squeezed Emma as they walked to the gallery's front door.

"I'm so excited for tonight; it's been too long." Emma hugged Brandi before slipping her arm through Matt's again.

A hand touched Emma's back as they entered the gallery. Turning she found Jenna standing behind her in a bright red dress. Then her eyes averted to the man standing next to her caterer. He wore a black suit with a purple and red striped tie.

Emma sucked in a deep breath; she slid her arm from Matt's. Her folds tingled as she caught a fresh clean scent tickling her nose. She scanned him from head to toe and back, greeting him with a sweet smile when their eyes finally met. She didn't think Jack could look any better than he had that first night she met him, but he did. He made her body feel things she hadn't felt in ages. She had a staggering desire to be with him. Talk to him, spend time with him, touch him in ways she knew she shouldn't, but at that moment, she had to find out what it was about Dr. Jackson Bryant that held her under a spell.

Jenna's voice interrupted Emma's fantasy about Jack as she greeted them. "Good evening, everyone."

"Hi Jenna, Jack. So happy you could join us," Emma spoke first, stretching her hand to Jack and skipping Jenna.

"Luckily, I'm not on call." Jack squeezed Emma's hand softly and held it longer than a normal handshake.

"Nice to see you again, Jack. This is my husband, Bennett." Brandi introduced Ben.

"It's just Ben, great to meet you, man." Ben shook Jack's hand.

"Yeah, you too, - Matt." Jack nodded toward Matt, and he acknowledged him with a nod back.

"Your wife and her team have done a fabulous job for us." Brandi and Jack shook hands quickly.

"I'm proud of Jenna and her team. They worked hard to build this business." Jack lovingly kissed his wife's cheek.

Jenna blushed and said, "Thanks, babe. The night's going to be great. I need to go and change. I'll catch up with you later Jack." Jenna walked toward the hallway where the restrooms were located.

Emma's eyes settled on Jack; his gaze met hers. Heat crept through her, stimulating every nerve when she saw his charming smile. He nodded and walked toward the tables of food and drink.

"We should mingle, Em." Brandi patted Ben's arm, then turned to leave with Emma.

"Sure, let's go." Emma kissed Matt. Then she and Brandi walked to the other side of the main room.

Out of her side vision, Emma caught Jack watching her. She didn't turn toward him, she couldn't let Brandi see her paying attention to another man, especially this other man. She'd already given her grief after their afternoon at Jenna's catering kitchen. She couldn't let Brandi catch onto her and Jack's cat and mouse game. *It's just flirting,* she kept telling herself as she walked alongside Brandi.

"I'm going to mingle with our guests in my room. You, okay?" Brandi asked.

"Of course, why wouldn't I be?" Emma faced Brandi, yet she felt Jack's eyes upon her.

"Just checking. I'll find you later." Brandi squeezed Emma and left her alone.

Something called to her, she spun around, Jack's smile sent torrid heat through her. She panned the room, making sure Matt or

Jenna wasn't around. She spotted Jack, then lifted her hand, and slowly tumbled her fingers into her palm.

He raised his glass and nodded, then turned back to the bar as Jenna came up to him and encircled his waist.

Emma's blood perked at seeing them like that. She didn't understand what it was about that young man, but she knew they had a special connection after their first encounter. She shook her head to clear her thoughts. She was working after all.

Her phone sounded and she brought it out of the small clutch she carried. "Hi, Shea."

"Hi, Emma. I'm sorry I didn't call before your big exhibition began. Work is crazy."

"No worries, baby sister. I wish you were here to enjoy it with me. Maybe next time." Emma smiled into her phone.

"I wish so too. We'd all love to be there with you and Brandi. I hope your night goes well. I won't keep you from your guests. Tell Brandi I sent well wishes. And say 'hi' to Matt. I love you, Em."

"I will and I love you too, Shea. Bye." Emma closed her phone and slid it back into the clutch. She walked over to speak with guests that showed some interest in her paintings.

"Welcome to BE Unique," Emma said to the family standing before her painting of a city skyline.

"Thank you." The young woman turned to speak with Emma. "This is a stunning painting. Is this your work?"

"Yes, I'm Emma, the E in BE Unique." Emma extended her hand to the young woman. She clasped Emma's hand tight.

"Oh my gosh. I'm honored to meet the artist." She turned to the young man next to her, "Honey, this is Emma Taylor."

Emma smiled sweetly and offered her hand to him as well.

"And who do I have the pleasure of meeting?"

"I'm Mia and this is my husband, Scott. These are our children, Kim, and Davey." Mia corralled her two children close to her to meet Emma.

"It's nice to meet all of you. Do you live in town?"

"Thanks, and yes we live in the subdivision off Traver Street," Scott answered. He held his young son's hand.

"Emma, we love this painting and want to purchase it tonight," Mia chimed in holding Kim's hand.

"Of course, we will mark it sold and when you're ready to leave, stop at the front desk, and either I or Brandi will take care of you. Thank you."

"No, thank you, Emma," Mia said.

"Please excuse me, I see someone I need to speak with. I hope you enjoy the rest of the exhibit." Emma noticed Joe and Sophia with Matt at the bar, she also had seen Jack walk toward Brandi's room, so she knew she'd stay calm while visiting with the Thomas's.

***

Emma smiled as she approached Joe, his arms open wide for her to walk into. "Emma, dear. How are you?" Joe embraced her and kissed her cheek.

"I'm great, Joe. You and Sophia look wonderful. Thanks for coming tonight. It hasn't been long, but I know Matt misses you at the office already." She grasped Matt's hand and squeezed, throwing him her sweet grin.

"That's a fact, Joe. Work has exploded since you retired. I'm interviewing for an assistant." Matt threw back a swig of his beer.

Tamara from Jenna's crew came up to them and held an empty tray. "I can take that for you, Mr. Taylor."

"Thanks. I'll have another when you get a chance."

"Right away. Anyone else?" Tamara panned Emma, Sophia, and Joe.

"A water, please," Emma replied. The Thomas's each passed.

"I'm glad you both came tonight. I have your special gift in my office. I'll be right back."

"Emma you're too nice." Sophia brushed Emma's arm as she turned to make her way to the long hallway which led to her office.

She scanned each room, feeling Jack's eyes upon her. She caught him in the main room near a painting of a beach cabin, the young couple in the photograph were newlyweds when Brandi had done their photoshoot. They asked Emma to do a painting of their cabin.

Their eyes met just before she turned and walked toward her office. She heard the sound of his dress shoes on the wooden floor coming closer. *What am I doing.? This is crazy. What kind of spell am I under?*

She paused at her door, not knowing exactly why, but she couldn't move, she wanted him to touch her, she wanted to feel him press against her. Her face flush, her insides molten lava, her palms damp.

She gasped when his clean scent entered her nose. Her lips curved upward; her body filled with anticipation of his touch. She waited, hand on the knob. *Oh, dear God.* His breath swept across her bare shoulder; she felt his lips whisper across her skin. She froze, waiting, hoping for what, she did not know.

Emma turned the handle, the door swung open, and she entered her office. She turned and faced Jack. She smiled sweetly. His grin was sinful as he took a step toward her.

"Are you enjoying the exhibition, Jack?" She finally found the words to end the silence between them.

"I am, thank you. I like this private exhibit better though." He took another step closer to her.

Her chest rose as she tried to step back, her legs wouldn't move. *What the fuck?* She tried to keep more than an arm's length between them. *He's only flirting, he's harmless.* Ran on a loop in her brain. Another step and he'd be close enough to touch, another after that, and… *Oh, Christ no, I can't, I want to, but I can't.*

"Um, um Jack," Emma stammered and dropped her gaze to the floor. She had to break whatever spell it was he had her under.

"It's okay, Emma. I won't do anything you don't want me to do."

She lifted her eyes back to his, a jolt from her head to her toes went through her.

"I need to get a painting for friends." She quickly changed the subject. Her body trembling fiercely inside. She had to put more space between her and Jack, or she'd do something she'd regret. This man was alluring, desirable, and much too tempting for her.

"Are you sure that's all you need?" Jack's sensual voice rolled over her. She felt an incredible heat between her thighs, she knew he caused.

"Yes. Jack. I'm sure. I need to get the painting and give it to my friends. I'll catch up with you later. Maybe we can share a whiskey. I've been told that's your drink. So later, okay?" Emma managed to right herself. Still wanting to touch Jack but knowing a touch would lead to more and more would lead to...*Oh, fuck, just fuck me, please.*

"If you're sure, I'll see you later." Jack pushed one last time.

"I'm sure." She shook her hands as they hung by her sides and walked to the closet to retrieve the painting. She knew Matt would wonder where she'd been.

When she came out from the closet with the painting, Jack had left. She blew out a deeply held breath, ran her hand through her hair, then headed back to Matt and the Thomas's with the painting she'd done of them.

When she emerged from the hallway and began walking to where Matt, Joe, and Sophia waited, she glanced around, still sensing Jack's gaze following her.

She didn't see him until she approached her room. He stood close to the archway she had to pass through. She avoided his eyes as she walked by. Carrying the painting made it difficult to not skim Jack's arm when she passed by him. He placed his hand on her elbow as she went by. She peered up at him and smiled, then nodded. She didn't stop at all, she walked over to Matt.

"Here you go." Emma lifted the bubble wrap from the portrait she'd painted of Joe and Sophia. "Thanks." she said to Matt as he handed her the tall glass of water.

"Geez, Em. Where did you go to get that?" Matt asked glancing at his watch.

"I had buried it under some other things in the closet. That's what took so much time. Did I miss something?" Emma managed to cover her absence with a question.

"No, but I was getting worried."

"It's all good now. I hope you both like this. I took the liberty of painting this from a picture at the company's holiday party two years ago," Emma told Joe and Sophia.

"It's beautiful, Emma. We love it," Sophia said as she hugged her.

Joe hugged Emma as well and wiped a tear from his cheek. "Thank you for this. We will cherish it," Joe said, wiping his nose with his handkerchief.

"You're welcome. Matt, will you help them carry the painting to their car when they're ready to go?"

"Yeah, no problem, Em." Matt agreed to help, although he seemed distant to her. She didn't bother prodding him. She didn't want her night to be ruined if Matt got upset with her. He was usually more enthusiastic about her work. He appeared to be heavily distracted the entire evening of the exhibition.

"I hope you'll excuse me. I should mingle with our other guests." Emma waved her arm around the room. Catching sight of Jack, who moved into her area and stood by one of her cityscape paintings. She didn't meet his gaze, not this time but she knew he'd been watching her.

"Of course, Emma. Thank you again for this lovely painting. I think we'll head on out." Joe took Sophia's hand in his. Emma's heart softened when she saw the love between them. She smiled and nudged Matt.

"Yep, I'll get this for you. Lead the way, Joe." Matt picked up the painting, kissed Emma's cheek, and followed the Thomas's out of the gallery.

***

"May I join you?"

Emma froze at the sweetness of his voice. She hesitated for a brief time. "Of course, Jack." She turned to face him and at her short height, her eyes met his chest. She remembered him wearing the unbuttoned crisp white shirt under a sports jacket the evening they met. She knew under his buttoned-up shirt was soft brown hair laying nicely on his delicious pecs. Her tongue wet her lips as she breathed in his clean scent, not yet meeting his gaze, but feeling it penetrating her.

Jack's soft fingers grazed along her face, lingering on her chin, tenderly tilting it upward. *He's just flirting.* She finally looked into those fucking gorgeous sea of blue eyes. He held her chin so gently, caressing her with his thumb.

She wondered what it felt like for his thumb to caress her clit, for his lips to kiss her nipples, for his face to be between her thighs as she fisted his perfectly quaffed deep brown hair. She quivered and stepped back from him. She had to release the trance he put on her every time he stood close to her.

She took a sip of water and said, "Let's find a place to sit."

"I'll follow you, Emma." She skipped a step when his hand rested on her lower back. She led him to a group of chairs and a table in a corner.

Taking a seat, she crossed her legs, allowing her dress to fall open at the slit. *Now, who's flirting?* She giggled inside and side glanced to see if she caught Jack's full attention. She had.

"How long have you been a doctor? You look too young to have been practicing for long." She sipped her water, wishing it were whiskey.

"For eight years now. How long have you been painting?"

"Since I was a child, which was eons ago. Do you work at Seren's Hospital?" Asking him another question to keep the subject on him and not her.

"Yes, but more at the physicians' offices in the area. I do have privileges at Seren's and perform surgery there twice a week."

"What kind of surgery?"

"Hey, y'all. Hope you're enjoying the show, Jack," Brandi interrupted as she placed herself between Jack and Emma.

"I am. Thanks."

Awkward seconds of nothingness filled the air around them. Emma panned the room, looking for Matt, for anyone, a guest eyeing her work. She wanted to avoid Brandi dressing her down again as she had in her car.

"How long have you and Emma had the gallery, Brandi?" Jack asked, breaking the silence.

"We've had this place for five years now. Our husbands supported us when we were struggling at the beginning. Honestly without Ben and Matt, I don't think we would've made it this long, right Em?" Brandi nudged Emma's arm and in turn, her water splashed onto her bare leg. "Sorry Emma, let me get that." Brandi reached for a napkin, but Jack was ready with one as he reached in front of Brandi and wiped Emma's thigh, peering up at her with a tiny, but sinful grin.

His hand grazed her knee, she shivered when their skin touched.

Her chest expanded, then collapsed. Her heart pounded, trying to escape her chest. "Thanks, Jack, I can manage." She took the napkin from his fingers, softly swiping him.

"Anyway, as I said Matt and Ben, are our biggest fans. We absolutely love them." Brandi gently touched Emma's hand this time and gave it a soft squeeze.

Emma threw her friend a look, guilt twisting in her gut. "Yes Brandi, we love them," Emma admitted in a low tone as she balled up the napkin and laid it on her lap.

"It sounds like a great partnership you two have and the best part is your husband's complete support. Jenna and I are like that as well."

Emma shifted in her chair. Her nerves pulsing, her heart pounding, her core on fire. She knew she had to find Matt. Jack drove her body insane for him. She didn't understand why, she knew she loved Matt, but she fiercely wanted to fuck Jack.

Her mind and heart fought back against the urges for Jack that her body emitted constantly. Two against one, she felt she would be able to control herself around him, around Jenna, around everyone. She could hide this primal attraction to this extremely gorgeous, younger, married man.

"I need to go find Matt. He's probably huddled with the guys from his office. He is such a workaholic. Y'all behave." She winked at Brandi as she rose from her seat and headed toward a group of men.

Coming up behind Matt, she slid her arms around him. She squeezed him warmly. "There you are. Please tell me you're not talking shop. That's not permitted in my gallery."

"Never, my love," Matt assured Emma as he turned into her embrace and draped his arm over her shoulders.

***

As the evening wore on, there were many 'sold' tags on hers and Brandi's pieces. Ben and Matt helped wrap, while Emma rang everyone out. Brandi made sure the right pieces went with the right guests.

With only two customers waiting to be taken care of, Jenna popped out from the hallway, "We're about done with breakdown. Do y'all need anything?"

They all nodded 'no' and she left to finish. Emma noticed Jack helping Jenna while she rang up her clients. She'd seen him clear tables and carry trays for the girls. She made sure no one noticed her staring at Jack.

With the last guest rung up and Matt helping carry the painting to their car, Emma started down the hallway to her office. She knew Jenna and her team were using the extra storage room for their stuff. She passed by the door, sensing Jack's presence, she avoided looking into the room but knew he saw her.

"I'll be right back, Jenna." Emma heard Jack call out. She kept her steady pace. "Hey, beautiful."

Do not turn around, keep on walking.

She stopped, spun to face him. Her hands landed on his chest to right herself. Her heart exploded, her blood so hot, her center smoldering.

He topped her hands with his. *He's flirting*. She wanted to do all sorts of naughty things with that man. *Like hell he is*. She tried to free her hands, but Jack threaded their fingers together. She felt his velvety soft tongue as he grazed her fingertips with his mouth.

A tiny moan escaped her as her knees went weak. Jack's arm caught her and folded her petite body into his.

"I've got you, Emma," his lips whispered into her neck.

She couldn't move, she had to move. "No, please. I'm fine, Jack. I need to get my purse from my office. I hope you enjoyed the exhibition." Emma freed herself from Jack's embrace, she didn't want to, she had to. She quickened her pace as she went to her office and shut the door behind her. She leaned against the door, *oh my God, oh my fucking God. That wasn't just flirting.*

A wicked smile formed on her face, then she jumped from in front of the door. She reached for the knob and opened the door. "Hey Brandi, I was just getting my purse. Are we all set to close up?"

"Nice try, sit down." Brandi nudged Emma toward her desk chair. She sat in the one across from her.

"Okay, what did I do now?" Emma asked, puffing a breath out.

"You know damn well, Em. You spent a lot of time staring at Jack Bryant. I saw you. Yes, he is attractive, but damn girl, Matt's here. Be careful, I'm just saying."

"Christ, Brandi. I was only enjoying the view." *And what a delicious view he is.* "He's very married. His wife is catering our show. I'm not stupid. I won't risk my marriage for a piece of ass.

Although that ass is beautiful, even you can admit that." Emma teased, her eyes sparkling.

"Okay, yes, Jack's incredibly good looking – as well as married, too young, and married. Take a cold shower or fuck Matt when you get home. Do something to settle yourself."

"Okay, Mom," Emma said sarcastically.

"I mean it, Em. Don't do what I did, please. Stop anything before it becomes something. Promise." Brandi stood and leaned on Emma's desk, holding out her pinky.

Emma rolled her eyes. "Really? Pinky swear? How old are we?" Emma resisted.

"Really." Brandi stared into Emma's eyes.

Fuck. Emma relented and hooked her pinky around Brandi's.

"Say you promise to stop messing with Jack, now. Say it Em and mean it." Brandi now glaring at Emma.

"Okay. I swear I will stop messing with Jack," Emma said in a sarcastic tone.

"No, promise." Brandi pushed harder.

"Jesus, fuck, Brandi. Fine. I promise I'll stop messing with Jack." *For now.* She spoke quickly, shook her pinky from Brandi's, and walked to the door. "You act like I'm ten. I know what happened with you and that guy." Emma used air quotes around the word guy. "I won't do what you did, I promise," Emma stated emphatically. Jack wasn't Keith or whatever his name was. She knows she'd never do what Brandi did and that was the promise she just made. She opened the door.

"Please don't." Brandi walked by her and stopped. "I'm going to set up a meeting on Monday with Jenna to settle up. Does that work for you?"

"Yes, of course. We have a lot of work to do then."

Emma watched her best friend turn into the room Jenna was finishing up in. She grabbed her things and went back to the main room. She waited with Matt and Ben for Brandi, Jenna, Jack, and the team to say goodbye. She avoided Jack's stare. Her eyes followed him when he turned to leave. The view from the backside was almost as fabulous as the front. She quivered.

Brandi and Emma turned off the lights and locked the door to their gallery. A successful exhibition ended.

CHAPTER 9

Emma and Brandi began the day deciding which pieces they would rehang, and which would be stored. It was a big job for the two of them. Some smaller pieces were already down and ready to wrap.

"Hey, I have to meet Ben before lunch today, will you be okay here alone?"

"Of course, I will be. I don't need to be watched. I'm fifty-five years old. Is everything okay?" Emma asked.

"Yeah, he wants to go over some things for our weekend away, nothing major."

Emma nodded as Brandi collected her purse and jacket. As her friend headed for the door, Emma grabbed two small paintings and headed to the storage room when the bell over the front door clanged. Turning she said, "Did you forget—" Emma paused when she noticed it wasn't Brandi entering her gallery; it was Jack Bryant.

"Hi, Emma, are you open for business?" Jack asked as he rubbed his square jawline.

"Yes, we are. Well, I am. Brandi went to meet Ben. What brings you here today?"

"It's Jenna's birthday today. She had pointed out one of your sunset paintings to me at the exhibit. I'd like to get that for her if it's still available," he informed Emma. His smile was beautiful. It pulled at the strings of her heart. For a second, everything stilled. Captured by the heat in his eyes.

"Please show me which one. Is it out here? Or I may have wrapped it already. Do you see it?" she asked, speaking quickly as she always did when she was nervous. She glanced around the gallery.

"I don't see it," Jack said after he scanned what remained.

"It must be in the storage room, follow me. We can look through my paintings."

"Okay. Lead the way." Walking up to her, Jack placed his hand on her lower back.

She nearly fainted at his touch. His heat seeped into her, and her center became wet.

His hand gently nudged her forward. Needing to put space between them, she took several quick steps and tripped herself.

"Oh no." Emma grasped at the air in front of her, in slow motion she saw the door coming too close to her face. She sensed his hands on her, holding her right before her face smashed on the door.

"Jesus, Jack, thanks." A wave of erotic tension flowed through her while being in Jack's arms.

"I wouldn't want that pretty face of yours to get marked up." Still, in Jack's arms, he turned her to face him. His lips curved upward. He showed her his gorgeous smile.

As she breathed him in, her heart began a rapid beat. A delicious heat covered her. He was too close. No, he wasn't close enough.

Their bodies touching fully, *oh, dear God,* she froze in his blue orbs. Her core ached for him to touch her there. Taste her there.

Jack's smile grew as he moved his lips closer to Emma's.

She wanted to kiss him, she wanted to do so much with him, to him. She reached to brush his smooth face and suddenly stopped.

"You did say a sunset painting, right?" Emma breathed, quickly pulling free. She hurried into the storage area.

Standing by the door, Jack replied, "Yes, it was one with the purples and pinks. Jenna loves those colors in the night sky."

"I think I know where it is, let me see now…" Emma held her chin and panned the room. She walked to the other side and flicked through the bubble-wrapped stack of paintings. "Found it, I think. Come here." Emma waved her arm for Jack to join her.

"That's the one. Jenna will love this, thanks."

"You're welcome. Anything for a paying customer." Emma bent over to resecure the wrap she loosened so Jack could see the painting.

His hands wrapped around her waist again. Stilling instantly, she relished in the fire spreading through her, starting from the pads of his fingers. She finished securing the bubble wrap and grasped Jack's forearm. Feeling his soft skin again ignited every nerve ending in her body. She slowly stood straight, her body folding into his.

Jack tightened his embrace, she sensed his hot breath on her neck, his hard cock against the small of her back.

She froze, not wanting to move away. Wanting to turn, strip her clothes and fuck him for hours. *No, no, no.* She pushed free again and took several steps away from Jack. She turned; her head bowed for a second. Emma raised her head, "Jack…" She couldn't find the words to say.

"I'm sorry, Emma. I didn't want you to fall over." Jack shrugged innocently. He held his hand to her, his eyes inviting her to accept it.

She ran her hands through her hair, prolonging the moment, thinking. She laid her hand in his and shook it.

"It's fine, Jack. Thank you for caring. Now let's get you rung up and on your way." Emma's tone changed to the professional business owner she was. She didn't know exactly when Brandi would return and didn't want Jack there when she did.

"Will you carry this for me?" Emma leaned the painting toward Jack.

"Sure. Anything for you Emma." Jack's smile returned and his eyes sparkled.

"Thank you." She returned his smile.

Rounding the corner, putting the desk between them, she punched in the total in the till. Tearing off the receipt, she handed it to him, looking up into his blue eyes, her mind wondered for a nanosecond. *No!* Her brain yelled. Ducking her head, she said, "Thanks for your business, Jack. I need to get back to work."

"Of course, thank you. I'll let you know how Jenna likes her surprise. Take care, Emma," Jack said before walking away.

Lifting her head, she watched Jack walk to his car. She locked the door.

***

As Emma finished wrapping one of her pieces, her thoughts drifted to Jack when he wrapped his arms around her. She longed to feel that again.

There was a knock on the door. Peering through the glass, she sighed when she saw Jenna. She needed to compose herself, get her head straight for her meeting with Jenna. She had to remove Jack from her mind. Whatever he did to her, he did it good. He lived in her brain twenty-four-seven. It took great effort to concentrate on her work and off of touching, holding, kissing, and fucking Jack Bryant.

Jenna was a decent and nice woman. Their marriage seemed good. Jack was supportive, he even helped break down when her events were over. Was he just a flirt? Did she have boundaries for Jack, or did she just tell Emma that?

Emma had to find out more from Jenna and she needed to control her thoughts about him. Jack could be her fantasy; she couldn't have him in reality. She didn't want to hurt anyone; she didn't want to ruin a new and seemingly good working relationship. She didn't want Brandi up her ass, but mostly, she didn't want to hurt Matt.

Jenna knocked again, louder, and longer this time.

Emma shook her whole body and walked to the door. She stood at the door and inhaled deeply, composing herself, bringing out her inner businesswoman. She put a sweet smile on her face as she opened the door to let Jenna in. "Hi, Jenna. Hope you weren't waiting long." Emma closed the door.

"Hey, Emma. No, I was a few minutes early. I see you're in the middle of rehanging the gallery, so I won't take a lot of your and Brandi's time. Where is Brandi?" Jenna looked around before sitting in one of the seats around the small coffee table.

Emma watched as Jenna laid out her invoice from the exhibition. She stood behind her trying to wrestle with her attraction to Jack and her business relationship with Jenna. It was just flirting, maybe a little petting, but nothing to share or confess to either Jenna or Matt. She and Jack wouldn't go any further. They just had fun flirting. Innocent flirting.

She walked around and took a seat across from Jenna. Smiling brightly, she said, "You and your team did a fabulous job for us. Our social media pages are blowing up with mentions of your business and how wonderful the food and drink was and the friendly service."

"Oh, my goodness. That's so great to hear. I hope they loved your and Brandi's work as well. I know I have my eye on a couple of paintings of yours. We can talk about them another time though."

"Hey, Jenna." Brandi came out from the back.

"Hi, Brandi." Jenna waved.

"Are we ready to settle up?" Brandi asked, sitting next to Emma with the business checkbook in hand.

"Yes. Y'all are my last stop today. Jack called me and asked me to meet him for dinner. He said he has a surprise for me. It's my birthday."

"Oh geez, happy birthday," Emma said gleefully, even though she already knew it was Jenna's birthday.

"Thanks, Emma."

"Yes, happy birthday. Let's get this done so you can meet with your husband. I'm sure he has something really special for you."

"Jack loves to spoil me with surprises. Even on regular days. He's so romantic," Jenna gushed.

Emma began coughing as she hated hearing happy shit about them. The jealousy bug bit her. "Excuse me. I need to grab a water. I have something caught in my throat." She stood and quickly headed to her office.

She entered her office and slammed the door. Leaning against it, she grabbed her chest. She bent forward, feeling the pain of guilt or jealousy. She pulled at her hair. *What the fuck, why me, why did Jack pick me to fuck with? Why can't I shake him? Why do I want him so goddamn much?*

These questions and more ran through her mind all the time. She had to stop; she knew she must stop messing with Jack. *Why? It's just flirting. Everyone flirts. It's harmless, have fun.*

Emma went to her desk and pulled open the bottom drawer. She brought out the whiskey bottle and tossed back a good shot or more. Her belly warmed when the booze flowed down. She took one more swig, then replaced the bottle and joined Brandi and Jenna back in the main room.

"Are you okay, Emma?" Jenna asked first.

"Yes, thanks. I get this tickle in my throat every so often. It's annoying as hell. A little water and I'm good as new. So, what did I miss?"

"Jenna was telling me about her and Jack's engagement and wedding. They both sounded so perfect."

"Oh, that's sweet. But you need to get going, right? Maybe you can tell me about it another time. I don't want to keep you. Jack's waiting. And it's your birthday." Emma sounded rushed. She wanted to get Jenna out of her gallery. She certainly didn't want to hear about their damn engagement or their wedding.

"Yes, I do need to get going. Here's the invoice. I'm sure it's all in order." Jenna passed a paper to Brandi.

She looked it over and passed it to Emma. Emma did a fast pan of the list and nodded to Brandi. She didn't care at all if there was something wrong, she wanted Jenna to leave before she gushed about Jack again.

"Okay, Jenna. Here's what we owe you. Have a great birthday." Brandi gave Jenna a check. Emma sat silently as Jenna gathered her things.

"One more thing," Brandi began, Emma rolled her eyes.

"Yes, what is that?" Jenna asked.

"We'd like you and your team to be our caterer for our next event, right Em." Brandi slapped Emma's knee.

"Oh, yes."

"It's going to be a while, but we'd like to meet with you and your team and talk about options. How's Friday at KCs?" Brandi continued.

"That's good for me. See you both Friday. Is six good?" Jenna asked as she stood.

"Good for me, Emma?" Brandi nudged Emma to get her attention.

"Yes, that works for me too," Emma replied.

***

Emma approached Brandi in her office, "Hey, are we good?"

"Yes, we're good." Brandi looked up from her pile of single photos.

"Okay. We had a great exhibition, didn't we?" Emma's smile grew.

"Yeah, I've heard a lot of great feedback from the guests I spoke with. I think your idea of painting my photos is where we need to take our work. I have a lot of photoshoots scheduled for the next six to eight months and most are already asking if you will paint a photo they choose from their sitting."

"I love hearing that. Painting the photos will take longer, but if I can figure out a sustainable schedule, I don't see why I can't make it work."

"Great, Em. I think we should focus more on these groupings instead of separate displays. Next time the entire gallery will be our pieces paired up."

"I love it. We're going to need at least six months or more to build an inventory. And we'll be borrowing the pairings from the people who've bought them. We'll need a contract, right?" Emma asked.

"Probably, I'll check with our lawyer. Shouldn't be a difficult contract to draw up. We'd mostly need permission to display their image. Like I have for my photos. Nothing to worry about."

"Well, I'm beat. Going to head home. Tell Ben thanks again for all his help. I'll catch up with you tomorrow."

Brandi nodded to Emma, and she left the gallery for the night.

CHAPTER 10

Emma sat waiting for Matt at home alone again. Since Joe's retirement, Matt's workload had exploded. Emma let it go, she busied herself at the gallery. She was excited about her and Brandi's new idea for their next exhibition.

Matt supported her and she knew how important being promoted meant to him.

But she was lonely. She missed their quiet evenings together, she missed having Matt at home, she missed their routine sex in the bed. She never thought she'd feel that way, but she did. She missed Matt.

Emma tried to convince herself to concentrate on her marriage. She felt it slipping away.

Matt's work was slowly taking more and more of his time.

She hoped a new assistant would give him time to be with her. Time to rekindle that love she knew they shared and relight their passion for each other. It was a love no one could deny.

"Emma." She rubbed her eyes, then slicked her hair from her face.

"Hey, baby. What time is it?" She squinted, trying to focus on her watch.

"It's late and I'm so sorry." Matt sighed, his hand resting on her knee.

"Let me guess, another work crisis?" She yawned and stretched her arms above her head. She glanced down to her lap when she felt Matt place a box there. "What's this?"

"Open it, babe." Matt nudged the box.

Emma gently tugged the ribbon; removed the lid. A grin formed when she saw the deep purple dress. She peeked underneath and saw matching heels. Lying beside the heels was a sparkling clutch. She lifted the mini fringe dress and shook it. She'd wanted one for months but didn't have the time to shop. She peered up at Matt and reached for him. Her hands cupped his scruffy cheeks as she drew him closer to her. Their lips met. "Thank you, the dress is beautiful. I love the heels and matching purse. Purple is my favorite color." Emma's eyes glowed.

"Let's go for dinner and dancing tomorrow. I'll finish up early, I promise."

"Are you asking me out on a date, Mr. Taylor?" Emma ran her hands through his wavy locks.

"Yes, I am, Mrs. Taylor. Dinner, drinks, dancing, and…" His smile grew as he pulled Emma into him. "I love you. We need a night together before my work gets even busier than it is."

"So, it was work that made you this late?"

"Yes, I needed to schedule site visits, line up interviews for my assistant. Finish paperwork on upcoming jobs. I'm going to be extremely busy for the next several months."

"Please hire someone fast, maybe you need two assistants."

"I'm looking for the best candidate. And you're right, I may need more than one. I'll mention it to Troy tomorrow."

Emma yawned and stretched again, "We can talk about this later. I'm tired, let's go to bed."

***

Dinner, drinks, and dancing were exactly what Emma and Matt needed. Their long days apart wore on their thirty-year marriage. It was something she didn't like. Matt had always been there for her, never missed an exhibit. Answered her texts in a timely fashion. She worried a lot. Not about Matt, no, she worried about her self-control.

At the upscale restaurant, Matt spared no expense. He ordered the best whiskey for Emma. He knew her well. Steak, vegetables, salads, and her favorite, creme brûlée for dessert. Her evening with Matt showed her where she belonged. A pinch in her heart when her mind tried to drift. *Stop, not tonight. Not ever. Focus on Matt.*

"Matt, this is perfect. You even remembered my favorite dessert. It's been too long since we had a date night. We need to do this more often."

"It is. Baby, I know everything about you. I know all your wants and needs. I'll always be here for you, never doubt me. I love you with all I am, forever." Matt reached across the table. She laid her hands in his. He raised her ring finger.

"Matt, what are you doing?" She gave him a funny look.

"I saw this at the jewelry store and knew it would look perfect on your finger."

"Matt—"

"Emma, let me finish. It's been crazy at work, and there's going to be some nights I may not be home. And there may be some trips I have to go on, but I'll always come home to you."

Emma cupped her mouth, she gulped back tears, sticking her ring finger out straight and watching Matt as he slipped a princess-cut amethyst on her right ring finger. A tear escaped, Matt stretched across the table and softly brushed it away.

"Oh, Matt. It's beautiful. I love you so much." She leaned across the table as Matt joined her in the middle and their lips met in a delicate kiss.

"Not as gorgeous as you, Emma." Matt rose from his chair, came around to her, and offered his hand to her.

Her lips curved upward as she slid her hand into his.

He escorted her to the dance floor, drew her into him, and glided around to a waltz. He led her with perfection.

She loved to dance, but mostly to fast and crazy songs. Being in Matt's arms, she sensed his love and loyalty for her. She melded into him. Wanting them to never part.

A full set of slow songs followed the waltz, and they danced the night away. Matt tugged Emma closer, she smiled when she felt his bulge.

"Time to go home. I want you inside me for hours, baby, hours." She breathed against his neck.

They made their way back to their table. Matt waved for the server. "Check please." In a matter of minutes, the check was paid, the valet brought their car and Matt drove home unusually fast.

As she entered the house, Matt scooped her up, rolled her into him, and rushed to their bedroom. At that moment, Emma didn't care that they went right to their bed. She missed Matt. It had been too long.

After stripping her naked, he removed his clothes. He drew Emma close to him and pressed his mouth to hers. They kissed passionately; it was hot, wet, and delicious. He placed his hands around her waist and eased her petite body onto him.

Her mouth turned upward, she blinked slowly as his manhood thrust into her hot middle. Tossing her head back, she rode him to heaven.

He throbbed inside her.

Emma leaned back, reaching for Matt's calves for support as his thumb rubbed her clit. She wiggled as sensations traveled to every nerve ending.

"Oh God, Matt, yes, yes!" Emma gasped as she reached her climax.

Matt hugged her tight, flipped them over, and pumped fast and furious. His shaft bulged in her hot tunnel. The friction gave her multiple orgasms while Matt's cum sprayed into her.

"I love you, Emma." Matt breathed against her slick neck. "Only you baby." Their lips met as they ended the evening.

CHAPTER 11

"I love you. See you tonight." Emma headed toward the bedroom.

"Hey, Em, I almost forgot, I have to go out of town next week for a couple of days. Let's plan a beach weekend when I get back – east coast? We haven't been over there in a while. What do you think?" Matt called out.

Stopping short of their bedroom, Emma turned around. "You know how I hate it when you go out of town for work."

"It's a new client, I'm sorry, babe. It'll only be two days, promise. I'll make it up to you on the weekend. Pick a place, make reservations, and I'll take Friday off as well, okay?" Matt pleaded with her.

"Alright, just this once."

"Thanks for understanding, Em."

"You're lucky this time, Matt. I need to find a unique beach location for a couple of sunrise paintings. I've got to get ready; Brandi and I are setting a schedule for me to paint her photography clients today. I'll see you later."

Emma hated being alone. Not because she needed Matt to take care of her, she was quite capable of living alone.

He had traveled for work when they first married. It put a strain on their young marriage. Matt worked his way up at Marcus Construction to not have to travel, he promised that type of work was over. He was next in line to be the department's supervisor. Joe never traveled, he always sent the guys under Matt.

Emma felt Troy expected too much from Matt for a job he deserved and shouldn't have to prove anything to be promoted.

The late nights were one thing, at least Matt came home to her, eventually. Working out of town, that part wasn't part of the plan. She'd try to understand, try to keep busy with her gallery. She'd sketch more, paint more, think of Jack more. *Uh, no, not a good idea at all.*

She hoped Matt working out of town wouldn't become his normal routine.

***

Emma entered the gallery with a pep in her step. She and Brandi had a big day of scheduling planned before they meet with Jenna later. She carried her coffee in one hand and a Diet Coke for Brandi tucked against her as she opened the door.

"Hey girl, let me help you." Brandi came to her when she saw Emma's arms and hands full.

"Thanks. Are you ready to go?" They were heading to the local mall to set the plans in motion.

"Yep, let me grab my phone and appointment book. Will you drive?"

"Sure. My stuff is in my car anyway." Emma waited by the front door for Brandi to gather her things. Her thoughts went back to when Jack stopped by. She wondered how he was, what he was doing. Maybe she'd see him around town soon.

"Emma?" She heard Brandi's voice in the distance, but continued in her daydream, seeing Jack in his open white shirt and sport coat. Her fingers fell upon his soft brown chest hair…

"Emma!" Brandi yelled.

"Yeah, sorry. Ready?" Emma smiled and opened the door to leave. As she took a step, Brandi held her elbow and stopped Emma's movement.

"Are you okay? You seemed a little distracted."

"I'm fine. Matt told me he has to go out of town next week for a couple of days. I was thinking of what I could do while he's gone." The partial lie fell right from her mouth with ease. She knew not to mention Jack around Brandi. She didn't want Brandi getting any more suspicious than she was.

"You can have dinner with me and Ben. Don't worry. The time will go by fast. I'm sure he hates leaving you as much as you hate it too."

"I know you're right. C'mon, let's go make plans." Emma and Brandi walked to her car and went to the mall.

With both their appointment calendars full, they packed up and went to KCs to meet Jenna and her team.

"Hi, Mrs. Taylor, Mrs. Davis," Pete called out as they sat at the bar.

"Hi, Pete, our usuals, please," Emma said, pulling her phone from her purse.

"Coming right up. The misters joining you ladies tonight?"

"No, we're meeting Jenna Bryant," Brandi said as she watched the door.

Pete sat their drinks on the bar for them.

Jenna and her team arrived and joined Emma and Brandi at the bar. "Hey, Pete, we need some drinks," Emma called out.

"Be right with y'all," he shouted over the crowd.

Each one ordered a cocktail; Tessa, the host, escorted the group to a table in the back, quiet enough for them to talk business.

When Pete came over to take the food orders, Emma raised her glass, "Another round for us, please."

"You got it, Mrs. Taylor," Pete replied after taking everyone's dinner orders.

"Okay, ladies, cheers to a fun night," Jenna said, raising her glass. They all reached to the middle of the table and clanked their glasses.

"Jenna, what options have you brought for us?" Brandi asked.

"We have four themes to offer up. The first is Italian fare. It will feature traditional Italian food and a special dessert or two. The second is Mexican night. We can do a piñata to add some excitement, with a nice prize inside. Our third option is Greek style. We all enjoy a good Greek salad, right? And finally, we think a fancy French night would be interesting. It's lots of wine and cheese, and probably the most unique of the four. We can make it a play on the gallery's name, like 'Welcome to BE Unique and enjoy a unique dining experience.' So, Emma? Brandi? Do you like what we've offered?" Jenna asked as she laid out the brochures she and her team had put together.

"Wow, I'm blown away. I like them all. Brandi, what do you think? Can you pick one?"

"I think we need to take your brochures with us. We'll choose one or two and get back to you. We have time. Is that okay, Jenna?" Brandi asked.

"Absolutely. We didn't think you would choose tonight right girls?" Jenna looked around the table at her four friends. They all nodded in agreement.

Pete was back with the second round of drinks and their food. He and a new server handed out the plates to each one. They all began eating, but the conversation still flowed between them.

Emma didn't want to, but she asked, "Hey, Jenna, did you like your birthday surprise?"

"Oh, my God, yes, Emma. Your work's amazing. I love the painting. I'll treasure it forever. Do you remember where you were when you painted it? I'd love to go there with Jack."

Emma swallowed hard, her face felt hot, her heart tightened when Jenna mentioned Jack. "Um, I think it was in the panhandle, maybe. I'm not exactly sure. That painting was one of my older ones." Emma smiled weakly and downed her whiskey. She knew damn well where she was when she painted that sunset and every other painting in her repertoire. She wasn't going to tell Jenna Bryant where to take Jack. Maybe she wanted to take Jack there herself. Maybe she wanted to share her special places with him.

"It's okay, Emma. I'll plan a romantic weekend with Jack in the area and hope we can see a sunset that beautiful while we're there," Jenna said as she took a sip of her drink.

Emma's heart ached, she needed to remove herself from Jenna's presence. Jealousy reared its ugly head inside Emma again. She didn't understand why. Jack was Jenna's husband. She and Jack were acquaintances at best. He did pay attention to her and flirt too much with her, but she was sure he was harmless.

"Excuse me, ladies." Emma pushed back from the table and made her way to the other side of the restaurant and down the long hallway to the restrooms. She desperately needed air and to splash chilly water on her face.

She took care of her needs and washed her hands. Pulling her phone from her back pocket, she checked her email. She walked slowly down the long hallway to return to her table. She'd only taken a few steps when she bumped into a body. "Oh, I'm so sorry, I—"

"It's okay, Emma," a familiar sensual voice said.

She looked up and into Jack's blue eyes. A wave of intense heat filled her body. His smile was radiant.

"Jack, when did you arrive? Have you been here all this time? Where are you sitting?" Emma rattled off rapidly. She glanced around Jack, making sure none of the girls came down the hall to the restroom. Especially Jenna or Brandi, but for varied reasons. She knew Jenna would touch Jack like she wanted to touch him, and her jealousy would show. Brandi would accuse her of something they weren't doing, not yet anyway. Her eyes came back to his. She didn't know why she felt so nervous around him. *He's just a flirt, just a flirt, just a flirt.*

Standing straight and holding his strong gaze with her own, she shook off her nervousness and put her phone back in her pocket. She released the breath she'd held and leaned against the wall.

"I haven't been here long. How are you?" Jack stepped closer to her.

"I'm great. Finishing up some business with Jenna. We wanted to get some ideas going for our next event. Hope you can make it." She smiled playfully as her heart raced.

"I wouldn't miss a show of yours. Your work is beautiful... but not as beautiful as you, Emma." His hand brushed her cheek.

Against her better judgment, she pushed her face into his incredibly soft palm, her body heating up, his touch electrifying her soul. Peering deep into Jack's blue eyes, she felt her knees go weak.

He coaxed her down the hallway a few feet. Placing his hands over her head, he leaned in.

Her heart bursting from inside her chest, she slipped out from under his bicep, turned toward him, and tilted her head up. Her body was an inferno, but she knew he was trouble.

"It's nice to see you again. I've got to get back to the girls and finish up for the evening. Take care."

"You too, Emma." He winked at her before going into the men's room.

When she saw Jenna from the back, she stopped in her tracks. The tightness in her chest returned. She felt guilty for allowing Jack to flirt with her. It didn't matter that Jenna was okay with his flirting. She shouldn't be. Emma knew if Jack were hers, she wouldn't be okay with him flirting with other women.

There had to be some other reason for Jenna to excuse his playful behavior with Emma. She didn't know how to ask or even if she should bring up the subject of Jack. Not with Brandi there. She'd find a way to ask Jenna straight up when they were alone, or she'd ask Jack what his game was.

Her heart was dangerously close to going all-in on this man, she had to put a stop to it, or she'd lose everything.

She shook her hands as she stood back from the table. Ran her fingers through her long blonde locks and drew in a deep breath, then blew it all out. She touched her cheeks to be sure the heat Jack caused had left her. Brandi would certainly know something was amiss if her cheeks were red. Another deep breath in and out; she marched on back to her table and returned to her seat.

"Did I miss anything?" Emma looked around at everyone, smiling at Brandi.

"Not much, what took you so long?" Brandi pried.

"I checked my email when I was done in the restroom. That's all." Emma shrugged and waved for Pete.

"Pete, I'll take the check and an ice water, please."

"Emma, it's my turn to pay for dinner. Brandi picked up the last one," Jenna said.

"You can get the next one, and the one after that. No worries, Jenna. I wouldn't pick up the check if I didn't like you." Emma winked and smiled Jenna's way.

"Thanks. I think it's safe to say we all like you too." Jenna held her hand across the table to Emma.

Emma hesitated for a beat or more, then held Jenna's hand. A cold sensation plowed through Emma. She quickly pulled her hand free and grabbed the napkin in her lap. The coldness lingered for several minutes. It was a sensation she never wanted to experience again.

"Here's the bill and your water, Mrs. Taylor," Pete said.

"Thanks." Emma handed him her credit card and took a sip of the water. She wanted another whiskey to warm her insides up.

They continued to discuss the four viable options for their next exhibition. Jenna went over the lists in more detail.

Kaitlyn excused herself as the rest finished their drinks.

Emma sat back, still feeling the chill from Jenna. She panned the restaurant when she saw Brandi checking out one of the fliers in detail. She found Jack at the bar, with Kaitlyn.

His hand rested on her shoulder, they were laughing, enjoying a drink together.

Kaitlyn reached and brushed his cheek. Emma's chill was gone, her jealousy sent a heat rod through her.

Her cheeks were warm again. She caught his gaze and grinned sinfully, hoping he would leave Kaitlyn at the bar, but he just winked, then turned into the bar and resumed the conversation with Kaitlyn. Emma ran her hand through her hair and turned back to the table. She didn't want to see Jack flirting with Kait or anyone.

CHAPTER 12

At the park, Matt spread the blanket out and Emma placed the plates and utensils on the blanket. She laid out the ham and Swiss sandwiches, the cheddar cheese chips, she knew were Matt's favorite and a bowl of fresh fruit. She handed Matt the champagne bottle to open while she held the glasses.

The afternoon sun shone brightly in the cloudless bright blue sky. The park was alive with families and a lot of children running around. Emma wanted to spend as much time with Matt as she could since he would be gone for a few days. She wasn't looking forward to being alone.

After enjoying their lunch, they walked around the park to where a makeshift stage was built.

Emma panned the area for information on what the setup before them was for. She found a flier on a post and headed over to it.

"Matt, there's a concert this afternoon. Let's stay and enjoy the bands. I'm sure there are people involved that have supported the gallery."

"Sounds great, Em. We should grab our folding chairs from the car."

"Good idea." They walked back to their car, placed the picnic basket in the trunk, and retrieved the two chairs.

When the afternoon concert in the park began, Emma and Matt found spots for their chairs. They flicked them open, grabbed their drinks, and sat back and enjoyed the bands.

She noticed some familiar faces in the crowd and waved to those she knew.

The bands played music from the nineteen fifties to the present day. Each band consisted of a drummer, a keyboard player, a bass guitar player, lead guitar, and the lead singer. The concert lasted about two hours.

She glanced at her watch and realized the sun wouldn't be up for much longer and she needed that light for her drawing of Matt.

"Are you ready to go?" Matt asked as he folded their chairs and tucked them under his arms.

"There's one more thing. We can take the chairs back to the car so I can get what I need." She smiled mysteriously.

At the car, Emma brought out her sketchpad and pencils.

"Hey, Em. You're going to work?" Matt pointed to her sketchpad.

"That's part of my surprise for you. Do you see that bench under the big oak tree across the lake?" She pointed to their south.

"I do, but what kind of surprise do you have in mind?" Matt shrugged.

Emma laughed inside. She knew Matt worried she'd want to do something risqué here in the park. "It's not a surprise if I tell you." She tucked her sketch pad under her arm and hooked her pencil bag around her wrist. She threaded her fingers with Matt's and tugged on his arm to walk with her.

"Okay, Matt. Take a seat please." She directed Matt to the bench.

He sat right in the center.

"Um, no, honey. Move to one side, please." She waved her arm right to left.

"Emma, what is this major surprise?"

"It's not a major surprise. I want to sketch you, then I'll paint you on canvas. You're a trial-and-error piece for me. I don't work much with people, and I need practice. So, babe, you're my test subject." She walked over to Matt and helped pose him as she wanted him to be. She placed his arm across the top of the bench. She stepped back and took in her handsome husband. "Cross your leg on your knee, please," she instructed him.

"Like this?" he asked as he placed his left calf on his right knee.

"Perfect." She flipped open the sketch pad, unsnapped the pouch that held her pencils, she looked around for a place to sit. She saw a medium-sized rock and sat down. "Don't move, Matt," she reminded him as he looked around the park.

"Sorry." He smiled brightly as Emma began sketching.

With the sun still bright enough, Emma had plenty of light to capture Matt in her drawing. She studied him for several minutes, holding the pencil against her lips. Her eyes traveled along his scruffy jawline, then took in his wavy dirty blond hair.

She put pencil to paper, drawing his handsome face, his big round eyes. Shading in his mustache and beard, his thick eyebrows. "Matt!" she yelled when she saw him turn toward the sirens driving by.

"Sorry." He grinned and reset himself.

Emma drew Matt's chest with his cotton shirt, then his shorts. Making the lines crisp, straight. She'd fill in the colors later. She glanced up at him again and studied the positioning of his muscular legs.

Matt's calf muscles were amazing for a man in his mid-fifties. All of Matt was amazing for his age. He took excellent care of himself as did Emma.

"Matthew!" Emma yelled when Matt moved, again.

"Shit, I'm a terrible model for you, Emma. Sorry, I won't move again."

She used short strokes to sprinkle the hair on Matt's legs. She finished with his boat shoes, sketching slowly, making sure she had captured all of him. Satisfied with her work, she flipped the pad closed.

Matt went to move, and she raised her hand.

"No, wait. I need a picture for when I paint this. Please sit back down on the bench." She smiled at him.

He took his place back on the bench in the pose she had asked him to sit in.

Emma snapped several photos, then slipped her phone back into her pocket.

"Can I see?" he asked walking to her.

"Sure, it's only a sketch. It's not the finished product." She flipped the sketch pad open for Matt to see.

"Wow, Em. You make me look great. Thanks, baby." He kissed her cheek. "My turn," he announced with a huge grin.

"What?" Emma's voice raised. Her eyes like saucers.

"I want to draw you." Matt held his hands out for the pad and pencils.

"Matt, you don't draw." Emma held onto the pad and pencils, thinking he was joking around with her.

"How do you know I don't draw? Maybe I can." He stood tall as he pushed out his chest.

"Okay, have at it. Where should I sit?" Emma passed the pad and pencils to Matt and looked around the park.

"I want you to lay on the bench." Matt pointed to the one he had been sitting on. "Lay on your back, your hand on your forehead and your one leg bent at the knee, the other out straight," Matt instructed Emma.

She giggled because he sounded like a professional director. She threw him a quizzical look. She hadn't seen this side of Matt before, but she did as he said and positioned her body just as he instructed her.

Laying on the bench, she looked his way, she giggled again as she observed him studying her.

"Look at the sky, Emma," Matt said and pointed with the pencil in hand.

She did as he wanted. She laid still for what she thought was ten minutes. "Are you almost done?" she asked, keeping her eyes on the sky.

"Yes. I'm finished."

Turning, Emma sat upright on the bench.

Matt sat next to her, sketch pad closed, and handed the pencil to her.

She smiled sweetly and asked, "May I see your drawing?"

"Sure," Matt sounded greatly confident. He pushed out his chest again and lifted his chin.

Emma slowly peeked into the pad, lifting the cover a little bit, then glancing at Matt. She flipped it open and cupped her mouth when she saw his rendering of her on the park bench.

Matt broke out in a full belly laugh and hugged Emma. They both laughed so hard, tears streamed down their cheeks.

"Oh my, God, Matt. I love it." She held his chin and moved closer to him. Reaching with her body, she kissed his soft lips. "I'm going to frame this and hang it in my office." She held the sketch pad out in front of them.

Matt's drawing was Emma in stick figure form laying on four lines, which was his bench. Her long hair looked like a bunch of straggly lines falling toward the ground. Her one leg looked like an upside-down V.

"I doubt I'll ever win a prize in the arts, but I'll draw you anytime, Em. I love you." Matt kissed her softly and hugged her tight.

"I love you too, Matt."

CHAPTER 13

Emma kissed Matt before he left early Monday morning for his trip. She spent all day making lists of supplies she needed to pack for their mini vacation.

She wanted to find a beach with rocks or some formation she could paint along with the sunrise. After a Google search, she found the perfect beach on the east coast of Florida – a resort with a suite and a view. She made reservations for Friday and Saturday.

The gallery stayed quiet all day. A few lookers came and went, but no one bought anything. She thanked each one as they exited, but her mind was on the weekend away with Matt.

Emma tapped on her phone to pan through some old photos from their last vacation away from home. When she read the dates, she realized how long it had been.

"Over a year, wow," she said aloud. She smiled when she remembered the wonderful time she and Matt shared at the cabin on the lake.

She thumbed the photos back further to a Christmas with her sister, Shea in South Carolina. "Oh my, they were just babies," she spoke aloud again.

Her niece, Amelia, and nephew, RJ were teenagers now. Amelia would graduate in the spring. She made a note to be sure to clear her calendar and be there when she graduated. That was one event she and Matt wouldn't miss.

She came across some photos of her and Matt's wedding. Digital cameras weren't around back then. So, she had taken pictures of pictures to have them on her phone. She panned through them.

Noticing how handsome Matt was then. A bit thinner thirty years ago, but still the man of her dreams then and now.

A tear splashed onto her phone screen. She sniffed back several more realizing how much she loved Matt.

He'd only been gone since morning, and she missed him already.

She brought her phone to her lips, feeling a bit silly, she still kissed Matt's photo and whispered, "I love you, always only you."

***

Emma met Brandi at KCs for dinner. She hated eating alone and was happy when Brandi agreed to join her. If Matt didn't make it home tomorrow, she'd deal with eating alone then.

They each had their usual drinks and meals before them.

"So, when did Matt start going out of town for work again?" Brandi asked.

"This week. He said it's a new client and may only be this once if he can hire an assistant soon." Emma puffed out a breath in frustration.

"I remember how you hated it when he had to travel right after y'all got married. I hope it doesn't come to that again." Brandi reminded Emma of a time she truly didn't enjoy.

"Once he's promoted to the boss, he can delegate all this travel work to someone else, like Joe always did. He's waiting on Troy to make his decision. Matt's frustrated but will do what he needs to do to be promoted." Emma sipped on her whiskey.

"Oh, shit, I almost forgot. Ben and I want to go to North Carolina for two weeks next month. Can you oversee the gallery alone?" Brandi dragged her hand through her hair and gave Emma an apologetic smile.

"Yes. I'll be fine. Things have been quiet since our exhibition and should stay quiet. I can work on some of your photos while you're gone. We have that week scheduled out already. Go, have fun. Have lots of sex with Ben." Emma teased Brandi.

"Ha, ha. You're so funny, but yeah, I knew we scheduled those weeks for you. Ben mentioned this trip out of the blue. I could use some time alone with him. Away from here. Thanks, Em. I'll owe you one." Brandi reached for Emma's hand and gave it a soft squeeze.

"You don't owe me anything." Emma smiled.

Brandi and Emma waited for Ben to join them before ordering dinner.

"About time you get here," Brandi said to Ben when he took his seat next to her.

"Sorry, a last-second call came in just as I was leaving. I can't wait to get away for our vacation. Oh, you did mention it to Emma, right?" Ben looked at Emma.

"Yes, Brandi told me about y'all going to North Carolina for two weeks. I think it's a great idea. You both deserve a nice quiet vacation alone. If I need help at the gallery, I'm sure Matt or someone will help." Emma assured Ben and Brandi. "Let's enjoy dinner."

***

Sitting in her office while Brandi watched the front desk, she propped her feet up and leaned back, closing her eyes, her mind wondered what Jack was doing. Was he at the physician's office or was he in a long hard surgery? She never did find out what type of surgery he did. As hot as Jack was, she thought he was probably in plastics, specifically breast implants. Those doctors were all hot as fuck, well at least the ones she recalled from the TV commercials.

Emma never had an interest in having plastic surgery to enhance anything. With her small frame, her breasts were the right size. Matt never complained. At her age, she wasn't going to mess with what nature gave her. She had it and she flaunted it when she felt like it.

A knock on her office door brought Emma back to reality.

"Hey, Brandi. What's up?"

"I'm going to close for the day. There's been no one in today. We can go over the paintings scheduled for next week if you want. I have three photoshoots on my calendar next week too and all three are interested in you painting one of the photos."

"Okay. Sure, we can check my schedule and see what days I have open. I know I'm pretty full, but I'll squeeze them in if there's an urgency to them wanting the paintings."

"Great. Thanks, Em. They didn't sound like they wanted the painting right away. Maybe pencil them in and I'll get more from them next week."

"Sounds good." Emma brought out her daily planner.

"I'll be right back." Brandi went to lock the front door.

Emma kicked back in her chair waiting for Brandi to return. A vision of Jack in a white doctor's coat flashed in her mind. No scrubs, just the white coat, buttoned at his navel. Remembering his brown chest hair from their first encounter, in her vision she imagined his full chest with just the right amount, soft and silky as she kissed him starting with his neck, his pecs, and below...

"Emma!" Brandi startled her as she nearly fell from her desk chair.

"Sorry, I was daydreaming again." Emma smiled wickedly and shook the visions of Jack from her mind.

"You can daydream about Matt later. Now let's go over your calendar starting next week." Brandi pulled up a chair and opened her planner with her photoshoot appointments.

Emma let out a soft laugh knowing her daydream was of Jack and not Matt. "Okay, I've got Monday, and Thursday set aside for the Owens and the Patels. Did you have them choose what kind of painting they want? Oil painting, which will take much longer to dry, acrylic, which dries fast, or watercolors. I can do a pencil sketch in black and white or color if they want a rawer look. All of these options have different prices as well." Emma looked across the desk at Brandi.

"Yeah. The Owens want an acrylic painting. They may want more than one, but I told them they'd have to discuss that with you. The Patels want an oil painting, and they want it on a 20×24 canvas. You know they are both doctors at Seren's, so money isn't an issue." Brandi made a note and slid it to Emma. She wrote in the specifics under each name and a side note to ask the Owens which size they wanted.

"That's good for us, isn't it?" Emma grinned.

"You're right. It's great for us." Brandi agreed. "Do you want to go over the weeks I'll be gone or wait until we see how next week's appointments go?" She leaned back and bit on the end of the pen.

"Let's wait. I want to be sure I can manage the new workload. Especially the oil painting. I can figure out how long that will take to dry and go from there. I'm not worried about the acrylic ones," Emma said and closed her planner. "Dinner?" She hoped Brandi would say yes.

"Sorry, I can't tonight. I promised Ben the night. Call and get takeout. Go home and resume your daydream of Matt, or video call him." Brandi gathered her things and pushed back her chair.

"No worries. I'll go and hang out with Pete at KCs. He's always good company. Say 'hi' to Ben. See you next week."

**

Emma's phone buzzed as she locked up for the day. Glancing at it, she saw it was Matt. "Hi," she answered. "Please tell me you're almost home."

She stepped slowly toward the back exit of the gallery. Listening, hoping Matt would say he's waiting for her in their bed.

"Hi Em. Oh, don't be mad -"

Her heart sank, she squeezed her eyes tight.

"- I have to stay one more night. I promise I'll be home Wednesday by lunch. I have an early morning meeting, then I'll be on the road home, I swear."

Defeated, she wrapped an arm around her tiny body and swayed side to side. Not listening to Matt yet hearing him tell her he won't be home to her. She sighed deeply, then shrugged it all off. "I knew it. I guess I'll have dinner alone."

"Why don't you have dinner with Ben and Brandi?"

She paced the hallway before she answered Matt. "Because they are having a night together, just them. I already asked Brandi before she left the gallery." She balled her fist. Matt's assumption that she could always have dinner with their friends irritated her. She drew in a deep breath to stifle what she wanted to say, then exhaled slowly, counting to lower her elevated blood pressure. "I'll be fine. I'll grab something quick at KCs. I miss you; I love you."

"I love you too. I'll see you Wednesday for lunch. Be ready in bed. Can you arrange that for me?"

Emma hesitated for several seconds. She puffed her hair and squeezed her forearm, allowing the silence to go on longer. She missed him already but refused to give in. "I guess you'll have to wait and see when you get home."

"Oh Emma, don't be mean, babe. I can't help this," Matt pleaded his case.

"See you tomorrow, Matt." She ended the call.

***

As she walked into KCs, Pete called out to her from behind the bar.

"Hey, Mrs. Taylor, where's Mr. Taylor tonight?"

"Hi, Pete, he's out of town 'til tomorrow. I'm solo tonight. Can I get my usual?" Emma asked, taking a seat at a small table away from the dinner crowd.

"Here's your whiskey," Pete said, placing a menu down along with her drink.

Emma pulled out her phone from her purse. She checked on her social media and the gallery's page for the latest reviews. Lost in her reading, she twitched when she felt a familiar presence beside her. Her body shuddered.

"Hey, Emma, are you having dinner alone?"

She tilted her head upward and took a few deep breaths before speaking. "Hi, Jack. Yes, I am. Matt's working."

"May I join you?" Jack asked as he stood close to her, his hand scratching his perfect jawline. His tongue slipped out and wet his full lips.

Emma quickly averted her gaze back to her phone. Her thoughts fighting with the other. Of course, he could join her. Why did she even hesitate? For looks, to make him beg for her attention.

"Where's Jenna? Shouldn't you be having dinner with your wife?" Emma's eyes remained on her phone.

"She's at a meeting with a new client across town. I'm solo tonight too, so may I join you?" He placed his hand on her shoulder.

Emma relented quickly as his touch instantly melted her. She looked up into Jack's baby blues, she breathed in his clean masculine scent as he slipped a hand through his hair.

Her face warmed as she waved toward the chair across from her. "Sure, have a seat."

What the fuck am I doing? He's trouble and I know it. But he's surely a lot of fun and exhilarating sex.

This is wrong, Matt's busy working and here I am, sitting next to this crazy hot younger man. I should go, no I need to go.

She smiled as Jack took a seat beside her and not across from her as she expected him to do. She placed her phone in her lap and clasped her hands. She didn't want any temptation to touch Jack. That was already in her head, driving her crazy. The attraction to him was unyielding. The desire for him, insatiable. *What. The. Fuck.* She didn't know. She shook her head from side to side.

For Christ's sake, she worked with his wife. Jenna's a nice girl, beautiful, successful, kind. Was all this just Jack flirting with her? It seemed like a lot more than just flirting. She knew how to flirt, she didn't touch those she flirted with, she used her smile, her eyes, her sense of humor, but never touched them as Jack has touched her.

Emma abruptly sat forward as Jack's knee touched hers. Her phone dropped to the floor. "Oh, shit." Reaching for her phone with her fingertips, she glanced up. Her gaze landed on his bulging crotch. A wicked smile formed as a thought of how she'd love to take him with her lips, suck him, taste him…

"Emma, are you okay?" Jack appeared below the tabletop.

She brushed her hair from her heated face. She grinned at Jack as her tongue circled her soft pink lips.

"Yes, thanks. My phone slid from my lap. I have it." She showed Jack her phone.

"Hi, Dr. Bryant. Sorry for the wait. What can I get you to drink? Mrs. Taylor, another?" Pete asked.

"Sure, Pete. Thanks." Emma held her empty glass for him to take.

"Bourbon, thanks," Jack said.

"I'll be right back with those and take your dinner order."

While Pete was gone an awkward silence sat between Emma and Jack. She side glanced at him and smiled sweetly but didn't offer any conversation. All she had on her mind was the image of Jack's large cock wanting to be free of his scrubs. She squirmed in her seat and squeezed her eyes closed and pursed her lips to keep her tongue inside. She needed to erase that fucking hot image.

"Here we go, guys." Pete handed them their drinks. "What'll it be for dinner?"

"Chicken Caesar, please." Emma handed Pete the menu.

"I'll have the sirloin, medium-rare. Steak fries and a side salad with Ranch. Thanks, man." Jack gave Pete his menu. He left them alone again.

"Cheers, Jack."

"Cheers, Emma."

They clinked their glasses and sipped their drinks.

Emma placed her tumbler on the table, still holding it, watching Jack as he took another sip. His tongue appeared again, swiping around his lips.

Thinking, if only it were her nipples his tongue swiped around, her curves would love to feel how velvety soft it had to be as her eyes followed his movements.

He slowly placed his glass beside hers.

Her gaze lingered on his hand as he rolled the amber liquid in circles.

His glass inched closer to hers, close enough to graze her fingers.

She pinched her legs closed. Practically tied her legs into a knot to try and keep the wetness from escaping her panties. Emma let out several fast breaths.

Their fingers wove together while holding their glass. She couldn't move. She didn't want to move. She enjoyed touching Jack. Feeling his soft skin against any part of hers. Emma looked at Jack.

When he smiled devilishly, the edges of her mouth turned up slowly and she chewed on her lower lip. Electric pulses shot throughout her body, her middle ablaze.

"Okay, y'all, here's dinner," Pete said as he arrived with a server and a tray full of food, bringing Emma back to Earth.

She jerked upright in her chair. Her hand grabbed the cloth napkin and flicked it open, placing it across her lap. She handed Jack the other set of utensils and a napkin.

"Thanks." Jack held his palm up as Emma placed the items in his hand.

Her fingertips dotted his palm quickly. "Thanks, Pete," Emma said.

"No problem, Mrs. Taylor. Y'all enjoy now," Pete said before walking away. He didn't seem to notice the flirtatious interaction between her and Jack.

She hoped if Pete saw something that bothered him, he'd talk to her. She thought she'd stop by one afternoon and talk with him, let him know she and Jack are just friends.

Trying to cool herself off, she turned the dinner subject to Jenna. "You said Jenna was across town tonight. Why didn't you just go home and wait for her there, Jack?"

Jack gave Emma a quick look, then shrugged, "I don't like eating alone. Jenna's business is picking up and she's busy most nights. KCs is close to my office, so I stop in here often. I don't know about you, but I'm starving," Jack said, cutting into his steak.

"Me too." Emma began to eat her salad.

He nudged her with a smile. "You don't look like you're starving. You're just poking at your food."

"Okay, so I'm not starving. I'm a little upset with Matt. I came here to blow off some steam."

"I don't want to sound flippant, but I'm glad he's out of town. That gives me a chance to have dinner and spend time with you." Jack wolfed down a bite of steak and shrugged again.

"Jack, that's selfish of you. I'm drowning my sorrows in whiskey and you're happy about it?" Emma huffed.

"His loss is my gain." He placed his hand on her leg.

Emma glanced down, hesitated for a second, then removed Jack's hand. "I want my husband home with me, not in some hotel having dinner alone. I'm sure you want the same with Jenna, right?" She pushed on. "I know you're a flirt, Jack. Jenna as much as told me. And that's fine. If it's just flirting. I can play that game too." She smiled as she reached for his hand that lay on the table. She gave him a friendly pat.

What a fucking fabulous lie that is, who are you fooling, you want him as much as he wants you. But go ahead and play hard to get. This will be fun.

"You caught me, yes, I love to flirt with beautiful blonde women. Especially those with stunning blue eyes." He touched her chin and tilted her face up to his.

She jumped in her seat when her phone sounded in Matt's tone. She answered. "Hey baby, I miss you." She gave Jack an evil grin. He turned and finished his meal and drink.

Her smile grew as Matt spoke, "I miss you too, Em. The meeting in the morning was canceled, I'm on my way home. I was going to surprise you but thought better of it."

"That's great news. I'm just finishing dinner at KCs. Jack Bryant was kind enough to join me. Seems Jenna was busy tonight too. I hope you don't mind, me eating dinner with another man." Emma stared at Jack as she spoke to Matt.

He paid her no attention as he thumbed away on his phone.

"I'm glad you didn't have to have dinner alone. Jack's a good man. I'll see you very soon. I love you." Matt said.

"I can't wait. I love you too." Emma ended the call and turned to get Pete's attention.

"What else can I get you two?" Pete asked.

"Will you please box this up? Mr. Taylor is on his way home. I need to go. Thanks," Emma said, still watching Jack for any reactions. Nothing. Maybe he is just flirting with her.

"Sure, can I bring you anything, Dr. Bryant?"

"Just the check. Dinners on me, Mrs. Taylor," Jack said in a sharp tone.

Oh, how she wished dinner were on him, better yet, he was her dinner.

"Thank you so much, Dr. Bryant." Emma smiled sweetly. "Next time dinner's on me, if there is a next time."

Jack's mouth curved upwards in a mischievous smile.

She knew his exact thoughts and those thoughts weren't just flirting, *dammit.*

Her imagination went off the rails in that split second. Jack and her, a round king-size bed, black satin sheets, food all around her, on her. Jack's perfect white teeth nibbling on a snack of her nipples before wildly lapping up whiskey in her navel, his tongue traveling methodically to her folds…

Her body swayed a bit too far as she sensed Jack's hands on her elbow and shoulder.

"Excuse me, Jack." Emma grabbed her purse as she pushed back from the table.

Jack stood and helped her with her chair. Smiling politely, she walked to the other side of the restaurant and down the long hallway to the restroom.

She splashed ice-cold water on her face. Jack Bryant drove her insane. She wanted him, but it was wrong. *He's a married man. You're a married woman. He's so young... He's so delicious, so damn hot.* She shook her head to rid herself of her mischievous voice.

Standing in front of the mirror, her playful grin reflecting, she splashed chilly water onto her cheeks again. Patting them, she smacked some sense into herself. Then grabbed some towels and dried her face.

As she left the restroom, she pulled her phone out of her purse and checked the location app. She sighed, still an hour until he'd be home. Leaning against the wall, she slipped her phone into her purse, closed her eyes, and massaged her temples.

The waft of fresh cotton sheets blended with his natural scent that Emma knew too well, trailed into her nose. She held her hands on the sides of her head. Her stomach clenched. Her heart yelled. *No!* Even as her knees weakened with the knowledge that Jack hovered above her.

Emma breathed him in. Basked in the warmth of his body heat, she tried to move. The brush of his hand on her shoulder caused her skin to shiver, but inside she was an inferno. Her chest rose and fell with each breath she took. Slowly opening her blue eyes, she tilted her head upward.

His sky-blue pools of pure lust grabbed hers, she couldn't even blink to break free.

The heat glided through her folds, her clit aching to be kissed, sucked, and licked by his plush tongue. She shifted against the wall, trying to meld into it, put space between them, although space wasn't what she wanted.

His hands cupped her face, it warmed as his thumbs glided upon her cheeks.

She stood like a statue again, caught in his web, not able to or wanting to move.

His hands dropped. One to her waist, the other took her hand and brought it to his lips.

She finally blinked and held her eyes shut for a second, thinking she had to be dreaming. She opened them to see him moving in slow motion closer to her. *Oh my God, oh my God.*

"Jack—" she began, but his mouth covered hers before she could finish. Every inch of her brain yelled for her to pull back, to stop kissing a married man. But she couldn't. She didn't want to stop.

His tongue swept across her lips.

She wanted to open her mouth, to taste him. She wanted to reach up and grab him, but her arms stayed glued to her sides. She fought every desire she had at that moment.

Jack's soft tongue teased her again, she knew better, but she had to taste him. She stood on her tiptoes, pressing her mouth firmly against his as her tongue shot into his warm delicious mouth. She moaned inside him. Her hands dying to feel his hair, his body but she shook them at her side as they tingled with the erotica sensations coursing through her.

Two women stumbled into them, breaking their kiss; they looked at one another.

Jack stepped back; Emma slid slightly toward the main room.

"Excuse us," one of the women laughed out and yanked the other into the restroom.

Emma smiled curtly at them. She looked back at Jack as he took steps toward her. She lowered her head. She touched Jack's arm and whispered, "I can't."

"I know, I can't either, but—"

"But what?" Emma jumped at Brandi's voice. Turning, she watched her friend walk toward them.

"But nothing," she sighed, taking a step away from Jack. "What are you doing here? You said Ben wanted a night at home with you."

Brandi's eyes narrowed as she looked between them. "Ben decided he wanted wings and KCs has the best, so we hopped in the car and drove here."

"I'll leave you ladies alone." Jack excused himself and went to the men's room.

Brandi grabbed Emma's wrist and dragged her into the restroom. The two drunk women that broke Emma and Jack apart stumbled past Emma and Brandi.

"What the hell were you two doing?" Brandi leaned on the vanity, hands-on-hips, lips pursed.

"Talking... that's all. It wasn't... what you think," Emma stammered as she massaged her wrist.

"Talking in a dark hallway, sure Em."

"What's wrong with that?" Emma held her hands palm up looking around the room.

"Nothing, if that's what happened. Dammit, Emma. We've talked about my mess-up with the guy who wasn't. How I fell for it all. He hooked me like I see Jack hooking you."

"Stop it right there. Jack is fucking real."

"Oh, so you're admitting you're messing with him?"

"No, not at all. I'm pointing out that Jack is a real man." *And a damn gorgeous one at that.* "He's not on the internet pretending to be one."

"It's still messing around and cheating. Same difference. Please, Emma, don't do this to Matt. You miss him. Jack pays attention to you, he's a flirt. You know this, from his wife. Emma!" Brandi yelled.

"What?" She realized she'd been smiling inappropriately when she caught her reflection in the mirror behind Brandi.

"You were thinking about Jack just then. Jesus Christ, Emma. Trust me on this. If you mess with that married man, you will regret it. You'll lose the man who loves you more than anything." Brandi shook her head and ran her hand through her hair.

"I'm not messing with Jack, we were talking. You and I pinky promised, remember. I won't break that. I won't do what you did. I promise." Emma swore again, knowing what she and Jack were doing wasn't anything like what Brandi went through. She knew she'd never break her promise. Jack was real. Brandi's guy wasn't.

"I remember. I'm going to hold you to that. You belong with Matt. Now get your phone out and have an Uber drive you home. I can smell the whiskey. Unless you want to have Ben and me take you home," Brandi's tone turned to concern.

"No, I'll get an Uber." Emma brought out her phone from her purse and sent for the Uber. "Look, Mom." She held her phone for Brandi to see. "Only five minutes out. Happy?"

Brandi smirked, "Yes, now go home. I love you, Em."

Emma hugged Brandi, "Yeah, yeah. Love you too."

CHAPTER 14

Emma laid across their bed in her black sheer robe Matt had bought for her a few birthdays ago. A feather boa lay between her breasts; she also wore her black silk thong, giving Matt a small barrier to remove. She couldn't make it too easy for him.

She wanted him to know that traveling wasn't going to be something she could accept.

He had to talk to Troy and be sure Matt's assistant did all the out-of-town jobs. He was needed at home.

Emma held the whiskey she poured before laying across their bed. She sipped on it. She gazed at her hand on the glass and saw Jack's hand graze hers.

No! fucking no. A thundering sound rattled through her brain. She gulped down the whiskey and forcibly erased the memory of Jack.

***

At the creak of the kitchen door, her skin tingled. Her heart raced as it warmed knowing her husband was home. She missed him terribly. Missed kissing him every day. She missed the damn simple things they shared daily. Emma needed all that from Matt.

Her lips curved upward when he appeared in the doorway, holding a dozen multicolored roses. The roses tumbled one by one onto the floor.

Matt's eyebrows raised as his tongue lapped around his lips. Quickly stripping, he tossed his clothes into a corner of their room.

"Come here, baby, I need you," she said. "I missed you and your—"

Matt kissed Emma before she could finish. His tongue dove into her mouth. He took her breath away with his passion for her.

"God, Emma. You taste so damn delicious," Matt moaned into her warm neck.

She slid her hand down his chest, searching for her prize, his rock-hard shaft. Smiling, she took Matt into her hand. Stroking him slowly, he hardened more as she moved up and down. "I've missed you, baby." She breathed into his slick shoulder.

Matt tenderly massaged her breasts, teased her with his thumb on her hard nipples. He gently crept his hand down her ribs, her stomach. Finding his way to her clit, thumbing her softly, he slid one finger in.

She moaned, "Oh God."

He plunged a second into her wet core, circling her clit with his thumb.

Her body twitched beneath him. "Baby, baby, please fuck me." She groaned loudly while stroking his hard cock faster.

"Anything for you, Em." Matt moved between Emma's soft thighs, placing his hands on her knees, spreading her wide. His shaft penetrated her hard and deep. Their bodies smacked together.

She lifted her hips to meet him. They moved fast and furious, each wanting the other more.

"Matt, oh dear God, Matt. I love you so much. You make me feel so good. You feel so fucking good inside me. I only want you. I promise." A tear escaped her eye, but in the dark Matt couldn't see. Her chest filled as her body released an incredible orgasm. She brought Matt to her and squeezed him tight. "Oh fuck." She clamped her legs around Matt as she hit her bliss.

"Damn, Emma." Matt exhaled as he came inside her. "I love you, baby."

Afterward, they laid spooning, sweat dripping between them. Emma threaded her fingers through Matt's, kissed his hand, and pulled him as close to her as she could.

He squeezed her breast with his free hand, letting her know he'd missed her too.

***

Matt's phone woke them. Emma glanced at the clock, *six a.m., what the fuck?* He wasn't home twelve hours and work called him.

She grabbed his arm hoping to keep him in bed.

"Em, I need to take this. I won't be long, promise."

Relinquishing her hold on his arm, she rolled over to her side of the bed. She wondered if Jack would take an early morning call after being gone. Of course, he would, he's a doctor, he'd have to take every call. His job is life or death. Matt's job isn't. He didn't have to take that damn call.

Throwing on her robe, she stomped to the home office, barging in.

"We need to talk, now," she demanded. Emma caught a glimpse of a woman on the phone screen.

"Emma, please. I'll only be a few minutes," Matt pleaded with her.

"No, now. You can talk with her later." Emma pointed to the phone screen, then placed her hands on her hips. Her robe opened revealing her naked body.

"Christ, Em." Standing, Matt reached for her robe belt. He turned back to his phone. "I'll call you in a few." He closed his phone. "Okay, what the fuck?" He faced Emma; cheeks red and he shoved his hand through his messy hair.

"You're not home for twelve hours and work calls? Seriously? I thought you took the rest of the week off." Plopping into the other chair in his office, her robe fell open again.

"Well technically I took off on Friday, not today, so I am working. I've hired an assistant." Matt's eyes took in all of Emma. "That's who you saw on my phone. She had some questions about the job I gave her to handle."

"She?" Emma sat forward; legs spreading wide.

"Yes, she as in Miranda Grey."

"Tell me more. What does she look like? How old is she? Will she be handling the out-of-town work?" Emma rattled off several questions.

"Emma, you have nothing to worry about." Matt moved closer and hugged her.

"I know, I'm curious, that's all. Tell me about Miranda Grey, please."

"Okay, she's twenty-eight. A green-eyed brunette. I'm not sure how tall she is, or what she weighs. I didn't take notes like that. She's trainable and that's what I need. Yes, I made it clear she'd be traveling a lot."

"She's young enough to be your daughter, so I'm not worried." Emma smiled. She knew very well Matt wouldn't cheat on her.

He barely noticed anyone other than her.

She did her best to only notice Matt.

"Now, please will you let me get back to work and finish with Miranda? If I don't get her completely on board, I'll have to set up calls on Friday or even the weekend," Matt pleaded again with Emma.

"No way. This beach getaway is for us. I want you all to myself. No work, no Miranda." Emma switched her legs, purposely showing Matt her pussy. Her smile oozed trouble.

"So now you're using your body to entice me. Not fair. And aren't you working while we're at the beach?" Throwing her plans to paint back at her.

"I'll be getting up early to sketch and paint the sunrises. It won't interfere with our beach vacation. Not like your work could. And yes, I'll use all my resources to entice you to be with me and not work." She sat forward again with her legs open, and her smile wide.

"Goddammit, I don't want to fight, not now. I have to take care of this little bit of work, then I'm all yours. Please Em." Matt adjusted his hard cock in his shorts. "Christ." Matt rubbed his bearded face, shot his hands through his hair. "Fuck work, I want you." He stomped to her, lifted her from the chair, and playfully tossed her onto the twin bed.

She fell into a pile of pillows, her ass raised.

Matt smacked against her.

"Yes, baby, mad fuck me, give it to me hard," Emma begged. She whipped her head around to see Matt.

He lunged toward her and fisted her messy hair, pulling her head back.

She screamed again, "Yes, harder, Matt, harder."

His cock grazed her clit, he slid two fingers into her core and pushed deep.

"C'mon, fuck me," Emma demanded, her head bobbing up and down.

She felt his shaft near her core. She pressed back against him, he plunged hard into her.

Grasping her hips, he pushed and pulled on her. Loud smacks of their bodies hitting reverberated throughout his office. His powerful thrusts lifted her off her knees, causing him to go deeper into her than he ever had.

"Oh my God, baby. Don't stop, please don't ever stop. Ah!" She screamed one last time as her pussy clenched his throbbing cock.

"Fuck, Emma. Dammit, woman. I'm so mad at you, but I fucking love you." He kissed her glistening lower back.

Emma collapsed onto the small bed. She rolled over, swung her legs off the bed, tied her robe. She smiled like a satisfied woman. She kissed Matt's sweaty cheek, strutted out of his office, and went to shower.

CHAPTER 15

After settling into the suite, Matt and Emma walked along the beach. The waves splashed around her ankles as she searched for the perfect spot to sketch and paint in the morning. They walked a little past the next hotel to their south before Emma jumped and ran toward a large boulder.

"Emma, wait for me," Matt yelled, running after her.

She stopped when she got to the location, she knew was perfect. "Matt, this is the spot. Look at this view and imagine it from up on top of this rock."

"Oh, no way are you going up there without me with you."

"Not tomorrow morning. Tomorrow I'm setting up back there." She pointed to an area of about ten feet behind the rocks. "I want to have these rocks in the foreground with the sun coming up from the ocean. Oh my God, it is going to be the most gorgeous painting." She jumped in place, her hands clapping, her lips smiling wide, and her eyes sparkling with excitement.

"Emma, please don't climb up there. It's too risky." Matt's brow furrowed as he walked to where Emma stood.

"I'll be extra careful, babe. I promise. Just picture the sun rising from the ocean from up there." She pointed to the top of the boulder in front of them. "I have my rubber-soled shoes and I'll bring along a tie-down rope. Don't worry. Nothing bad will happen." She grabbed his hands and spun them around. They fell onto the sand, rolling around until the sand covered them.

Lying on top of Matt, Emma's lips brushed his. She gazed into his big brown eyes. "I love you." She pressed her hips against his, feeling his hard erection.

"I love you too. C'mon, let's head back to the room." Matt rolled enough as Emma slid off him.

She'd hope to make love on the beach, but alas, she knew Matt wanted to go to the room and make love on the bed. She didn't push, this weekend wasn't about trying to be more daring with Matt. She wanted to be alone with him, and away from home and his work.

As she slowly brushed the sand from her body, she wanted Matt to help her, she watched him smacking the sand from his body and shaking his head to try and remove the sand from his hair.

He ran his hands through his hair several times.

She thought if it were Jack, they'd be naked, and rolling in the sand. She knew he wouldn't hesitate to fuck her on the beach or anywhere. She knew he'd take her wherever she wanted him to. She imagined Jack's hands softly wiping the sand from her body.

His big, soft hands gently caressed every inch of her, those hands lingering between her thighs.

"Oh God," she said aloud as her cheeks warmed and her body shook.

"What Em?" Matt came up behind her.

"Nothing." She wiped the vision of Jack from her mind. She had to stop thinking, dreaming about Jack Bryant. *Fuck! But he's so damn gorgeous and fun, you know he'd be so much more fun than M...No!* Emma squeezed her eyes tight and held them closed for several seconds. She shook her hands, then her body, doing all she could to release the thoughts of Jack from her.

"Emma, are you okay?" Matt asked with a worried tone.

"Yes. I'm fine. Let's go." She grasped his hand, and they went back to the suite.

***

After dinner, Emma lay across the king bed in the hotel bathrobe. She had an early alarm set and was excited to paint in the morning. Matt came from the bathroom wearing the other bathrobe and laid with Emma. He tucked a wild piece of her hair behind her ear. His hand traced along her soft cheek, and to her full pink lips.

"This was exactly what we needed, Em. A weekend together, away from the hectic everyday routines we live."

"I knew you'd enjoy this. You've been working so much. I miss our evenings together." She placed her hand on the back of his neck, drawing him closer to her. She kissed his soft lips. "I miss us." She tugged on the belt holding Matt's robe closed. Her tongue wet her lips when his robe fell open revealing his manhood, hard, erect, and ready for her. "For me?" She asked innocently, smiling shyly.

"Always babe." Matt yanked the cloth belt on Emma's robe. It fell open and he pushed it off her body. Sliding his hands down her arms, then drawing her to him. "Emma, you feel so good," he whispered as his lips found hers.

Her arms embraced him as he moved between her legs. She kissed him passionately while she felt him enter her with his hard-erect cock. They held each other's eyes as they made love.

His body gently met hers, his shaft creating hot friction in her middle.

She moaned with each thrust into her. Emma released her grip on him as he pulled out and laid beside her. She cupped his scruffy face, looking deep into his brown eyes, her heart beating rapidly, her heart also ached.

She knew after the weekend Matt would be back at work and too busy for her. She sometimes wished Joe never retired. The added responsibility Matt took on as supervisor would be enormous. She knew he was capable of doing the job well but was scared of what it may do to them. Matt had never put work before her in all their years together.

***

Emma rose before her alarm sounded. Hoisting up her duffle bag, she slung it over her shoulder. After skimming Matt's lips with hers, she left their room.

Pulling out the small flashlight she'd packed, she turned it on. Darkness engulfed everywhere but her as she made her way to the spot on the beach. Placing the flashlight upright in the sand, she began setting up her easel and side table for her paints. She'd brought every color she had, wanting to capture all the different hues of the sunrise.

Flicking open her chair, she waited for the first rays of the sun to poke over the Atlantic Ocean.

Within minutes the sun peaked on the horizon. She stood and began sketching quickly, she pulled her phone from her back pocket and snapped several photos to capture the colors of the sunrise. Once the sun fully rose, she propped her phone on her easel and brought her paints out.

This morning's sunrise had oranges and yellows with streaks of white. Emma had her acrylic paints with her knowing that type of paint dried fast. She mixed the red and yellow to make an orange shade to match the photo she had taken. She opened the white and blue and green for the ocean water and brown and black for the boulders in the foreground. Lastly, she mixed brown and white to make a tan shade for the sandy beach.

Emma looked around at her setup and began painting. She picked up one of her larger brushes and started with the ocean waters using long strokes of mostly blues, a few thin streaks of green, and some white dotting on the edges of the waves as they crashed onto the sand. With a different brush for each color, she filled in the tan shades of the beach using thick long strokes.

She loved the beach, the calmness it gave her, the salty aroma tickling her senses, and the wide-open spaces.

Finishing the ocean and beach, Emma painted the large rocks, saving the sunrise for last. She made sure the texture of the large stones came through in her painting. Mixing the brown gray with just the perfect amount of black.

She checked her work to be sure she showed the shapes and dimples of each one.

Emma picked up another brush and with long strokes, she filled the canvas with a beautiful light blue hue. Looking at the photos, she had captured some morning puffy clouds. She used a smaller brush to dot the sky, replicating those clouds, wanting this piece to be exactly as the photo and her memory.

She took a few steps back and viewed her work. She inhaled and exhaled quickly, then shook her arms and hands out by her sides. The feature of her piece needed all her energy centered.

Emma began with yellow and filled in the orb a little more than halfway above the horizon. She brushed a little orange around the edges of the sun, very lightly as she remembered it. The rays were mostly orange as she used long strokes to create those beautiful lines, placing soft yellow rays every three or four spaces apart. She finally added a few white strokes of sun rays, they appeared like flashes from an old camera flashbulb from her childhood. She smiled remembering having specks in her vision after each flash went off at picture time at every family holiday.

Emma finished her sunrise painting by signing the bottom left corner, *EB Taylor*.

She stepped back again, held her phone, and compared the photo with her painting. Pleased with how she'd captured the sunrise, she snapped a picture, then closed her phone and slid it back into her pocket.

"Oh!" She jumped when a set of lips touched her skin. Dropping her brush, she turned to see Matt.

"Good morning to you too," he said. "Wow, that's amazing, Emma. Are you sure you want to sell it?"

"Good morning. Sorry for jumping. You snuck up on me. Of course, I'll sell it. I don't paint these to keep them."

"It's stunning. What's on the schedule after this?"

"Let's just wing it today. Go into the village and walk around. Find a nice local place for lunch and dinner. Just spend the day together."

"Sounds perfect."

After packing up her supplies, they headed back to the hotel. Matt carefully carried the wet painting for her.

***

While walking through the small beach town, Matt's phone rang. By habit, he answered it. "This is Matt Taylor." Silence, as he listened.

Emma couldn't hear the other end of his conversation. She knew it was work-related. She stopped walking and crossed her arms. She stared at him while he spoke into his phone.

"Yes, I'll have my assistant handle this issue and check with her on Monday when I return to the office. Thanks, bye." Matt turned toward Emma. "Sorry babe." He reached for her, and she recoiled from him.

Her lips were drawn in a tight line, her eyes throwing darts. "You promised," her voice was angry.

"I know and I made it quick. Emma, I can't ignore clients. As potentially the next supervisor at Marcus, I can't be unavailable like you want. Please understand, baby. This promotion will give me a huge raise; yes, more responsibilities, but the money will outweigh the extra work." Matt took a step closer to her and brushed her arm.

"You know I don't care about the money. Our time together is more important than any amount of money," she bit at him.

"I know how important our time together is, but this is what I've worked all these years for. Please don't ask me to give up the promotion. I'd never ask you to ignore a client's call or sell the gallery." Matt came back at her angrily.

"Fine, Matt," Emma sighed, she didn't want to fight with him. She was tired of talking about his damn promotion. She looked to her right and noticed a store featuring wind chimes. "Let's go in here. I've always wanted a big wind chime for our lanai."

She took his hand and led him into the wind chime store. Walking the aisles, Emma found the exact wind chime she wanted and two smaller ones.

A few doors down, Emma saw an adult store. Inside her body heated up. She grabbed Matt's hand and walked straight to the store.

Matt suddenly stopped before entering the sex shop. "Really Em?" Matt's hands ran through his hair.

"Why not. Maybe we can find something fun to use later." She teased and patted his ass.

"We don't need anything to use later. I'm all you need." He squeezed her round ass and pulled her past the door of the store.

"C'mon, Matt. I want to look around, please. Pretty please?" She begged and ran her finger across his lips.

"Okay, a quick browse." Matt relented to her persuasive touch. He placed his arm around her waist as they entered the adult store.

Emma walked to the aisle with the vibrators, then the aisle of dildos. She found a cock ring and held it up for Matt. "Want one?" Matt's face reddened and he shook his head, covering his face with his hand.

She walked ahead of him and to the aisle filled with oils and lotions. She imagined going to a sex store with Jack. She knew he wouldn't hesitate to buy and use anything that made her happy. Doing anything with her that made her happy. He'd never tell her no.

Her mind imagined them on the beach. A blanket laid out surrounded by tall beach grass, it was dusk. Their bodies pressed together so close they felt like one.

Jack held her, kissed her, caressed her.

She smiled at him. She framed his face and kissed him deeply.

His lips glided to her breasts and his tongue teased her stiff nipples. Emma moaned as she feathered his soft brown hair. His tongue followed her rib cage and she quivered…

"Emma, why are you shaking?" Matt's voice startled her.

"Oh." She hid her face from Matt as she felt her cheeks get hot. "You caught me dreaming of what our night will be when you massage my body with one of these oils. And use this vibrator on me. And shove this—"

"Okay, I get it," Matt interrupted her. "Get whatever you want and let's find someplace for dinner." He nudged her toward the front of the store and the cashier.

Wanting to go directly back to the hotel, Emma said, "We can get room service."

***

With dinner and drinks finished and the argument from earlier all forgotten, Emma whispered in Matt's ear, "I want you, baby." Grinning, she kissed him, her tongue slipping into his delicious mouth. "You taste so sweet."

"I want you so much. You make me ache for you." Matt breathed into her neck. He licked a trickle of sweat from her soft skin, kissed her shoulder, and walked her back against the hotel room wall. Pressing himself into his wife, he caged her in.

She brought her leg up and wrapped her calf around his ass. "Fuck me, Matt!" Emma commanded.

They stripped, tossing clothes everywhere.

He lifted her, turned, and fell onto the bed.

She frowned for a second, then his stiff shaft plunged into her. She was wet and ready as he glided into her. "Oh, Jesus, yes, yes!" Forgetting her disappointment of wanting Matt to fuck her against the wall, she made the best of her situation.

"Emma, baby," Matt mumbled as he covered her breast with his mouth. "You're so sweet." He licked her stiff nipples as she slapped the bed and grabbed the sheets, ready to scream out. His tongue drove her insane.

"Keep going, don't stop." She fisted his wavy locks, pulling him to her, pressing her mouth to his, her tongue swirling around his. She dug her fingertips into his shoulder blades, holding him tight, wrapping his body with her legs, squeezing with all her might. "Oh, dear god, Matt, Matt!" She arched her back as her climax exploded.

"Jesus, baby." Matt kissed her hard as his body thrust hers when he came. "You're my queen, my everything." His breath wisped across her collarbone, sending sweet chills to her toes.

They kissed softly, lying together afterward.

***

Emma rolled over when her alarm blared. Gathering her supplies in her duffle bag, she leaned the easel by the door and tiptoed to the bed where Matt still slept, snoring loudly. She kissed his cheek. A smile appeared on his face when she whispered in his ear, "I'm going to paint. Meet me on the beach when you get up. Love you."

Carrying her easel under her right arm, she left the hotel. Stopping at the base of the rocks, she pulled out her flashlight. After tucking her easel and duffel bag of paints out of sight of any passersby, Emma made her way up the steep incline with just her canvas and sketching pencils.

The rocks were soaked from the spray of the sea. Her body pulsing with adrenaline from fear of falling as she carefully began to climb. But as soon as she shifted her weight, her foot slid on the wet rock.

Oh shit! She grabbed onto the upper rock to avoid falling, her heart racing in her chest, taking a deep breath, she waited a few minutes until she calmed down. Slowly, she made it to the top.

Placing everything down, she unpacked her pencils and the canvas. As the sun's rays appeared, Emma looked at the eastern skyline. She sat up on her knees, getting into a position where she felt secure.

She waited a few minutes until the rays were lighting up the sky in a beautiful array of colors. Drawing on the canvas, she sketched a quick outline. The warmth of the sun made her skin tingle. The beauty of the colors and the sea made her feel alive.

Bringing her phone out of her pocket, she snapped some quick photos to capture the mixture of colors. This morning's sunrise shone light and dark pinks with touches of orange and a blush of purple. It was a cloudless morning; the sky was a few shades richer in blue than yesterday's. Her eyes widened as she took in the extreme beauty before her. Watching the tide go out and the waves calming, she sketched her piece. Her heart pounding in anticipation of the creation she would produce once she climbed down from her position on top of the boulder.

When she was pleased with her sketch, she took a few more pictures with her phone to view back at her easel. After securing the canvas under her arm, she made her way to the edge of the rock formation.

As she started to climb down, a familiar voice called up to her. She looked over in his direction automatically. She was just about to call out a greeting when she lost her footing. "Fuck!" she screamed as the ground rushed up to meet her.

She hit hard on her left side, a lightning-like pain making her scream. But as she started to slide down the side of the massive rock, she clenched her teeth through the agony and scrambled to grab hold of what she could. Her fingers clasped around part of the rock, holding her still. Keeping her safe.

Her shoulder hurt like hell as she lost her grip and slipped down the side of the rock, landing on her left shoulder.

"Emma!" Matt yelled, scrambling up to her side.

Tears in her eyes, she looked up at him. "Matt, it hurts a lot."

"What does? What hurts?"

"My shoulder. I landed on my shoulder. I think I injured it worse this time."

"Oh shit. Let me take you to the ER."

"No. Not the ER. Just a clinic, please. You know I hate hospitals." Needing to focus on something else, she looked around for her canvas. Her eyes widened. "Shit, where is my sketch?" Emma cried.

"Just forget about it. Let me take care of you."

"No! Matt, please…"

"Em, you can sketch another sunrise somewhere else."

"Matt! I don't want to sketch another."

"You need to get medical attention, now let me help you."

"Not until you find my fucking canvas." Her body writhed in pain, but her eyes shot bullets at Matt.

Sighing in defeat, Matt stood up to look around for the canvas. He had to climb a bit to get it, but he did so without issue. "Here it is," he said once he was back beside her. "It's going to need fixing, but I think it's patchable." He shook his head. "But don't worry about it now. We need to get your shoulder looked at, please Em."

"Goddammit. It was such a perfect sunrise, dammit." Emma sat on the sand, holding her face in her right hand. When she tried to get up by herself, she winced.

"Easy, babe." Matt helped her stand and gathered her things.

"No ER. Promise me, Matt."

"Okay, an urgent clinic it is." He relented to her wishes as he assisted in lifting Emma from the sand.

CHAPTER 16

They sat in the dull waiting room of the orthopedic office, waiting to see a doctor and find out the results of her scan. She checked her phone, and it was ten minutes past her appointment time. "Ugh." She hated to wait, especially for doctors, and the pain in her shoulder wasn't making it a pleasant wait.

"Calm down, baby. They'll call us soon."

"Whatever. You know how I hate it when I'm not called on time."

"Yes, I do, but—"

"Mrs. Taylor?" a voice called out.

"That's me," Emma said, rising from her seat. She bit her lip at the sharpened pain in her shoulder before she and Matt followed the nurse back to the exam room.

After asking Emma a few routine questions, the nurse headed for the door. "The doctor will be in soon."

Fifteen minutes later, the orthopedic doctor entered and began to introduce himself. "Good morning, I'm—" He stopped talking when he saw her. "Emma? Matt?"

Oh, fuck me. Emma smiled inside when she heard Jack's velvety voice, then his clean fresh scent filled her nostrils. She twitched her nose and erased her smile. She feared Matt would see and ask her about it later. She wasn't sure if Jack being her doctor was a good thing or bad. She kissed him, he kissed her, passionately, as she recalled. Another smile, a bit more sinful appeared, she quickly shook her head.

She sat straight and moved closer to Matt, placing her hand on his knee. She had to send Jack a message, especially now that he was her doctor.

"Jack? I didn't know you were an orthopedic doctor."

"I am. Small world, isn't it?" He smiled and made eye contact with Emma. "What happened? Did you fall recently?"

"Yes. Twice, but the first time was just a stinger, the pain passed in a few days." She shrugged and winced. "Then we went to the east coast so I could paint a couple of sunrises for my next show and, well, I fell again while climbing down a rather large rock." Her eyebrows pulled closer as her lips drew in tight.

"You fell how long ago?" Jack's voice rose an octave as he looked Matt's way.

Matt shook his head. "She's stubborn and determined. Is my wife going to be all right?"

"Let's take a look at what's going on," Jack said, waking up the computer. He swiveled the screen around for Emma and Matt to see the image of her left shoulder. "The MRI scan shows me you have a deep partial tear in your rotator cuff and your bicep tendon is ruptured."

"Really? Do I have that much damage? Am I going to need surgery?" Emma asked, clutching Matt's hand when he placed it on her shaking thigh.

"So, Jack – oh, sorry, man, I mean Dr. Bryant, is that what Emma needs – surgery?" Matt piped in.

"It's okay, Matt. I won't force Emma to have surgery." His gaze moved to Emma. "But it'll be your best option if you want to have full range of motion and strength of your arm again. Followed by occupational therapy for several months."

Emma turned to Matt, her face pinched. He squeezed her hand gently, reassuring her that he'd be here for whatever she needed.

"Why don't you take a moment to talk about this?" Jack said. "I can give you a cortisone shot for some temporary pain relief," he offered.

"Thanks. Just don't show me the needle, or you'll be picking me up off the floor." Emma smiled at Jack.

"I'll tell the nurse to get the shot ready and be back to administer it. I promise to be gentle." Jack placed his hand on

Emma's shoulder. A delicious heat spread through her insides. Her chest expanded, she twisted a lock of her hair and swallowed hard.

Now that Jack Bryant was her doctor for the foreseeable future, she needed to focus on Matt, her marriage, her art. Their flirting had to cease. What the hell had she thought? There was absolutely no fucking way she and Jack could be together. No matter how strong their attraction was, or any feelings that had begun to manifest. When she could, she'd speak with him and set him straight. She'd never allow him to lose his medical license for her. She'd never forgive herself. For now, Jack, Dr. Jack Bryant was her doctor and would repair her shoulder. Nothing more than friends outside of the physician's office.

She turned toward Matt with a mild panic look as her brow furrowed, her eyes glassy.

"Everything will be okay." Matt squeezed her hand again as Jack left.

"I hope you're right." She laid her head on Matt's shoulder. "But Matt." She sat forward and faced him. "I have a torn shoulder and a ruptured tendon. That fall was bad."

"Yes, it was, and you need to have the surgery. I'll take care of you. I'm here for you, I promise, babe."

"That's going to be a lot on you. I don't know. Jack didn't say the surgery was my only option. Let me see how this shot does. Maybe if the pain isn't too bad, I can rehab the injury with therapy instead?" Emma tried to look hopeful.

"No way, Emma. You heard Jack. Your shoulder has a deep tear, and your bicep tendon is ruptured. You're having the surgery; no more arguing." Matt held her hands tight.

"But Matt—"

"No buts." He raised his hand and shook his head from side to side. "I'll speak with Troy tomorrow about a leave of absence if I have to. We'll talk with Brandi, Ben, Shea, and Rob. Let them all know what you need and ask if they'll be able to help. That's final." Matt held Emma's hands together between his.

Emma looked away meekly. She hated being a burden. She knew his job was important. His promotion was important. Sighing, she gave in. "Let me call Brandi then and see if she's okay with handling the gallery on her own."

She lifted her purse onto her lap and fumbled through it. She brought out her phone and thumbed to Brandi's number. She smiled at Matt as she called her best friend to share her news.

"Hey, Emma, what's up?" Brandi asked.

"I'm at the doctors. I need surgery." Emma informed her.

"What the hell? Why? What happened?"

"Well, I have a torn rotator cuff and a ruptured bicep tendon. I fell when we were at the beach. I guess I shouldn't have gone on the rocks without Matt there."

"Holy shit. So, do you need me to cover the gallery? When are you getting the operation?"

"I don't know. Jack—"

"Whoa, who?" Brandi interrupted Emma.

Her cheeks burned as she stood up to walk a bit away from her husband. She hoped Matt didn't notice she was moving away so he couldn't hear their conversation. Ducking her head, a bit, she said, "Oh yeah, um, Dr. Jackson Bryant is my orthopedic doctor. Isn't that nice?"

"No, it's not nice," Brandi scolded. "You know he has the hots for you and you him."

She glanced at Matt trying to see if he'd heard her, but he just stared at her lovingly.

"How are you going to handle that?" Brandi asked.

"It'll be fine, I promise," Emma said. Needing to switch subjects, she added, "I think we'll need to postpone our next event. Will you call Jenna and fill her in?"

"Yes, I'll talk with Jenna. I'm sure she'll understand about the surgery." Brandi's voice rose on her last word. "Let me know when it'll be. I want to be there for you and Matt."

"Thanks. I'll let you know. Talk later." Emma ended their call and returned to Matt's side.

"Is Brandi on board with you having surgery?" Matt asked as he placed her hand in his again.

"Yes. She's going to call Jenna and handle everything. Let me give Shea a quick call before Jack comes back." Matt nodded and opened his phone.

Finding Shea's number, she listened to the ringing. "Hi, Emma," Shea answered.

"Hey, I don't have long to talk but I'm at the doctors. I need surgery on my shoulder."

"What? Emma, what the heck happened?" Shea's voice sounded full of concern.

"I slipped and fell when Matt and I were at the beach. I'll be fine. I'll fill you in on the date and time when I schedule the surgery."

"Okay, Em. Take care of yourself. I'm sure Matt will take care of you too. Call me later."

"I will. Bye." Emma ended the call and put her phone back in her purse. She leaned into Matt.

"While you were talking with Brandi and Shea, I thought about us taking a trip before you go under." Matt smiled.

"Where?" Emma perked up. She'd love to get away from here with Matt and away from Jack.

"How does Las Vegas sound?"

"Oh, my God, yes." Emma threw her arms around Matt and screamed out in pain. She released him quickly after she hugged him and grabbed her arm.

She bent over massaging her shoulder as the door opened to Jack. Seeing the capped needle in his hand, she swallowed hard and pinched her eyes tight.

CHAPTER 17

They landed in Las Vegas in the wee hours of the morning. Emma was excited to get far away from Matt's work schedule that got busier and busier every day. It took him away from her more and more.

As Emma stepped off the escalator, she saw a man dressed in a suit with an iPad that read, 'Mr. & Mrs. Matthew Taylor.' She let out a tiny squeal of delight. "A limousine." Turning to Matt, she hugged him tight.

"You spoil me so much, Matthew Taylor," Emma said as she grinned.

A sadness washed over his features before he smiled. Her heart clenched, knowing he was thinking of his mom. She was the last one to have called him by his proper full name.

"You're worth it, besides, we don't splurge often enough. Let's make this trip the best one yet," Matt said softly before walking up to the man in the suit with the iPad. "Hi, I'm Matthew Taylor. This is my wife, Emma."

"Good morning, Mr. & Mrs. Taylor. Welcome to Las Vegas. I'm Pauly. Allow me to assist you with your luggage, sir."

"Thanks, Pauly," Matt replied, following him outside.

Emma cozied up close to Matt. Her shoulder ached with enormous pain; the shot Jack gave her wore off. She tossed back some Tylenol with her first sip of champagne.

While the limo made its way to the Bellagio, Emma watched the casino buildings passing by. Excitement bubbled up inside her. She couldn't wait to hit the casino floor and play.

Pauly drove the limo up to the front of the Bellagio Casino and Hotel. He opened Emma's door and greeted her once again. "Welcome to the Bellagio, Mrs. Taylor. I hope you enjoy your stay."

"Thank you, Pauly."

"You're welcome. Good luck; you too, Mr. Taylor."

Matt nodded as he took their luggage and handed Pauly a tip. They waited for the bellhop to assist them.

A man in a red uniform walked out the large doors of the hotel. "Welcome to the Bellagio, I'm Jose. I'll help you and your wife get checked in and up to your room."

"Hello, Jose, nice to meet you." Emma extended her hand to him. Matt shook Jose's hand before walking into the lobby. Looking up, Emma spun herself around. The Chihuly ceiling arrangement amazed her. She brought out her iPhone and snapped several photos.

After checking in and getting settled in their room, Emma turned to Matt and said, "Let's go play."

"Sure, babe. Give me a few minutes to check in with the office and I'll be all yours, promise."

Her smile fell. "Wait, what? It's too early for anyone to be at your office. Who are you checking in with?" Emma's arms folded across her body.

"I'm just checking in with Miranda. I need to touch base with her daily. Remember that promotion is on the line. It'll be a few minutes tops."

"Whatever. This is supposed to be our vacation. It's not a vacation if you're checking in with work." Emma pushed her lower lip out and plopped onto the end of the bed. She thought this vacation would be different. No work, but alas, it was going to be like all the others. Sighing, she fell back onto the bed while Matt made his call in the other room.

Closing her eyes, she drifted to a field of roses. The rich, soft aroma tickled her senses, the petals felt like feathers on her skin. His fingertips gently drew along her curves. His face was in shadow, but she knew by the clean fresh scent who he was. Her tongue wet her lips as her chest filled when his hand traveled between her thighs.

His soft lips grazed hers. His breath was warm, sweet like sugar.

She wanted to touch him, feel his body, but she couldn't move. She just smiled as she watched him, felt him cause wave after wave of orgasms...

"Emma." She bolted up at the sound of Matt's voice and grasped her arm as knife-like pain shot through her.

"Why did you yell?" she asked with an ache in her voice.

"Because you didn't answer after calling out your name three times. Are you okay? Your shoulder hurts, doesn't it?"

"A little." Annoyed she asked, "Are you finally done talking to Miranda?"

"Yes, I'm done with work for the day. Now I can play. Are you ready?"

"I was ready thirty minutes ago. Matt, you promised this was our vacation. No more work, I mean it. Promise me, no more work."

"I promise I'll try. You want me to get that promotion, right?"

"Of course, I do. I can't believe you even asked me." Emma puffed out a hard breath.

"Well, then I'll need to check in with Miranda daily. I'll do my best to keep it under thirty minutes. That's my promise." Matt leaned to kiss Emma, but she turned away. "C'mon baby, let's go play." He kissed her cheek and pulled her up from the bed. He coaxed her into a better mood when he patted her ass and kissed her neck.

"You keep that up and we'll play right here in the room, fuck the casino." Emma smiled seductively and pinched Matt's ass.

"Later, baby. That's a promise I can keep."

Emma slid her hand into Matt's, and they went down to the casino floor. She needed coffee first, so she waved to a server nearby. "Coffee, please. Matt do you..." She looked to her left he wasn't beside her where he'd been a second ago.

She smiled at the young woman. "I'm sorry. I seemed to have lost my husband. Just the coffee, for now, thanks." The server left Emma. She blew out a breath. "Matt." She yelled. Nothing. Her face grew hot as she stood with folded arms waiting on her coffee. She walked around a bank of slot machines, not wanting to wander far from where the server would return. No Matt in her general area. Her blood boiled. She plopped into a seat and waited for whichever came to her first, the coffee or Matt.

After several minutes, the young woman returned with Emma's black coffee. "Thanks." She handed her a tip and decided to search for Matt. He couldn't have gone far and what the fuck was he doing?

She went up and down several banks of slots when she finally heard Matt's voice. "Yeah, Miranda. I won't be back for several more days. I'll call you as soon as we land."

What. The. Fuck! She gripped her cup tight; her knuckles were white. Her face heated up. She stayed behind the machine until she saw Matt end the call, then walked up to him. "You're still working?" she bit out. Her lips pursed.

"Sorry, babe. It won't happen again. Let's go play." Matt tried to distract Emma as he looped his arm around hers and began walking.

She stopped dead in her tracks. "No sir. I'll give you the early morning check-in with Miranda, but no more calls during our fucking vacation." Emma pulled away from Matt. Her shoulder writhed in pain; tears slipped from her eyes. Her heart hurt.

Jack would never do this, a voice whispered. "No, he wouldn't," Emma said aloud.

"What, Em. Who wouldn't?" Matt asked touching her uninjured side.

"Nothing. Please no more work, Matt. I want us to share the trip. If you're working, then we should've stayed home." She crossed her arms and pouted.

"Okay, and you're right. No more work." He slid his phone into the back pocket of his jeans. "Let's find a slot machine we can play together." He locked his fingers with hers and they walked around until they found a machine to share.

***

After dinner on their third night in Las Vegas, Emma heard Matt on his phone again. "Okay, thanks so much. She's going to love it." That was all she heard him say.

"Really Matt." Emma stood in the doorway between the living room and the bedroom of their suite.

"What. It wasn't work," he whined.

"Okay, sure." She turned and went into the bathroom. She needed to soak to escape on her own if Matt continued to work. She turned on the water faucet in the big bathtub and poured in lavender oil, then some bubble bath. While the tub filled, she called Shea.

"Hi Em. How's Vegas?"

"It's fine," Emma sighed.

"What's wrong. I thought you loved Vegas. Are you losing your ass on those damn slots?" Shea laughed.

"No, I've won some money this time."

"Then what's wrong. You sound like you've lost your best friend. Talk to me," Shea coaxed.

"It's Matt. He's on his phone with work every morning for check-in with Miranda and then I've caught him on it several times during the day." She ran her hand through the bubbles forming in the tub.

"Emma, you're overreacting. Enjoy your time out there with your husband. Stop fretting the little shit."

"It's not a vacation if he's working, Shea," Emma argued.

"Yes, it can be. Rob takes calls when we vacation. It's no big deal."

"Maybe to you it's not a big deal. For me it is. I wanted this vacation for us, before my surgery. Before I'm completely dependent on everyone." Emma blew out a breath as she sat on the edge of the tub, testing the water temperature. "I'm sorry to bother you. My tub is waiting."

"Please, Em. Enjoy the couple of days y'all have left there. We'll talk when you get home. I gotta run."

"Okay, bye Shea." Emma pressed the red phone icon and laid her phone on the vanity.

She let her robe fall to the floor by the tub. She tipped her toe in the hot water and slowly submerged herself into the soft bubbles and lavender oil-water.

Resting her head back on a pillow, she drew in a deep breath and closed her eyes. She faintly heard Matt talking again but didn't bother trying to discern what he said. She went searching for a young, tall, brown hair, blue-eyed man in her dreams. That man she knew wouldn't allow her to ever bathe alone.

"Jack," she whispered as her hand slid between her legs. Her fingers gently rubbed her clit. "Jack," saying his name aloud. She rubbed herself faster, harder as Jack appeared in her mind. He climbed into the tub with her, took her hand from her, and slid his fingers into her. In her fantasy Jack made her come many times. She released all the anger and frustrations she had bottled up inside from Matt's incessant work phone calls.

***

On their last night in Las Vegas, upon their approach to their room, Emma slowed her pace.

Matt slowed, waiting for her to catch up to him. When he placed his arm around her, she gazed into his eyes.

"I hate that this is our last night here. Back to reality tomorrow and the unknown of how I'll recover from my shoulder surgery. I won't lie, Matt. I'm scared as hell. You know how I hate anesthesia, how I always have a tough time waking back up. Why did I go up on those damn rocks? What was I thinking? All for a sunrise painting."

"I promise you'll be fine. Good as new once the surgery and therapy are done. I trust Dr. Bryant. Have faith in him."

"Okay, I'll try to have faith in him, but I'm scared. Not just about the surgery. I'm scared your work will pull you away from me. Miranda will call and you'll leave me. Matt, please don't do that to me. I'm going to need your undivided attention. If you can't do that, then I need to postpone the surgery." She faced Matt with a stern look of worry.

"Of course, I'll be there for you. My God, Em. You're my world. You come first. Always." Matt embraced Emma softly, kissed her forehead.

She cringed. "I hope so Matt. I do."

Walking to their door, Emma waved her phone to unlock it. She opened the door, what she saw made her turn immediately around to Matt. "What the—"

His lips covered hers and his arms embraced her. He lifted her.

She encircled his body with her legs and arms as he walked them into the suite's bedroom, then gingerly placed her down.

"Surprise. I wanted our last night here to be special. This is what I was on the phone for yesterday. It wasn't work, baby."

She felt a pinch of remorse for being mad with Matt. He wasn't on the phone with Miranda after all, he'd been planning this for her. "I'm sorry I was mad at you." Sorrow crossed her face. "This is amazing, so many rose petals." She breathed in the aroma as she sat on the edge of the bed. "Matt Taylor, what do you have planned for me?" Emma lifted Matt's chin as he knelt on the floor before her.

"Close your eyes, baby. Let me make love to you." Matt walked his hands between her thighs and to her panties.

She leaned down. Cradling his face, she touched his lips with hers. Her tongue entered his warm and delectable mouth, tasting him in a soft, tender kiss.

Reaching around her, he unzipped her dress and slowly stripped it from her body. He made short work of removing her bra and tossed it aside.

Sitting naked on the bed, her legs spread, she invited Matt to take her, do with her as he wanted.

As he kissed his way to her center, she squirmed under his grip. His soft tongue traveled to her folds, licking his way to her clit. He sucked on her softly. Sliding his tongue into her wet core, he tasted her as she moaned and screamed.

Clenching her thighs around his scruffy yet soft face, she arched her back and came apart on a cry.

After he wiped his damp face on the sheets, he moved onto her trembling body. She shook when his rock-hard member grazed her thigh.

"Oh, baby take me," Emma moaned.

Matt slowly entered her hot, wet tunnel. His body met hers with loud smacks.

She raised her legs straight over his shoulders.

He spread her wide into a V and thrust his hips forward and back.

"Matt, Matt! Oh, Jesus, baby, yes, yes," she groaned as he lifted her ass from the bed. She had pressure on her shoulder, but she didn't care. "Yes, harder baby," she screamed loud to let the pain out as well. She closed her legs around Matt's neck, crossing her ankles behind his head. She ignored the excruciating pain emitting from her shoulder pressing into the bed.

Matt plunged deeper and harder into her over and over. "God, Emma, I can't hold out, baby. I'm coming," Matt announced as she clenched her legs tighter around his neck. One last plunge and one last squeeze, they both climaxed and collapsed onto the bed. He laid to her side; their bodies bathed in sweat.

CHAPTER 18

They arrived at the surgery center on the morning of her surgery. Her nerves and anxiety ran high.

"Morning Matt. Emma, are you ready?" Brandi asked as she met them out front.

"Have to be. I'm glad you're here to keep Matt company. Jack said it would only take a few hours. I hope he's right."

"You're going to be fine," Matt spoke up as he held the door for the ladies. The three of them took seats after Emma checked in.

"I'm scared." Emma looked at Matt, her eyes filled with tears.

"It's going to be okay. I'll be here when you wake up. Dr. Bryant will fix everything, then your occupational therapist will get you through therapy. I'll be with you every step of the way, I promise," Matt said. He leaned over and kissed her.

"I'll be here. Ben too. We can postpone our vacation if you want." Brandi offered.

"Absolutely not. You postponed it once already. Y'all go and enjoy. We closed the gallery for the two weeks I'll be stuck to the ice chest twenty-four-seven anyway. Matt can help me at night, and I can care for myself during the day. Also, Shea wants to come and help, so we can call her if need be. Please, Brandi, don't postpone again for me."

"Okay, we'll go—" Brandi stopped as a voice called out.

"Emma Taylor?"

Standing, she answered, "Yes."

"Hi, I'm Tracy, your pre-op nurse. If you'll follow me, I'll be getting you ready for surgery." Looking at Brandi, she added,

"You'll have to wait here. I can only take one person to be with Emma in the pre-op room."

Taking a deep breath, Emma hugged Brandi before following Tracy through the double doors and down a long hallway that led to the pre-op room. A curtain-enclosed bay with a hospital bed sat in front of her, a gown on top of it.

"Okay, change into the gown, open in the front, please. Do you need a warm blanket?" Tracy asked Emma.

"Yes, please, it's kind of cold in here." Emma hugged her tiny body.

"I'll have one brought over. Now let's get you settled and ready for the anesthesiologist. He'll be here in a few minutes. Mr. Taylor, you may have a seat over there." Tracy directed Matt to an empty chair near the top of Emma's bed. She left Emma to change. Matt placed Emma's clothes in the plastic bag, and they waited on Tracy's return.

"Here you go, Emma." Tracy held a warm blanket for her.

"Oh, thanks so much." She wrapped herself uptight.

"I need to get your vitals before they put you on a relaxation medicine." Tracy placed the blood pressure cuff around Emma's bicep, then took her temperature and pulse.

Lying back, Emma did her best to remain calm.

Matt squeezed her hand and relief filled her body.

She smiled at him.

He leaned down and kissed her softly.

"All done. Your anesthesiologist will be in shortly. Dr. Bryant will be in as well," Tracy said as she left them alone.

Several minutes went by before she heard his familiar voice.

"How's my patient?" Jack appeared before her, dressed in his green scrubs, holding her chart, and writing something.

Emma managed a weak smile. "I'm okay, a little terrified, but okay."

"Don't worry, Emma. You'll be done in a few hours and home by dinner, I promise. Now, what am I doing for you today?" Jack asked.

"You're repairing my rotator cuff and bicep tendon on my left shoulder and arm," Emma said.

"That's right. I need to initial your shoulder and then I'll see you in my O.R. in a few minutes. I'll come to get Matt as soon as

I'm done and explain how your surgery went," Jack said. When he glanced at Matt, Matt nodded.

Emma looked over at Matt, worry all over her face as Jack initialed her arm. Moving his seat closer to her bed, he brushed his fingers across her cheek. He held her hand as Jack left and the anesthesiologist came in.

"Hello, Mrs. Taylor. I'm Tom, your anesthesiologist for your surgery today. I'm going to give you a little relaxation medicine, then a nerve block in your neck. You won't be able to feel your left arm afterward, so don't be alarmed. It's completely normal."

Her hand tightened on Matt's. Once she had a terrible reaction to anesthesia and worried each time after that she'd have that same reaction. She worried about her recovery from this huge surgery, would she be okay? Would Matt be there for her? When could she draw and paint again? All these questions and worries floated through her mind. Her face filled with angst, her lips closed tight, her chest rose and fell quickly.

"You'll be fine. Please stop worrying. Dr. Bryant said it'll only be a few hours at most. Breathe slowly, baby, breathe." Matt stroked her arm. Holding on to the comforting feeling of his presence, she gave a small nod.

As Tom approached, she closed her eyes tight to avoid seeing the needle. There was a tiny sharp sting in her neck, causing her to flinch. "There, I'm done. See you in the O.R."

She was a bit woozy and couldn't feel or move her left arm at all. Once Tom left, she said to Matt, "I'm scared. This is a big deal."

"Yes, it is, but I'll be here, and Brandi and Ben will be back to help in no time. I've got this covered even though I may have to work a week out of town every month—"

"Wait, what did you say?" Emma stared at Matt.

"I don't have the details yet, but I might have to work out of town more than I want. But I'll be here for you all I can." Matt pinched his face, waiting for Emma's response.

"Work out of town every month? You're telling me this now? Right before I'm going into major shoulder surgery. How long, Matt? How fucking long?" Emma's blood pressure monitors beeped.

Matt recoiled. He brought his finger to his face and covered his mouth to shoosh her. "Baby, calm down, not so loud. It's fine. I won't miss anything important. I've got this. It's part of the promotion I'm vying for, remember? I'll be sure to have Shea come down. We'll be fine. You'll be fine. Just calm down and let's get this surgery done, honey."

"No, I..." She took a deep breath. She wanted to continue their conversation, but the curtain flew open.

Tracy appeared and said, "We're ready for you, Emma. Are you ready?"

"As I'll ever be," Emma said, scowling at Matt.

He leaned down and kissed her forehead. "I love you, Emma. I'll be here when you wake up, I promise."

"You better be. We have a lot to talk about now," she said as Tracy and another nurse rolled her bed down the hall.

She couldn't believe Matt had dropped such news on her right before surgery. He'd promised her it would only be those two days. A week or more a month wasn't something she could live with. It was news he could have shared days ago.

Her bed hit the double O.R. doors as she was wheeled over to the operating table.

"I'm Rose, your O.R. nurse. Scoot on over here for me, Mrs. Taylor." Rose patted the operating table.

"Okay." Emma did her best to get onto the thin table. It was very cold, but she managed.

"Ready to go?" Tom asked. Emma gave him a weak smile. He placed a mask over her nose and mouth.

Just before Emma went under, Jack appeared above her. "I've got you, Emma. I'll make you all better, I promise. Now close those beautiful blue eyes for me so we can get started." He smiled as he touched her stomach.

She inhaled deeply, closed her eyes, and faded off to sleep.

***

Emma woke up in bed, her arm in a sling. She was attached to the ice chest with a pad on her shoulder that kept it cold to prevent swelling. She wasn't looking forward to being attached to it twenty-four-seven, but she knew it was for the best.

"Matt?" she called out in the dark of the room. The light switched on.

"Hey, you're finally awake. How do you feel?"

"Okay, I guess. I'm thirsty. Will you get me some water?"

"Sure, I'll be right back." Smiling reassuringly, he left. A few minutes later, he came back with a plastic cup of water, sat beside her, and ran his fingers through her hair. He leaned close and kissed her cheek. "Your surgery went longer than Dr. Bryant had expected, but he was able to repair your rotator cuff and bicep tendon. You need to keep the bandages on for five days, then I'll help you shower, and we can put Band-Aids on until you see him in two weeks."

"Did something go wrong? Is that why it took longer?" Emma asked, worried about what had happened to her.

"Nothing went wrong. Your tear was deeper than the MRI revealed. Dr. Bryant feels you'll recover fine."

"Okay." She struggled to keep her eyes open, and her entire body felt sluggish.

"And I called Shea. She mentioned coming to help. I told her I was taking a leave for these next two weeks."

She breathed out slowly, happy he wasn't leaving her. "Okay." Emma tried to roll onto her side, too tired to tell him thank you, but the connection to her ice chest stopped her.

"Em, you have to lie on your back. I know how you hate laying like that, but for now, you have to." Matt helped adjust her.

"Okay…" Closing her eyes, Emma fell asleep.

***

She woke up to darkness. She tried to move but couldn't. *Fuck, the ice chest.* "Matt," she whispered. He didn't answer. "Matt," she said, raising her voice. She heard him snoring. She hated waking him, maybe she could go by herself. She tried moving again and realized she wasn't in their bed. "Matt!" she yelled.

"What, oh, uh, what Em, what's wrong?" A light flickered as she heard a click.

"Where am I? Why am I not at home?"

"Shit, fuck," Matt said.

"Where are we?" her voice quivering.

"Em, you're fine. We're at the hospital. And before you go off on me, it was for precautions. I'm sure you'll be allowed to go home today." The light came on fully and she saw the recliner Matt was sleeping in. He stood by her bed gazing lovingly at her. "What do you need, baby?"

"I need to use the bathroom." She hated asking for help.

"Okay, hold on." He helped her slide her legs over the edge, then placed his arm around her waist.

She stood still for a few seconds. Her legs were weak, but she managed to move them. "Thank you," Emma said softly as she placed her hand in his.

He guided her to the bathroom. "You don't need to thank me; this is what I'm supposed to do." Matt held onto her as she walked slowly to the bathroom. He waited by the door for her to finish, then walked her back to bed.

***

The morning sun woke Emma. She heard voices on the other side of the hospital room door. "Matt," she called out.

The door swung open. Matt entered and Brandi followed. "Good morning, sunshine. Look who came to visit."

Walking over to Emma with a bouquet, Brandi held out her hand. Emma took it and squeezed it. She smiled weakly. "Hey, thanks for coming by."

"It's good to see you awake. Matt says you're doing surprisingly well." She placed the flowers on the table.

"I guess. It's a weird feeling being strapped in this sling and to this ice chest."

"I'm sure it is, but it's for the best."

Emma sighed. "I'm tired of this bed. When can I go home?"

"I'll go find Dr. Bryant; you visit with Brandi." Matt kissed Emma and left the room.

Brandi scooted a chair over and sat next to Emma. "You look good." She patted Emma's hand.

"I'm sure you're lying, but thanks." Emma rolled her eyes.

"And there's the Emma I know and love." Brandi laughed. "You can never take a compliment. You do look good for what you've been through."

"If you say so. I just want to go home and get better. I miss everything already." Emma pouted.

"You've got several months of therapy, so slow your roll girl. I'm sure Jack will give you all you need to get better soon."

Emma smiled sinfully, "Oh I know he will." She winked at Brandi.

"Dear God, Em. I didn't mean it that way. You just won't stop, will you?" Brandi dragged her hand through her hair.

"I'm playing. He's my doctor. I won't ever risk his medical license. I'm not that awful."

"I hope not."

The door opened with Jack followed by Matt.

"Good morning, Emma. Hi Brandi." Jack reached for Emma's good hand.

"Good morning, Dr. Bryant. Can I go home?" Emma glared at Jack.

"Oh, slow down just a bit. Let me go over your therapy instructions and medication. Sounds like you don't like me." He squeezed her hand and smiled shyly as he held her gaze.

"It's not you I don't like at all. It's this place." Emma looked around the hospital room.

"Okay. Now, you're going to begin therapy in a month. Twice to three times a week. Matt, please call and ask for Polly when setting Emma's appointments. She's the best we have, and I want Emma with her."

"You got it, doc." Matt stood beside Jack putting notes in his phone.

"For your pain, Emma. I've prescribed some Oxy, but if you don't want that, I can write you a script for Hydrocodone. You're going to have pain even with the ice. Don't try to tolerate it. Take the medication. When I see you in two weeks, we can see how you tolerated the opiates. If you want by then I'll have you take Tylenol Arthritis, it's stronger than regular Tylenol. Okay?" Jack scribbled on Emma's chart, then looked her in her eyes.

"Yes, doctor." She smiled and blinked slowly.

Brandi's phone sounded. She looked at Emma and said, "Hey I'm going to take this and check back with you when you're at home. See you later." Emma nodded as Brandi patted her leg and left the room.

"Any questions for me?" Jack looked at Matt and Emma.

Before they could ask Jack any questions, Emma's phone rang, she went to reach for it and looked to Matt for help. "It's Shea, will you talk to her?"

"Of course. I'll take it out in the hall. Be right back, babe." Matt answered the phone on his way out the door. "Hi Shea, yes…"

Jack pulled up a chair and sat as close to Emma as he could. He placed her hand gently into his. "You scared me, beautiful. How are you?" He raised her hand to his lips and kissed it.

"I'm sorry. I didn't mean to scare anyone. I never do well waking up from anesthesia. Can I go home? I want to go home." Emma smiled at Jack, allowing him to hold her hand. She knew she shouldn't, but he was asking about her health. He was overly concerned. *Yes, that's all it is. Sure, right. Yeah, okay.*

"I can't stop thinking about you, Emma. Our dinner, that kiss. Our kiss. You felt so right." Jack threaded their fingers together.

Emma knew in her heart she should pull back, but she couldn't. Something made her hold Jack's hand and not let go. "Me either. I remember the feel of your lips, the taste of you, but Jack, you're my doctor now. It's too risky for this." She tugged her arm free. A sadness crossed her face and settled in her heart. An ache rose within her to tell him how she really felt but she pushed those feelings down, way far down.

"I know." Jack bowed his head.

She softly touched his hair and traced around his ear to his smooth jawline. She raised his head and their eyes met. Her heart clenched as she noticed a sadness across his face. She saw tears in Jack's soft blue eyes. She fought the strong urge to try and hug him with her one good arm.

"Emma, I—"

She stopped Jack mid-sentence. "We can still be friends. Still have dinner. There's nothing wrong with that. We just can't be seen alone together. Not while you're my doctor." Emma grazed her thumb along his soft cheek. She desperately wanted to lean into him and kiss his full lips, taste his velvety tongue, and hold him forever.

A click of the door handle broke their trance. Jack quickly stood and held up her chart before him.

"So, what did I miss. Is my gorgeous wife able to come home with me, Dr. Bryant?" Matt walked to Emma's bedside and laid her phone on the side table. He patted her head. Something else she hated that Matt did too often.

"Yes, Matt. She certainly is. I'll have someone come and help you both. Emma, please don't do anything. Let Matt do everything. Ask for help. I'll call, to check on Emma, if it's okay." Jack looked at Matt.

"Absolutely. Let me give you my number and Emma's." Matt found a piece of paper and jotted both numbers down. He handed it to Jack.

"Thanks. I'll see you in two weeks." Jack held out his hand and Emma grasped it.

She smiled as he squeezed softly. "Thank you so much, Dr. Bryant. See you in two weeks." Emma blushed and tugged at Jack's hand.

"Take care of her Matt." Jack extended his hand and shook Matt's.

"Thanks for everything, Dr. Bryant. I'll take care of my girl. She's my everything." He leaned in and kissed her forehead.

Emma cringed. Her eyes trailed after Jack until the door closed and he was gone.

CHAPTER 19

Emma's two-week check-up went by without a hitch. Matt had taken the leave of absence as he'd promised. He took care of her every need. She wanted for nothing. This was the man she married over thirty years ago, the man she loved with all her heart and soul. The man she planned to grow old with.

Her next appointment with Jack was over a month away. Matt went into the office more and more as Emma was able to care for herself better as the days moved forward. She still wore the sling twenty-four-seven and cursed Jack when it got in her way.

She fiddled in her sketchbook while Matt worked. It wasn't easy to draw and control the sketch pad one-handed, but she managed to do small pieces to keep her mind from wandering. She missed going to the gallery.

Emma woke her phone and punched in Brandi's number. She needed to get out of the house.

"Hey, please come get me, I want to see the gallery. I miss it. I'll buy lunch or dinner, something. Come get me," Emma begged Brandi. She wasn't attached to the ice chest any longer. She only used it as needed.

"Okay, Emma. Ben will be there in a bit. I have a photoshoot at ten."

"Thanks, y'all are the best." Emma ended the call and managed to get herself dressed in normal clothes. She'd been wearing oversized shirts since her surgery. She found a thin-strapped dress to slip over her head and sling.

While she waited for Ben at the breakfast table, she sent Matt a text. **Ben is picking me up. I need to get out for a while. I'll be at the gallery, pick me up there when you're done. Love you.**

She watched her phone for Matt's response. She noticed that he read it, from the 'read' below her text to him. She wondered why he read it and didn't answer her. *Well, at least he knows where I'll be.*

Emma gathered her purse when she saw Ben drive into her driveway. She set the house alarm and met him at his vehicle.

"Thanks, Ben, for picking me up. I'm going stir crazy in there." She smiled as he helped her into his SUV.

"No problem, Emma. Did you let Matt know?" Ben asked when he got into the driver's side.

"I did."

***

Emma entered her gallery for the first time since before her fall. She breathed deep, glanced around at the familiar drapes, furniture, Brandi's photographs, and her paintings that were up on display since their last event. A tear trickled down her face, she brushed it away and tucked her hair behind her ear. She walked to her room and to the seating area where she and Jack had last been together during the exhibition.

She took a seat in the same chair. She leaned back as best she could. A few minutes passed when she heard Brandi working with her clients across the gallery. She rose from her chair and walked over to where Brandi had set up. She peeked in the doorway and waved.

"Hi, Emma," Brandi acknowledged her, then went back to her clients; Emma walked to her office.

It was the same as she had left it. Neat and organized. Her desk cleared, her blank canvases stacked in the corner, her paints lined neatly by type then color on the shelf.

She walked behind her desk and sat in her chair. Her phone rang, she fumbled with her purse, trying to remove it from her arm that was in the sling. "Fuck," she yelled. She dumped her purse on the desk and grabbed her phone. "Hello, this is Emma," she answered short of breath.

"Emma, It's Jack. What's wrong?" he asked, sounding worried.

"Nothing. I had a tough time getting my purse open and finding my phone. It's nothing, Jack. What can I do for you?" she asked, her voice calming down, her body heating up.

"I'm calling to check on you. And be sure your therapy has begun and is going well," Jack's tone sounded professional.

"Yes, Polly is wonderful. She's tough, but she knows her stuff and I'm sure I'll be fine. I have the best, right?"

"Yes, you have the absolute best in Polly. I'm happy it's going well. Jenna has asked about you. She said Brandi had called and filled her in on what happened. She wants to bring dinner over for you and Matt. I told her I'd ask you when I saw you."

"Please tell Jenna thank you. Matt's taking great care of me. He took time off to be home with me. He's back to work now. I can get around pretty well on my own." Emma's mouth turned downward when Jack mentioned Jenna. *Why did she have to be so damn nice?*

"I'll tell her after I see you next month. Take care, Emma. I'll check in again soon. Promise," Jack's voice softened.

"Okay and thanks. It means a lot that you care so much, Jack. You're the best doctor I've ever had. You may be my favorite." Emma giggled into her phone. She was glad he didn't Face-time her, as she felt her face heat up.

"I should get back to my patients. See you soon."

"Yes, Jack. I'll see you soon." She pressed the red phone icon and stared at her phone as it lay on her desk.

Oh my, God. Jack called to check on me. How sweet is that? Her face became hot, just as her body was. Jack turned her on through the phone, he was that incredible.

"Emma!" Brandi startled her and she bumped her legs on the underside of her desk,

"Yes? Why are you so loud?" Emma rubbed one ear with her free hand.

"Because you didn't respond to the other five times, I called your name. Where the hell were you?"

"I was remembering the last time I was here. Do you know it was before we went to the beach and my accident.?"

"Yes, I do know it's been that long. Did you let Matt know you came here?" Brandi came in and sat across from Emma.

"I did. I sent him a text before Ben picked me up." She glanced at her phone. "He's read it, but never answered me." She shrugged her one shoulder.

"He's probably swamped with work since his time off. I'm sure he'll pick you up when he's done. If not, we can run you home." Brandi sat back and opened her phone. "I think you should know, Jenna asked to schedule a photoshoot." She peered up at Emma.

Emma's heart tightened as she thought about Jenna and Jack posing close together for a photo session. "Yeah, did you put them on your schedule?" she asked acting as though it didn't bother her. Inside she screamed with jealousy and guilt for thinking about Jack that way.

"I told her I was booked for a few months but could put them down at my next available time." Brandi watched Emma closely.

"Maybe she'll ask me to paint a photo for them." Emma smiled wide. Inside, her smile didn't exist. She hoped to hell Jenna didn't ask her to paint her and Jack. How would she manage that clusterfuck, especially if it were an intimate pose? *Oh, fuck me, no, just no way will I paint them.* Emma shook her head from side to side.

"She'll probably ask you. I'd be ready for that request. I didn't mention that option to her, but by then, I'm sure she'll know it's an upgrade to their package." Brandi stared at Emma.

"I'm fine with painting them. Why wouldn't I be?" Emma met Brandi's gaze.

"Oh, I don't know, Em. You and Jack kind of have the hots for one another, so maybe that? I can't see you painting their photo if it's a nude pose. Can you?"

"Yes, I can, and I will. And I don't have the hots for my doctor. He's an attractive man and I enjoy looking at him and talking with him. That's all there is to it. I promise." Emma's toothy grin appeared on her face. She did her best to keep her real feelings hidden from Brandi. Her best friend had nearly caught her and Jack kissing at KCs. She had to be more careful, and for now, with Jack being her doctor, it would be easy to manage her feelings for him.

"If you say so, Em. Add their date to your calendar. It's four months from now. You should be well out of your sling and probably almost healed. I would hope you can start painting again in another two months."

"I get this damn thing off at eight weeks. But I'll be three-quarters of the way through my therapy by then. I don't know why Jack is insisting on keeping me in this sling so long. Oh, oh, maybe he's into bondage?" She smiled mischievously and let out a sinful laugh.

"Okay, Emma. Maybe he's overly cautious because you had two repairs done?" Brandi offered.

"You're probably right, but I like my idea better." She winked and giggled at Brandi.

***

"Emma, where are you?" Matt called out.

She didn't answer as she sat and thumbed through her Pinterest pins on her phone.

Matt never picked her up. Brandi and Ben had brought her home. He never answered her text from that morning.

"Emma!" Matt yelled again. "Em, why don't you answer me?" he asked standing in front of her.

A scowl showed on her face as she felt herself heat up with anger. "Seriously, Matt?"

"Oh, shit." He rubbed his forehead. "I did see your text and I forgot to answer. I'm sorry." He knelt beside her and reached for her right hand.

She pulled it back.

"Emma don't be that way. It won't happen again, I swear." He crossed his chest with his fingers and laid his head on her knee.

"I guess work is taking priority over me now," she bit hard at him. Wanting to make Matt feel awful about not answering her.

"No, never. It was a shitty day. It won't always be like this. I'll be giving Miranda more responsibilities soon and she'll manage the shit that comes in. If I have to, I'll hire her an assistant. You're always my priority." Matt did his best to convince Emma. "But I have some news you're not going to like." He held his breath and squinted his eyes shut.

Slowly laying her phone on the side table, she crossed her legs and leaned back in her recliner. She looked down at him. She didn't like the guarded look in his eyes like he knew he was going to upset her. "It doesn't feel like I'm your priority. So, just go ahead; tell me," Emma sighed.

"Troy wants me in Maine next week. I know you have therapy and an appointment with Jack, but this is important. This is the client that asked for me to lead this job, I have to go, Em."

"Christ Matt, you promised."

His words stung, she knew he didn't mean he thought his job was more important than her, but he promised to be there with her throughout all her therapy. Just like he promised to stop going away for work. What's the next promise he'll break? His promise to always love her, till death do they part?

She hung her head and sucked back the ache in her heart. She sat quietly as she waited for Matt to speak again.

"I'm sorry. It's only for a week," he said. "I'll be home Friday night, or Saturday morning at the latest." He pinched his face expecting Emma's wrath.

She didn't anger easily, but he knew this news wouldn't land well at all.

She shot him a look so sharp, she thought she saw him grasp his chest. Her eyes filled with a mix of anger and sadness. "The entire week? Seriously?" her voice rose to a higher octave.

"Yes." Matt's brow furrowed; his eyes filled with uncertainty. "Maybe Brandi can help us out."

"Whatever." Emma grabbed her phone and wakened it. She stared at the picture of them from their wedding. She swallowed hard and pulled in a deep breath. She looked back at Matt and said, "I'll call for an Uber. I can't miss therapy or my appointment with Jack. And I don't want to burden friends to take care of me." *That's what you promised to do.*

"I'm sorry, babe. I know the timing is the worst, please understand. I wouldn't go if we didn't have Brandi to help. Let's call Shea, she did offer when you told her about your surgery."

"Sure, Matt. Call Shea. Do whatever you need to do," Emma's voice was dull, her heart ached. She wasn't Matt's priority as he promised she'd be.

Matt stood and pulled his phone from his back pocket. He punched in Shea's number. "It's her voicemail," he said to Emma. "Hey Shea, Matt here. Will you call me or Emma tonight? It's important." Matt left a message for Shea.

Emma's eyes returned to her phone, she tapped it open to avoid seeing their wedding picture.

Jack wouldn't let her down like this. He'd move heaven and earth to be with her. He showed her that when they spoke alone in the hospital.

She believed he'd risk everything to be with her, but she wouldn't allow him to do so. She'd wait.

CHAPTER 20

"I'm so happy to see you, Shea." Emma stretched out her good arm to her sister.

Shea hugged Emma gently. "Well, when Matt called and explained he had to go out of town, I thought it best to come down and help."

"What about your family?" Emma looked troubled.

"They're fine. The kids have school, Rob's working. They don't need me. Where do you want me to put my things?" Shea looked around.

"Follow me." Emma slowly led Shea to the spare room in the back of her house.

"Thanks, now sit down," Shea said, shooing her toward the chair. "I can unpack. Tell me how you're progressing." Shea plopped her suitcase up on the bed.

"I'm doing well so far. It's early, but I feel better every day. I had several therapy sessions, but still not doing much on my own. That takes time according to Polly."

"I'm glad to hear that. Anyone who gets you to listen is a saint in my book." Shea gave Emma a soft bump and a big smile.

"Thanks for coming but this isn't your job, it's Matt's. He promised to be here with me." Emma's mouth turned downward; her eyes were glassy.

"I know what he promised. He told me everything on the phone. Emma, not everything in life goes as we promise. He loves you, don't ever doubt him. That's why he called me, to be sure you were taken care of. He's still fulfilling his promise, just in a different way. Now had he just up and gone to Maine and let you fend for yourself, then I could see you being mad at him. He didn't do that. He made sure you had someone; me, to help you." Shea sat on the edge of the bed and took Emma's free hand in hers. She wiped the tear that trickled down Emma's cheek.

Emma knew Shea was right about Matt, but she was still hurt by him choosing work over her. He may have gotten Shea to come down, but he still left Emma for work in Maine.

"I do love him, Shea. I always will. He has my heart but right now, it's a little bruised. When I need Matt the most, where is he?" Emma waved her good arm around in the air.

Shea hugged Emma. "I understand. C'mon, let's have some tea. Show me where you keep your stuff and I'll make us a cup."

Shea followed Emma to the kitchen. She made them each tea, then they walked out to the lanai.

"Tell me, when does your sling come off?"

"This week. I'll be able to drive myself then."

"Are you sure? I am here to help."

"I'll let you drive me to the gallery every morning. But enough about me, catch me up on your life. I hate that we're so far away. I miss too many major events."

"Amelia graduates in the spring. I'm sure you'll receive an invitation. RJ's driving and working when he's not playing baseball for the high school. Rob's still working a lot."

"I can't believe Amelia's graduating. I missed so much of her growing up. What are her plans after high school?"

"She's going to nursing school. I guess I rubbed off on her in an effective way." Shea shrugged.

"That's awesome. She'll make a great nurse, just like you."

"Thanks, Em." Shea covered her mouth as she yawned. "Hey, I'm beat. Mind if I take a nap?" She stood and picked up Emma's teacup.

"Go relax. I'll fill you in on our new project at the gallery when you're rested."

When Shea went to her room, Emma brought out her sketchpad and began drawing. She didn't usually draw people, but she started to sketch Matt, looking at their photo on the stand beside her chair. She reached toward it and ran her hands down the sides. She knew Matt was her home, so why was Jack embedded in her mind all the time?

What was it about him that drove her crazy for him? What the hell did he do to make her want him so fucking much? To risk everything to be with him. Was he a fun fuck? A no-strings just sex affair in the making? Or was he a new love? *Oh my God, No!*

Her heart skipped, jumped, began to race as she thought about Jack. It can't happen, they can't happen. She wanted him more than oxygen, her desire for him was the most intense feeling she'd ever felt in her fifty-five years of life.

He was her doctor now. Not only was he unavailable, but he's also married to Jenna, and he was off-limits. It would be extremely unethical for either of them to engage in an affair while she was his patient. She reminded herself of that daily. She hated that fact, but it was a fact of her life now.

Feelings for Jack had blossomed months ago. Not love at first sight. She didn't believe in that. But she knew she was falling in love with him, and she couldn't stop herself. She didn't want to stop. She wanted Jack Bryant.

Emma drew on her paper through misty eyes. Thinking she'd drawn Matt, she looked at her drawing and gasped when she noticed who she'd drawn. In her lap lay a rendering of Dr. Jackson Bryant. She held it close to her chest. She pressed the sketch into her heart. She whispered, "I love you," as tears streamed down her face.

Falling in love with Jack took Emma by complete surprise. How can that be? She loved Matt; she can't love two men. It wasn't who she was. "No, I can't, no, no, no." She began to sob. Her heart finding this new love and breaking at the same time.

Her phone rang. She wiped her face with her hand and glanced at the number, Jack's. "Hello," she answered meekly.

"Hi Emma, I'm calling to check in on you and let you know you can remove the sling. I spoke with Polly, and she updated me on your progress. I feel you're doing well enough to come out of it."

She tried to stifle her emotions, but she sniffled loudly. "Emma, are you okay?" Jack's voice was full of compassion and concern for her.

"Yes, Jack. I'm good. And thanks so much for calling. I'm happy to get rid of this sling." She took in a deep breath.

"You should wear it if you go out around people or to the store. To protect yourself. If people see a sling, they tend to be more cautious around that person."

"Okay. I'll wear it when I'm outside the house."

"Sounds good. I'll see you soon. I miss you," he said softly.

"Jack, please. I miss you too, but we can't," she said reluctantly.

"I know, but I still miss seeing you at KCs and around town. If there's anything you need, please call me. I'll come right over. I promise."

"I will, Jack. But I'm good. My sister is here, so I'm not alone." She sucked in a breath; she didn't mean to let Jack know that Matt wasn't home. Her body tensed all over.

"You shouldn't be alone, I'm glad your sister is there. Where's Matt?" Jack asked.

Shit, she messed up letting Jack know Matt was gone. "Um, he had to go away for work. He won't be gone long, but he didn't want me to be alone, so he called and made plans for Shea to be with me. I'm fine, Jack. Don't worry."

"I always worry about my patients. And especially you, Emma." his voice softens again. Soft, caring, and gentle.

"Thank you, Jack. I should go. See you soon," Emma said.

"Okay. I should go too. Jenna will be home soon. Take care, and I'll see you next week." Their call ended.

Emma picked up her sketchpad and looked at her sketch of Jack. It was perfect. Just like Jack.

CHAPTER 21

In the building where Jack's office was located, Emma arrived early hoping for a chance encounter before her appointment as she stopped in the small cafe on the ground floor for a coffee.

She'd given in and let Shea drive her one last time this morning. She was ready to be on her own again.

Emma ordered a coffee and bagel and found a seat in the back. As soon as she heard his velvety voice, her body exploded. She wiggled in her chair and watched the entrance of the cafe, hoping to see him.

His voice gets closer; her body temperature increasing.

Pretending to be preoccupied with her phone when Jack entered the cafe, she peered up without moving her head. Watching him as he ordered a coffee and danish, her breathing intensified, her core wet. Emma smiled when Jack turned and noticed her.

He spoke to his colleague and walked over to her table.

"Hi Emma, may I?" Jack pointed to the empty chair.

"Of course, Dr. Bryant." She smiled sweetly and waved her arm toward the empty seat.

Jack moved the chair so that it was beside Emma. "It's *so* good to see you." His hand touched her arm lightly.

She'd heard his emphasis on 'so', her heart warmed.

"It's good to be seen." She giggled and patted his hand.

"You know you should have your sling on while you're here. Please be careful. I wouldn't want you to re-injure your shoulder."

"I'll be extremely careful, I promise. I don't want to extend my time as your patient."

Jack's lips curved upward into a mischievous grin. "Where did you say Matt went for work?"

"I didn't say when we spoke on the phone last week. He's in Maine," Emma sighed. Her gaze fell to her lap.

"That's far away."

"It is," Emma stated flatly.

"Well, I'm glad your sister is here, how long is she staying?"

"She can't stay forever but probably until Matt's work settles down, or I send her home. He worries about me being alone, especially with my shoulder." She met Jack's gaze. "But you know how work can be."

"My work doesn't take me away from my priorities in life, so, no I can't say that I do know."

"Matt's vying for a promotion and his boss is testing him. It won't be long before he gets the promotion. I'm okay. I'm not a child. I can take care of myself if I need to." She averted her eyes from Jack's knowing she just fed him a line of bullshit. She hated being placed after Matt's work. She hated that he left her with her sister, she hated being a burden. She couldn't wait until her shoulder was healed and her life went back to normal. Whatever that normal would be.

Jack glanced at his watch, then said, "I'll see you in my office in a few."

"Yes. I'm ready for my next checkup. Will Polly be with you?" Emma wanted to know if they'd be alone.

"Not today, her schedule is jammed, and she's needed in the therapy gym. It'll be just us." His soft blue pools of pure lust grabbed her before she could blink.

Her body trembled; her eyes held him as though she were attached to him. Her heart boomed against her chest wall.

"Okay, I'll be there in a bit," her voice is a whisper, she felt stuck in his aura.

Jack placed his hand on her shoulder, she nearly fainted.

Emma sucked in a breath and finally blinked free of his gaze.

"Great, see you soon." He squeezed her shoulder and let his hand linger for a few seconds before walking away from her.

She leaned back in her chair and closed her eyes.

Jack was there smiling his incredibly gorgeous smile, holding his arms wide for her to walk into. Oh, how she wished she could, but she couldn't.

***

Waiting in the exam room, her insides jumping like live wires throwing sparks. She knew she and Jack would be alone. A dangerous situation she had to try and control.

A soft knock as the door swung open. Jack walked in with her chart in hand. He was stunning in his white coat, perfect hair, those fucking delicious blue eyes.

She'd known from their first encounter that he was trouble; fun, fuckable, delectable, sinfully luscious trouble, that she wanted to get into.

Emma clasped her hands in her lap as Jack sat on a stool and rolled over to her, right into her personal space. She didn't complain.

"Hi, again." He smiled and held his hand to her, palm up.

She didn't meet his gaze, she looked at his hand. She knew how soft his hands were. She hesitated, then slowly laid her hand in his.

His fingers wrapped around her small hand. Their skin touching gave Emma jolts of heat, pulsing all through her. He held her hand, he didn't shake it. With his other hand, Jack lifted Emma's chin.

She blinked and held her eyes closed for a beat. When she opened her eyes, he caught her.

His blue fuck me eyes grabbed hers and didn't let go.

"Emma, tell me, are you really, okay? Without Matt?" Jack asked.

"Yes, I'm fine," she reassured Jack.

He released her hand and pushed back a few feet. "I need to check your range of motion and strength. So, will you show me how high you can raise your arms?"

"Sure." Emma raised both arms. Her left one didn't go quite as high as her right.

Jack made notes on her chart. "Okay, that's normal for where you are in your recovery. Push against my hands as hard as you can without pain."

Emma placed her open palms against Jack's and pushed as hard as she could. "Oh, that's all." She winced and dropped her arms.

"That's good too. Your strength is much better than I expected. I'm sure you'll recover nicely. Now I need to take a look at those scars." Jack scooted back into her personal space.

She removed her jacket and slid her short sleeve down her shoulder. She felt his warm breath on her skin, he softly ran his finger over each of her scars. Her chest rose and fell rapidly, her toes curled inside her shoes. *Fuck,* she knew she was in trouble.

His charm was too powerful for her to resist.

Truthfully, Emma didn't want to resist Jack, she only said they can't to protect him, his career. She wanted that young man more than kids wanted candy on Halloween night, more than people in Hell wanted ice water.

She avoided his eyes while he examined her scars, looking right at his shoulder. His clean fresh scent entered her nose, she sighed and squeezed her legs together as tight as she could. Her panties were wet, her core hot, she ached for him.

Emma's eyes traveled to the V in his green scrubs. *My God, my fucking God.* She let a breath out and watched his soft brown chest hair flutter.

He turned his face slightly, their eyes met, and for a beat, they held each other's gaze.

Her hand touched his bicep, he moved closer to her. Her eyes fell to his full lips.

His tongue peeked out and wet them.

She shook in her seat. It felt as though time had stopped. She slid her hand up to his arm to his shoulder.

His smile grew wide as he inched closer to her lips.

Stop! A voice yelled, *no, don't fucking stop!* Sounded a different voice. She felt her heart thumping harder than it ever had.

Jack's hand rested on her cheek, softly inching her closer to him. Their lips met for a brief second. He pulled back and their eyes locked in a trance. Like magnets, their lips locked in a heat of passion she'd never felt in her life. His tongue plunged into her mouth, ravaging her, tasting all of her.

She moaned with sheer ecstasy as their kiss kept on. She longed to strip naked and take him in that damn exam room, on the table, on the floor, against the wall. Fuck him until he couldn't walk.

Oh my God, no! She suddenly pulled back from Jack. She bowed her head to avoid his eyes. She held her hand up, stopping him from moving closer to her. "Jesus, Jack. We can't do this. Fuck. Someone could've come in and caught us. You would've lost everything. Please." She met his gaze with glassy eyes, her eyebrows pulled up, her mouth drawn tight as she clenched her jaw. She held her chest as her heart ached for him.

"Emma." Jack lowered his chin to his chest. He laid his hand palm up again on his leg. "I know, but I can't help myself. I want you," he stated as his hand brought Emma's face up.

"That doesn't matter, not right now. I should go." Emma shook Jack's hand firmly and rose from her chair. She touched Jack's arm. "I won't be your patient forever. But for now, I am. I'll see you soon, Dr. Bryant." She pinched his bicep, and he placed his hand along her lower back as he opened the door for her to exit.

"Take care, Emma. See you soon." His hand lingered on her back when she walked out the door.

Before she left the orthopedic clinic, her phone buzzed in her pocket. She brought it out, looked down, and saw it was Shea.

As she went out the exit, she glanced back over her shoulder, Jack stood at the counter, watching her leave. Her arm raised, her fingers tumbled into her palm, and she smiled sweetly.

He smiled and waved back.

CHAPTER 22

"Emma, we need to talk." Shea came up to Emma on a Sunday after being with her for several weeks.

"What's up?" She poured them each a coffee.

"I should go home soon. You're much better and don't need my help. I can see that."

"You're right. I'm healing faster than expected. At my last check-up, Dr. Bryant was incredibly pleased. So, yes, go back to your family. Matt should be home soon." Emma's voice lowered.

"I'll check flights and see when I can get a reasonable one. I still have time I can take from work, so that's not an issue."

"Okay. Whatever you decide is fine with me." Emma's phone buzzed with the tone she assigned to Jack's number; a playful grin formed on her face. Then she remembered Shea was standing beside her.

"Who's Jack?" Shea asked.

"Oh, he's one of my doctors. He checks on me every so often." Emma brushed Shea aside with a half-truth. Jack wasn't *just one* of her doctors. He was *the* hottest doctor she'd ever known. "I'll answer him in a minute." She closed her phone and slid it into her back pocket. Sitting back down at the table, she sipped her coffee.

Shea remained standing and gave Emma a curious look. "Since when do doctors text their patients?" she asked, taking a seat across from Emma.

"I don't know. Several of mine have texted me before. I guess I don't think about it as unusual." Emma shrugged.

"Does Matt know this doctor?" Shea probed further.

"Of course, he does. Jack has Matt's number too. It's not a big deal, Shea," Emma's voice rose as she crossed her arms.

"It must be something they do here. Our doctors back home don't text their patients, they call."

"Oh, Jack calls too. Both of us, he calls me and Matt." Emma quickly covered her ass.

Shea gave Emma a suspicious look, then finished her coffee. They remained at the breakfast table, each reading. Shea on her phone and Emma paging through her monthly artist magazine.

The doorbell rang startling both Shea and Emma. They stood and walked to the front door. Shea waited back in the foyer while Emma answered the door.

She cracked the door to peek out and see who had rang the doorbell. As soon as she saw him, she quivered. Her lips tugged up into a bright smile as she opened the door fully. Then suddenly her smile lessened as Jenna came up the sidewalk to join Jack.

"Um, hi. Did I miss my appointment?" Emma joked.

"Hi, Emma." Jenna smiled wide.

"Hi, Emma. May we come in?" Jack asked.

"Yes, I'm sorry, where are my manners?" She glanced at Shea. *Oh shit.*

Jack and Jenna each carried deep metal pans, and Jenna had a sack filled with something. Jenna placed the pan on the counter along with her bag. She turned to Emma and reached for her.

Oh fuck. Jenna embraced Emma in a warm hug. She stepped back feeling quite awkward and a little guilty as the kiss she and Jack shared came flooding into her memory.

"What is all this?" Emma waved her arm to the counter and stove. An unsettling feeling crossed over her. She was excited as hell to see Jack, but at the same time, seeing Jenna gave her an anxious vibe. Her anxiety rose, she took in a deep breath, waiting for Jenna or Jack to answer her.

"This is dinner and whatever else you need, Emma. When Brandi told me about your injury, I asked what I could do to help. She insisted you didn't need anything, that Matt was taking care of you." Jenna looked around the open kitchen and living room of Emma's house. "Where's Matt?"

"Oh, yeah, Matt's in Maine. It's work. This is my baby sister, Shea Stevens. Shea, this is my orthopedic doctor, Jack Bryant, and his lovely wife and our caterer for the gallery, Jenna." Emma's face scrunched when she said Jack's name. She looked at Shea and saw her eyes grow to saucers. She knew then, her sister would interrogate her later.

"It's nice to meet you both." Shea nodded.

"Yes, it's nice to meet you too, Shea," Jenna said. "There's plenty of food here for you both and Matt. When will he be home, Emma?"

"Soon, I hope. It's a huge job and important," her tone became low, her lips drawn downward.

"Can I help you with anything, Emma? You have my number, just call. I spoke with Brandi last week; she didn't mention Matt was out of town. Whatever you need, please ask." Jenna placed her hand on Emma's. Her heart clenched with guilt. Jenna's offer of help sounded sincere.

"Thanks so much, Jenna. I will call if I need help. This food smells delicious. Are you and Jack staying for dinner?" Emma hoped they would. Any time spent with Jack was a bonus in her eyes and it would delay Shea's questions.

"We can, right Jack?" Jenna glanced at Jack, he nodded and stepped closer to Emma.

His clean, fresh, masculine scent drifted into her nostrils. She sucked in a huge breath of him. Delighting in having anything of Jack inside her.

"Emma, go sit down, let me and Jack take care of setting dinner out. Now, where do you keep your plates and silverware?" Jenna interrupted Emma's quick fantasy.

"The cabinet to the left of the microwave and the top long drawer by the sink." Emma hooked her arm through Shea's and led her to the dining room. They sat at the long table.

Shea gave Emma a look she knew was coming. Emma smiled and shook her head from side to side.

Jack walked into the dining room with everything to set the table.

Emma followed his every movement.

He stretched across the table, and she caught a glimpse of his abs as his shirt pulled up.

Her eyes trailed his tall firm fuckingly stunning body. She licked her lips and tightly crossed her legs. She wasn't sure how she'd manage to get through dinner with him and his wife, *Ugh!* But she'd find a way.

Emma looked at her sister and saw Shea had her hawk eyes on her, she swallowed hard. And with Jenna there, Emma had to behave as did Jack.

"Wine for anyone?" Jenna asked holding a bottle of Pinot Noir.

"I'll have a glass, thank you, Mrs. Bryant," Shea said with an emphasis on Jenna's married name. She gave Emma a stern look. Emma pinched her nose.

"Oh, please call me Jenna. Mrs. Bryant lives in South Florida." Jenna smiled and poured a glass for Shea. "Emma?" Jenna shook the wine bottle side to side.

"No, I don't like wine. But I'll take a whiskey." Emma smiled and pointed to the bottle of her favorite liquor sitting on the table.

Jack grabbed the bottle and two tumblers. He poured them both halfway and walked to Emma's side. His hand covered the small glass tumbler, there was no way Emma wasn't touching him. His back was to Jenna and Shea as Emma caught his stare.

She smiled sweetly, not wanting Shea to notice her insatiable attraction to that man.

His tongue circled his lips, his grin so fucking sinful.

She flipped her legs across the other way and squeezed hard. Her center boiled for Jack, but she controlled herself in front of her sister and his wife. "Thank you," Emma said softly and opened her hand for Jack to place the glass into. They touched, her core clenched, she drew in a deep breath and tried to turn her body off.

Jack returned to his seat beside Jenna, across from Emma.

Shea placed herself between them. They all enjoyed the lasagna Jenna prepared, along with salad and garlic bread.

"Emma, how long has Matt been away?" Jenna asked.

"A few weeks," Emma said and sipped on her whiskey.

"I'll be here until Matt comes back," Shea interjected.

"Emma's lucky to have you here with her, Shea. And I'm glad she's not alone," Jack said, his soft blue eyes meeting Emma's.

She smiled.

"Emma, may I use your restroom?" Jenna asked as she pushed back her chair.

"Sure, down the hall and the second door on the right."

Shea's phone rang. She glanced at it, "It's Rob, I better see what he wants. Be right back." Shea stood and went out the backdoor to the lanai.

Jack scooted his chair and looked down the hallway. He placed his hand, palm up on the table.

Emma slowly wet her lips, letting her tongue linger in the corner of her mouth, grabbing Jack's stare. She teasingly ran her finger across his palm and pulled away quickly.

His fingers begged for her to touch him, wiggling on the table.

She floated her hand down to his.

His fingers folded around her small hand, engulfing it.

Heat raged through her when their skin melded together. She blinked slow and held her eyes closed for a second, wishing they were alone, and she wasn't his patient. Her body pulsed with desire for him. She wanted him more and more each passing day.

"Are you trying to get caught, Jack?" Emma asked in a whisper as she held his hand, enjoying the softness of his skin touching hers.

"No, Emma, but I need to touch you. I need you." He tugged on her arm, inching her closer to him. He looked down the hallway again, turned toward the backdoor, then back to Emma. He placed his hand on the nape of her neck and drew her to him.

In an instant, their lips met. They kissed deeply until the sound of the bathroom door broke them apart. "I want you," he whispered as he scooted his chair back to where it had been. His breath sent chills of enormous heat from her head to her toes.

She pinched her legs together even tighter and mouthed the words, 'I want you too.'

Jenna and Shea returned to the table. "Did I miss any interesting conversation?" Jenna asked in her sweet bubbly voice.

Emma fidgeted in her seat, picking at her nails under the table, so no one would notice the intense guilt she held. She looked quickly at Jenna then to Shea, smiling weakly. She stared at her lap, her smile turning seductive as she peeked at Jack from behind strands of her hair.

"No, nothing exciting," Jack assured Jenna, then he placed his arm around her shoulders.

Emma clenched her jaw and balled her fists in her lap.

"What did Rob want, Shea." Emma tried to change the subject.

"He asked when I'd be home. I think he misses me." Shea smiled and shrugged. "I told him I'd be back soon."

"I'll call Matt tonight and get a time when he will be back. The assistant he hired should be managing this shit," Emma's tone turned sour, she frowned.

"He's probably getting his assistant up to speed, that's all. No worries, Em." Shea finished her wine and began to gather the plates to carry to the kitchen.

"Let me help." Jenna reached for Jack's plate and silverware. She piled them with hers and pushed back from the table.

"Thanks, you're sweet to offer, but you did all the cooking and brought it here for us. You relax, Emma and I can clean up," Shea insisted.

Emma glared at her sister. Seething inside for a missed opportunity to be alone with Jack, she threw her napkin onto the table and forced a smile. "Yes, sit down, Jenna. You and Jack did enough for me. We've got this." Emma placed their plates with hers and carried them to the kitchen. She puffed a deep breath out, mad as hell at her sister, but she couldn't say a word to Shea. She knew the questions were coming.

"Are you okay?" Shea asked Emma while putting the dishes in the sink.

"Yes, why?" Emma shot at Shea.

"You seem a little mad, that's all. Is he the same Jack who sent you a text?" Shea didn't wait until Jack and Jenna left to begin questioning Emma.

Emma rolled her eyes and said, "Yes. The very one. And no, he's just my doctor, he's married to my business associate. I know what you're thinking and no. Just no." Emma tried to stop Shea in her tracks.

"Really?" Shea pushed.

"Yes, Shea. Really," Emma insisted speaking in hushed tones. She went back to finish clearing the table.

"Jenna, Jack, thank you both so much for dinner and drinks. I can't thank you enough for this and for caring about me. I'm so grateful we can be friends as well as have professional relationships. I'm so lucky. I'll be sure to let Matt know he missed a delicious lasagna."

Jenna reached for Emma again as they stood by the front door.
She drew in a deep breath and hugged Jenna.

"Oh Emma, you're so nice. When I found out what happened, I had to help in some way. It's who I am." Jenna touched Emma's arm, and again Emma felt a tight pang in her heart.

She knew it was her guilt hitting her. She pinched her eyes and swallowed hard.

"Well, good night to you both. It was nice meeting you," Shea said and opened the door.

"Same for us. Take care, Emma." Jack touched Emma's shoulder, the one he repaired. He gave her a soft squeeze and his stunning smile.

This time her heart filled with warmth; her center exploded in heat. She ran her hand down his arm, their fingers meeting for a moment, she hid their touch from Shea with her body. Emma lingered in the doorway, her eyes following Jack.

He turned as he got into his car, and their eyes met in the dim light from the lamppost.

She waved quickly and went inside.

CHAPTER 23

Emma slipped into one of Matt's white button-down shirts and sipped on a whiskey waiting for him to join her for their video call. She'd sent him a text after Jack and Jenna left that she needed to talk to him, see him.

Staring at the blank computer screen, she woke her phone, checked her text messages, hoping Matt had sent one and she missed it. Nothing. Her heart tightened. She checked the time, their call was scheduled for eight p.m., it was now nine. She fell back into the pillows and tried to stifle the immense pain flowing through her heart. *Where are you? Matt, where the fuck are you?* She closed her eyes.

"I'm right here," she heard Jack's velvety voice as she had so many months ago.

She bolted upright, wiping her face, raking her hair over and over with her fingers. She twisted her long blonde locks and tied it into a messy bun. She sat crossed-legged as she breathed deeply. "I'm right here," she heard his pussy drenching voice again. *Oh my God, what am I doing, what has my life become? What's happening to me?*

Her computer startled her when the video chat box sounded, and Matt finally appeared on the screen. "Hi, Emma," he greeted her, but he wasn't focused on her, his eyes were distant, his hair a mess, his shirt had stains on the collar.

She smiled and ignored his appearance; she was happy to see him. "Hey baby, I miss you so much. Please come home," Emma's voice quivered as she spoke to Matt; it had been over a week since their last phone call.

"I wish I could give you a solid day, but this job is too complicated for Miranda to manage alone. I've been working with her to explain how certain things need to be done but she's getting a lot of flak from some of the workers. I need to stay a while longer." Matt kept looking to his side, she heard him leaf through papers, he turned from the screen for a moment.

Emma's heart stung; Matt clearly wasn't invested in talking with her. She felt a flash of irritation as anger rose within her. "Matt, is the promotion worth us?" Emma lowered her head; she hid her tears with loose strands of her hair.

"Emma, please don't talk like that. This is all temporary, you know it is. I'll be home soon. I promise."

Emma watched as Matt ran his hand through his hair. She didn't answer. A few seconds of awkward silence lay between them. "Emma...oh shit, Miranda's calling, I need to go."

"Baby, please don't—"

The computer screen went blank, her heart cracked open as she fell back against her wedge pillow. Her hands covered her face, stifling her cries. Her body ached from the feeling of her thirty-year marriage slipping from her.

She wondered when she became the second choice to Matt. She'd never put anything above him. She'd sell the gallery if that's what it took to save her marriage. But why was she the only one who seemed to care? He'd never ended a call with her without telling her he loved her. Her heart sank, it lay deflated inside her chest. She pressed her hands against her body, feeling her heartbeat slowing, almost still.

"I'm here," she heard his warm, tender voice again. She woke her phone and found Jack's number. She sat and stared at it, wanting to call or text him, wanting, no needing to hear his voice for real and not in her memories.

Emma slid her hand across her phone, *oh fuck!* She'd touched the phone icon and her phone began to call Jack. She quickly smacked the red icon to stop the call and tossed her phone across the bed so she wouldn't be tempted to call or text him. She turned onto her side and cried herself to sleep.

***

The sun's rays kissed Emma's face as she woke, her hair matted from her tears. She decided to put her marriage woes away until Matt came home. Hoping when he came back, things would return to their normal routine.

A knock on her bedroom door startled her from her aching heart. "Emma?" Shea asked.

"Yes, I'm awake, come on in," she called out and sat back against her wedge she still slept on.

"Good morning. How are you?" Shea sat on the end of the bed with her coffee and held one out for Emma.

"Good morning. Thank you. What's up?" Emma took the mug from Shea and sipped slowly.

"I booked a flight home." Shea peered over her mug.

"Good. Your family misses you. I'm fine," Emma said.

"Did you talk to Matt last night? I thought I heard voices in here later on."

"We had a video chat. It was cut short by Miranda." Emma rolled her eyes.

"Who's Miranda?" Shea asked.

"She's his assistant. The one he hired to manage the out-of-town jobs."

"Then why is Matt up in Maine if she was hired to do that?"

"Ask Matt because I can't seem to keep him on the phone or video. Maybe I should be naked next time?" Emma joked, but it wasn't a joke to her. She was mad as hell at Matt. He chose work over her.

"Emma, I'm sorry. I know his promotion means a lot to him and he deserves it. But you should be his priority. I'll cancel my flight and stay. Rob can oversee the kids. They'll understand." Shea moved to the bedside next to Emma and hugged her gently.

"No, Shea. It's okay. Matt will be back. I don't know when, but when he does come home, we'll have a serious talk. I need him here with me. I love him." Emma hid her tears from her sister. She swallowed hard and wiped her face dry before looking at Shea. "I'll be fine. I promise."

"Are you sure? Emma…"

"Yes, I'm sure. Brandi's around if I need anything. I want to get back to drawing and painting. I'll focus on my work until Matt comes home."

"Okay. I'll pack later. Let's have lunch with Brandi and you can tell me about your new project."

"Oh, yes. I'm so excited to do this with Brandi. It's a lead-up to our next exhibition in the fall. You're going to love it." Emma opened her arms and Shea embraced her. They hugged for several minutes. Emma realized the silver lining to Matt being gone was having Shea with her. She missed her sister more than she realized. "I'll text Brandi and have her meet us at the mall. Go get ready." Emma gave Shea a soft nudge.

***

At the mall food court, Emma, Shea, and Brandi found a table away from the crowd of people. Sundays were always busy there.

"Oh my God, Shea, you look great." Brandi hugged Shea as they each took a seat. "Sorry I didn't get over. I've been swamped with photo sessions."

"No worries, Brandi. I'm happy we got together before I go home this week," Shea said.

"What? Is Matt coming home?" Brandi looked at Emma.

"Um, no." Emma's eyes fell to her lap.

"Are you going to be okay alone?" Brandi asked.

"Yes, Mom. I'll be fine." Emma rolled her eyes and ran her hands through her hair.

"When's Matt coming home, Em?" Brandi pushed.

"I have no fucking idea," Emma said angrily.

"Wait, I'm lost. Isn't Shea here to help you while Matt is gone?" Brandi held up her hands.

"Yeah, she was, but I'm better now. Jack is happy with my progress. He said I'm ahead of schedule. Everything's good. I can take care of myself," Emma said.

"You mean your doctor, Dr. Bryant, right Emma?" Brandi bumped Emma under the table.

"Yes, Dr. Bryant. Shea's met him and Jenna. They came by with dinner," Emma told Brandi.

"They're a lovely couple," Shea added. Emma closed her eyes.

"Yes, I agree. Speaking of the Bryant's, Emma." Brandi looked directly at her, "I moved up their photoshoot."

"Why?" Emma asked.

"I had a cancellation, so I called Jenna and she checked with Jack. They were able to take the earlier time I had. Jenna didn't mention asking you to paint their photo though. Do you want me to offer it to them, Em?"

"Sure, why not? I won't be able to get to them for months with all the others in front of them. It may be well after our next exhibition till I can paint them," Emma said.

"Wait, is this y'all's new project?" Shea looked between Emma and Brandi.

"Yeah, Shea it is. We've decided to offer, as an upgrade to Brandi's photo session, a painting of one or more of the client's pictures. Done by yours truly." Emma waved her hand across her body.

"That sounds fantastic. I'm excited to see the paintings and photos displayed together," Shea said.

"That will be the title of our next event. 'Pictures to Paintings.' We plan on filling the entire gallery with those as long as Emma can handle the workload." Brandi looked at Emma.

"I've got this. I can paint again. I don't have full range back yet on my left side, but I have enough to draw and paint. Besides, I need to be at the gallery daily again. Working will help pass the time until my husband decides to come home." Emma's lips tightened as she gritted her teeth.

"When is this event happening?" Shea asked.

"Most likely in the fall. I'll let you know when we pick the dates. It'd be great if you and the family could come," Emma said.

"I'll see if I can make that happen." Shea smiled.

CHAPTER 24

Emma's schedule at the gallery kept her busy while Matt continued to work in Maine. She didn't know what happened to the one week a month, he said he'd be working as he'd been gone for much longer than a whole month.

"Goddammit," she yelled out and grabbed her left bicep.

Brandi came running into the studio area of their gallery, "What happened?" She stood beside Emma, her eyes open wide and lips tight.

"I reached the wrong way, fuck my arm hurts." Emma bent over and breathed deeply. The pain shooting from the spot she knew Jack had placed an anchor when he repaired her torn bicep; he called it a button; to her fingertips. She couldn't hold the paint tray or her phone. "Please text Jack for me. Tell him I've hurt my arm." Emma took short quick breaths to try and stifle the pain.

"Why not call his office and get an appointment like everyone else does?" Brandi asked with an attitude.

"Because he said to text him directly." Emma shot her a stern look.

"Okay. I'm sorry I assumed you just wanted to see him. You really are hurting." Brandi found Emma's phone and sent Jack a message to call ASAP.

Within minutes Emma's phone rang with Jack's sound. She held her good hand out and wiggled her fingers for Brandi to give her the phone. "Hey," Emma spoke softly.

"What's up Emma? What happened?" Jack asked.

"I've hurt my arm painting, well, no, I reached the wrong way and I think I pulled your button out." She smiled as she spoke with Jack. She watched Brandi leave her alone in the room.

"Well, you can't pull the button out by reaching for something. Come in later and I'll check you out. I'm sure you pulled an arm muscle, or you may have tendinitis. I'll let my nurse know you'll be in today."

"Thank you, Jack. See you soon." Emma ended the call and held the phone to her chest. Was Jack the man to heal her broken heart? Was he the one to fulfill her, take care of her, spend the rest of their lives together?

Emma put her phone in her dress pocket and went to find Brandi. She remembered Brandi had another photoshoot to set up and went to her room in the gallery. She stood in the archway and watched her best friend setting up the last of the props for her next clients. Emma cleared her throat.

Brandi turned and came to her. "What did Jack say?" She asked Emma.

"I'm going to stop by the office so he can check out my arm later on. He thinks I pulled a muscle or something, but I want to be sure."

"Okay. He's probably right, but it's good to be sure. Lock up when you leave. This photoshoot is going to take a few hours, it's a large family, and they want your services for a painting and a pencil sketch," Brandi said.

"I'll look at my schedule and see where I can add them. The painting will take longer than the pencil sketch. Have them call me so I can speak with them."

"Will do, I need to get this set up finished. Remember to lock up when you leave." Brandi brushed Emma's arm and walked back to her work.

***

Emma waited patiently to be called back to see Jack. She knew she'd have to wait longer since she didn't have an appointment. Her phone rang with Matt's tone as a voice called her name. She touched the red icon, then toggled it to silent, and put her phone in her purse. Her anger with Matt was still present, so she chose to make him wait for her. He put her second, this time she put him second. Second to Jack.

The nurse took Emma to an exam room and told her the doctor would be right in.

She took her phone from her purse and sent a quick text to Matt. **I'll call in a few. Busy right now.** She bent over and put her phone back in her purse just as the door opened and Jack entered the room.

His eyes grew to saucers and a smile covered his face.

Emma realized the dress she had worn had a scoop neckline and she was giving Jack a free show. "Oh, sorry." She covered her breasts as she sat straight in her chair.

Jack's smile softened as he sat on his stool and rolled over to her, laying his hand out for her to take. His eyes were bright as Christmas lights when she laid her hand into his.

"No worries, Emma. Now, show me where your arm hurts."

She straightened her left arm but winced as she tried to push through her pain. "That's as far as I can go, please tell me I'm going to be okay. I can't be your patient any longer than necessary." Emma's lips tightened; her eyes pulled together.

Jack felt her forearm, pressing every so often, watching her face for her reaction. When he pressed on the inside of her elbow, she leaned forward and cried out, "No, stop. Please."

"Okay, it feels like tendinitis. I want you to rest it. No work for a week. Ice and heat and take some anti-inflammatory medications. You'll be fine, it needs to rest." Jack massaged her arm gently. Going higher up her arm with each caress.

Emma pinched her knees tight. His hands upon her drove her insane. She didn't try to stop Jack's hand. She closed her eyes, to avoid meeting his blue magnets; she knew if she looked into his eyes, she'd give into whatever he wanted. Her willpower around Jack became weaker with each encounter.

She breathed Jack's clean fresh scent in. Making her center hot as hell. *Stop, no don't stop. Yes, stop! Don't you dare stop. Touch me, hold me, fuck me.* The voices fighting in her mind were like an angel and a devil. Today, the devil won, she allowed Jack to continue feeling her up.

His hand slowly crawled to her shoulder.

Her gaze remained lowered as she felt his soft palm on the nape of her neck. She pinched her eyes tight as she sensed his warm breath on her cheek, moving to her lips.

He skimmed her mouth with his. "Emma, open your eyes, I want to see your stunning blue eyes."

She hesitated as she took in a breath, ready to kiss Jack with all she had. Her purse lay against her calf, and she felt her phone vibrating. Knowing it was Matt, she didn't care. She kicked her purse away, opened her eyes, and fell into Jack's arms.

Their lips locked, tongues intertwining. Standing, he drew her tiny body into him as his white coat fell open. His arms embraced her tight.

Ignoring the shooting pain in her left arm she wrapped her arms around his firm body.

He walked her back against the door, she lifted her leg around him, he raised her with his hands upon her ass.

She pressed her wet center into him and felt his hard cock through his scrubs. They kissed passionately, wildly, as she tasted his delicious mouth.

A knock on the door broke their kiss. "I'll be right out," Jack announced as he did his best to straighten his scrubs and white coat. "I need to go, Emma. I don't know if I can wait until you're not my patient."

"I know, but we have to. We do. I'm sorry, Jack." Emma lowered her head as Jack brushed her cheek and lifted her face back up to his.

"I don't know, Emma." Another knock on the door and Jack's voice rose, "I'm coming."

"Go. You can't get into trouble. Go. We'll figure something out. Go, Jack." She touched his arm; he leaned down and kissed her mouth before leaving the exam room.

***

While getting ready for bed, her phone rang with Matt's ringtone. Lying across their bed she answered, "Hi Matt," her voice monotone. He wasn't trying, so why should she?

"Hi Emma, I'll be home soon," Matt's voice sounded light and happy.

"When is soon? I hope you're done with traveling," Emma answered with no emotion.

"Um, I can't promise that. I called and told Troy I needed to come home. I needed to see you, be with you. He granted my request for a week. I should be home in a few days. Let's do something special together. I miss you, baby," his voice begged for Emma.

"I guess I'll take whatever I can get. I'm not happy about any of this. You promised!" her voice rose as her heart thumped hard in her chest.

"You'll have my undivided attention all week, I promise. I love you, Emma Brooke Taylor. Things will settle down soon."

"I hope you're right, Matt. I do." She wasn't going to allow herself to get her hopes up. Matt had let her down too much recently and she knew something would fuck up their time together.

"Find us a romantic cabin somewhere away from everything, for the entire week."

"Matt, I can't go away like that. I have a business to run and portraits to paint. I'd love to go away with you, but that's not an option this time. I may be able to take a few days away, around the weekend, but I can't go away for an entire week. Did you forget I had shoulder surgery and couldn't paint for months? I'm backed up by six weeks maybe more. Moving everything another whole week isn't going to happen. If you were home, you'd know what I'm dealing with." Emma omitted the fact that Jack just told her to take a week from painting to rest her arm.

"Emma, it's your business, you can take whatever time you want—"

"No, I can't, Matt." She stopped him mid-sentence. "I have dates to deliver these portraits to my clients. The ones I had to postpone because of surgery, well, they all understood. I'm about a week from being all caught up on those. Since you haven't been home, you don't know about mine and Brandi's new project for our next exhibition we're planning." She puffed out a breath, leaned back on her wedge, and cradled her sore arm, remembering Jack's soft hand caressing her, holding her, kissing her.

"Emma!" Matt yelled through the speakerphone. "Did you hear me at all? You didn't answer me," his voice weak.

"Sorry, I didn't hear you. What did you say?"

"I asked how your recovery was coming along. How therapy went and how your appointment with Dr. Bryant was."

"Oh, so you want to know how I'm doing. I'm doing well, Matt. So, well that therapy is over, and my appointment went well. Jack's pleased with me," Emma said sarcastically as she grinned sinfully thinking about how pleased Jack was with her. She felt relief that Matt hadn't video called her.

"That's great news, Em. I knew Jack would take care of you and fix your shoulder for you. He's a great doctor. You're lucky to have him." Matt gushing about Jack made Emma's heart tighten. If Matt knew how Jack felt about her and her about him; his praise wouldn't be so high. She shook those thoughts from her mind.

"Yes, I am very lucky to have Jack." If only she could have Jack. Her body heat rose, and her heart smiled, thinking of Jack.

"I need to go, I love you, Em," Matt said.

"Love you too," Emma answered and closed her phone. She laid on her sore arm, pain shot through it. She jumped up, grabbed her arm, massaging it. She went to the kitchen searching for some pain pills and whiskey. She found both and swallowed.

CHAPTER 25

"Who was on Zoom?" Emma asked.

"A vendor for a new client. I can get back to them on Monday. It's time for me to quit for the weekend." Standing, Matt ushered Emma out of his office.

A slight chill overcame her at the touch of his hand on her lower back. She knew about Miranda, so why would he lie and say she was a new vendor? Emma abruptly stopped, and Matt walked into her. Turning to face him, she said, "I heard a woman's voice. Was it Miranda? Please, Matt, don't hurt me like that."

Matt went completely still as he looked at Emma with a flat gaze. "Yes, it was Miranda, okay? But oh my God, how could you even think I... I love you. We've been together for over thirty years. You're my world, my forever."

Shaking her head, she apologized, "I'm sorry. I don't know what I was thinking. I know you love me. I love you." Emma's arms hung at her sides; she bit her lip as she felt a tightness in her chest. She slipped her hand into Matt's. "I believe you." She leaned into Matt, he embraced her gently.

"Now that, that's settled, what should we do for dinner?"

"Order something to be delivered. I don't want to share you with anyone tonight." Emma brushed Matt's bicep.

"Sounds good, pizza?" He woke his phone and thumbed through the food apps.

"Yes, and salad." They sat at the kitchen table as Matt ordered dinner for them.

***

They'd just sat down to eat when Matt's phone rang. Emma glanced over and noticed it was Miranda.

"She's got crappy timing," Emma said.

"I'll be quick." He jumped from the chair and walked toward his office. "Yeah, Miranda what's…"

The door clicked shut, cutting off the rest of his words. Her curiosity getting the best of her, she walked over and pressed her ear to the door.

"Okay, I'll make the arrangements. Yes, it's okay. I'll be there soon, don't worry. I promise. It'll be okay." Emma's heart squeezed. She'd never heard him talk so warmly to another woman.

Heart hammering, she scampered back to her seat and pretended to eat. She let out a whimper as her eyes watered.

She pushed her plate across the table and folded her arms while she waited for Matt to finish his call. She didn't want to fight with him.

She thought she wanted to fix their broken marriage or did she? Emma laid her head on the table, her feelings for Jack flooded her. She felt his arms around her, holding her. His voice promising to never let her down. Her body warmed as she remembered her last appointment with him, their spontaneous kiss, the hot sensations her body went through when he lifted her and held her against the door. His fucking hard as steel cock rubbing on her aching wet pussy. Her body tingled wanting Jack to take her away from all this.

She hurt inside from being pushed aside. Being chosen second to a job. Her emotions ran the gamut from lust for Jack to her anger with Matt when she jumped to conclusions about Miranda. To disappointment, in herself and her husband as her heart felt like it was shrinking into nothingness. While she sat and waited patiently, her stomach clenched, she wrapped her arms around her small body and cried.

***

"Emma, where are you?"

She stirred when she heard Matt's voice calling for her. His call lasted so long; she'd fallen asleep. Her emotions tiring her mind, body, and soul.

"I'm in here, Matt," she called out.

"I'm so sorry. I'm all yours for the rest of my time off. I told Miranda not to call me. Call Troy, that I was off work for the next five days." He climbed into bed with her and snuggled next to her. His arms embraced her as though everything was normal.

Her body became stiff, she didn't take his hands into hers.

"Em, what's wrong?" Matt slid up and propped himself on a stack of pillows.

"You're asking me what's wrong when you promised when you were home, there was no work." She glared at him, her voice cracking, her face warm.

"I know and I'm sorry. No more work from now until I go back to Maine." His arms laid at his sides; his mouth drawn.

"Wait, what? When was this decided? C'mon, Matt." Emma's nostrils flaring, her voice rising. Sitting up, she folded her arms across her body.

"I never promised the traveling was over. Not yet. When I get the promotion, I can delegate that work to Miranda and the rest of the team. This Maine job, I have to be there. Please be patient with me, baby. I promise when it's done and Troy gives me the promotion, I'm home with you all the time." He leaned in and kissed her shoulder.

Her chin rested on her shoulder as she saw his bottom lip protruding out, then slowly his mouth turning upward. How could she stay mad at him? She didn't want this promotion shit to ruin their marriage, their life. *Fuck why is all this so damn difficult. I just want my husband home with me.* She turned away from Matt, slid her legs off the bed, and went to stand when Matt's arms stopped her.

"Emma, please, I love you. I want you. I've missed us," Matt whispered against her skin. His soft lips glided down her arm, giving her hot chills.

She faced him, her lips tight, trying to stay angry with him, but his pouty big brown eyes warmed her heart. Yes, she held feelings for Jack, deep feelings she'd have to figure out, but Matt was her husband, he deserved every chance to make it work.

"Okay, Matt. As long as the traveling is done when you say it will be. I'm going to hold you to that promise." Wanting to be with Matt; it had been much too long since they'd made love. She missed his touch, his kisses, his dick inside her. She tucked herself under his arm and walked her hand across his firm chest. "I've missed you, too. I need you, too."

Matt rolled onto his side, slipped his hand under her top, and unhooked her bra, pulling it off like a magician, he showed it off to her and smiled brightly. He nuzzled his nose against her soft neck and inhaled her. His warm breath made her wet, she trembled as he removed her clothes and stripped his own off.

She nudged his body down on their bed and crept onto him, kissing him. She felt his well-endowed member as she laid on him. She mounted her husband and had fierce sex with him. It was rough; she had complete control sitting on top of him, maddeningly gyrating on him.

"Jesus Emma!" Matt exclaimed as his wife's body moved with a wildness he'd never seen before.

"Oh God, Matt, fuck me, fuck me hard!" she yelled at him.

He wrapped his brawny arms around his wife and flipped them over. He pounded Emma's body, bit at her nipples and her lip. He turned her over and lifted her to her knees. He plunged his rigid manhood into her slick center. His body smacked against her smooth ass. They collapsed onto their bed.

Emma hid her face in some pillows as tears streamed down her cheeks. She sniffled and turned onto her back, wiping her hair from her face.

"Emma, did I hurt you?" Matt asked when he noticed her tears.

"No, you didn't." She laid her head on his glistening chest. She skimmed her fingers around his nipples and down his abdomen. She searched deep in her heart for the love she once held for him. It had to be there, it just had to.

"Baby, I'm going to need a few minutes," Matt said when her fingers walked playfully down to his groin.

"I'll make you hard, lay back, relax." She took his cock into her hand and began to stroke him. She kissed his chest, licked his nipples. She felt him stiffen as she stroked faster. Within minutes his rod hardened.

He cupped her breasts with his soft hands and caressed them. His hand slid down her stomach, to between her thighs. He massaged her clit with his thumb and slid his finger into her center, rubbing her swollen mound. He kissed her hungry mouth, playing tag with her tongue, sliding another finger inside her.

"Matt," she moaned against his shoulder as her orgasm was insane.

He moved on top of her with her legs spread wide and slid his hard shaft into her. His thrusts were smooth; in and out, harder, and faster as he kissed her. He throbbed inside her. They came as each squeezed the other tightly. He laid beside her, her head on his chest. Matt threaded Emma's long locks with his fingers, lovingly brushing her hair.

She searched again for that love for him, she searched her entire heart and soul.

CHAPTER 26

Emma paged through her email while waiting to be seen by Jack. This was her next to the last appointment. She sensed something different in the office when she arrived but shrugged it off, thinking she was just overreacting.

"Mrs. Taylor," a female voice called out.

Mrs. Taylor? No one here calls me Mrs. Taylor, something's changed. She stood. "Yes, that's me." She smiled at the new nurse and placed her phone into her purse. She followed her past Jack who was at the computer. Their eyes met briefly. Something felt different about that too. She shivered and wrapped her arms around her waist, continuing to follow the nurse.

She took a seat in the exam room as the nurse turned on the computer and asked Emma some ordinary questions. "It'll be a few minutes, then Dr. Bryant will see you," she said and left.

Emma's phone sounded and she fumbled with her purse to find it and silence it. It was Matt. Since he'd left her again for work, she left his call go to her voicemail.

A knock on the door and Jack entered with the nurse in tow. A frown formed on Emma's face as she caught Jack's eyes. His head shook slightly from side to side and shoved his hands into the pockets of his white coat.

Emma took in all his body messages loud and clear. She knew he'd let her know what went on later when he could.

She put on her best smile and sat straight in her seat. Jack rolled over on the stool but stayed well out of her personal space. The nurse stood by the door, observing every movement between them.

"How are you doing, Emma?" Jack asked.

"I'm great, thanks."

"No pain any longer in your arm or shoulder?"

"None at all. I'm painting again and no pain."

"That's great news. I don't need to see you again for six months. That'll be your last visit with me and your official discharge. If I were allowed, I'd discharge you today, but protocol won't allow me, so in six months, you'll get rid of me." He managed to turn his body from the nurse enough and smile sinfully at Emma, she bowed her head, her body all ablaze.

Jack began to jot some notes on her chart and dropped his pen; it rolled past her chair, she instinctively bent over to grab it.

Sitting up slowly, her eyes, shielded from the nurse by Emma's long locks, landed on his crotch.

He was conveniently sitting with his legs spread and she was awarded the view of his cock straining to be free of his green scrubs.

Licking her lips, she swallowed hard. Back in her upright position, she ran her hand through her hair and handed Jack his pen, "Here you go, Ja– Dr. Bryant." Emma caught herself before she called him 'Jack' in front of the nurse.

"Thanks, Emma." He stole a soft touch as he grasped the pen, she held out for him. "We're all done here today. I'll see you in six months." Jack rose from the stool and left Emma in the exam room.

She felt cold and unsure of what had just happened. A nurse was never in the room before. Did someone see them? There was no way anyone saw them kiss. Maybe it was a new protocol because another doctor was caught messing with a patient. Whatever it was, Emma left the orthopedic office the same she always did, a smile on her face and a pep in her step. She was six months from not being Jack's patient.

***

Without the gallery and her art, Emma knew she and Jack would've crossed that invisible unethical line long ago. Her drawing, paintings, and running the gallery with Brandi kept Emma grounded since Matt was gone so much of the time.

The weird feeling she'd had at the doctor's office still lingered. She tried to shake it off as she entered the gallery from the back.

"Brandi," Emma called out, stopping by her office, and leaving her purse on her desk. She walked into Brandi's office, looking around the empty room. She went down the hallway to the main room, searching there, then she checked her side, and finally she walked over to Brandi's room. No one. "Hmmph, Brandi!" Emma yelled, she reached around to her back pocket, "Shit." She glanced at the front and realized the closed sign was still facing outward. She left it as it was, needing to be sure Brandi was okay before opening the gallery.

Heading back to her office to grab her phone, the back door flew open, and Brandi walked in hands full with her two cameras, two tripods, and long lens, and her backpack across her back.

Emma ran to help her. "Hi, let me help you with something," Emma offered.

"Thanks, Em. Here take the tripods if they're not too heavy," Brandi warned.

"I can handle them. Did you have an offsite photoshoot?"

"Yeah, last night. The Campbell's out on Roxy Drive." Brandi blew out a breath when they got to her office. She laid her cameras on her desk and turned to Emma.

"That big family? Don't they have eight kids, and the grandparents live with them?"

"Yes, that one. It was fun and a mess all at the same time." Brandi pulled her hair into a ponytail and plodded into her chair. "The kids were fine and took direction better than the grandparents. Mom and Dad just shook their heads. I was glad Ben went along. I would've never been able to manage them alone." Brandi looked around her office.

"What are you looking for?"

"I don't know, my brain is all over the place this morning. That's why I was late. I need a Diet Coke. Want to walk to the deli and grab lunch before we open?"

"Sure, let me get my purse." Turning, Emma went and got her purse, checking her phone, she saw a text from Jack and Matt. She opened Matt's first. **I'm going to be a few more days in Maine. Sorry for the lack of communication. I'm swamped. I miss you.** Emma's heart ached, she lowered her head and took several deep breaths.

Jack's text read: **I'll explain everything. When can I see you?**

Her body warmed, thinking when she could sneak away and see Jack. She closed her phone and met Brandi at the back door.

***

Emma's phone vibrated in her pocket several times while she and Brandi had lunch. Knowing it was Jack, she didn't answer right away. Before leaving the deli, Emma turned to Brandi and said, "I need to use the restroom before we walk back to the gallery." Brandi nodded as she finished her Diet Coke.

Pulling her phone from her pocket, Emma smiled when she saw Jack's texts. He'd sent four. **Emma, can you meet me later tonight?**
Think KCs will be safe?
Should we meet someplace else?
Emma?

Thinking of where it would be safest for them to meet, Emma replied, **I don't think KCs is safe. Meet me in the park, by the lake. There's a bench under the big oak tree. 7 p.m.**

Jack texted her back immediately. **Sounds good.**

She rejoined Brandi and they went back to the gallery.

***

Walking to the park bench she'd told Jack to meet her at, she looked around and noticed more than the usual number of people in the park for that time of night. They'd have to be discreet with so many eyes that may be watching them.

As she approached the bench, she saw Jack sitting, waiting. A heat passed through her, and a smile formed across her face. She waved when he noticed her.

He stood and walked over to meet her.

Shaking her from head side to side as Jack's arms opened for her, she pointed around the park, then to her own eyes. They walked to the bench and sat close enough to touch without anyone being able to see.

"Hi." Emma ran her hand across the back of Jack's, then rested it on top.

"Hi." Jack's eyes gleamed as he caught hers. "I want to hold you, kiss you." He moved closer to her and leaned in.

Emma panned the area around them and turned back to Jack. Their lips met and she didn't want to talk anymore but she knew they couldn't do more. She gently pushed Jack back. Her eyes, pleading with him to be more careful.

"I want the same, just not here. So, tell me what's going on at your office? Did you get into trouble? Or was it someone else?" Emma placed her hand on his again.

"It wasn't me, or us. It was another doctor in a different division but the policy of a nurse with every doctor for every patient's visit was set across the entire practice. It's probably for the best. And it may change again, who knows." Jack shrugged his shoulders and picked Emma's hand up, brought it to his mouth, and threw her a sinful stare. His blue fuck me eyes, drove her body wild for him.

"I'm glad it wasn't you. But it was odd having someone in the room with us. I felt like I was being watched. I don't like that feeling." Emma's fingers drew along Jack's jawline, around his ear, and back to his lips.

He sucked in Emma's index finger, she moaned softly when she felt his velvet-like tongue. Wanting it to be licking her clit instead of her finger.

"I know how you feel. I never had a nurse stay for the entire exam until now. I'm sure I'll get used to it."

She pulled her hand back and sat with it clasped with the other in her lap to avoid temptation. "It's getting dark. I should go. Walk with me to my car?" Emma asked as she rose from the bench.

"Of course, I wouldn't let you walk alone, ever." He placed his arm around her, she snuggled into his firm body, and they walked to their cars.

CHAPTER 27

"Hi, honey." Emma forced her voice to sound happy.

"Hi, Emma. Sorry about the call dropping; the service here is spotty. I hope to be home soon. How are you?" Matt asked.

"I'm great. I can't wait to see you."

"I can't wait to see you too, but I need to go now. Miranda is calling." Matt ended their short call before Emma could respond. An ache in her heart struck her. Again, Matt ended their call without an I love you.

She stared at her phone, wishing Matt to call back, apologize and tell her he loved her. It had been much too long since she heard those three words from her husband. Why?

She laid back, her stomach feeling heavy, her skin tingled and hurt. Her throat tightened, as she tried to breathe through the pain ripping her apart.

Lying on her bed she gazed at the wall. She turned and caught sight of the whiskey glass on her bedside stand. She grabbed it. A wail escaped her as she threw the glass. She grabbed her arm and screamed in pain. *Fuck! Where did it go wrong? When did Matt stop loving me?*

After several minutes of forced meditation, she needed to clear her thoughts, be calm. Emma woke her phone and thumbed to Matt's number. She sucked in a few fast breaths, building her courage, thinking about the words she planned to say to Matt. He had to come home, it was important, they had to talk; immediately.

She pressed on the green icon and the speaker on her phone. One ring then voicemail. She didn't leave a message. Matt would see she had called. Holding onto hope, using her rational mind, she waited. Her marriage was important to her, Matt was important to her, why wasn't she important to him?

Emma sat crossed legged on her bed, watching her phone screen again. Begging for it to sound, with Matt's ringtone. Her pulse quickened as the minutes went by with no call from Matt.

She went to the kitchen and poured herself a whiskey, remembering the glass she threw and needed to clean it up.

Her phone pinged and she had hoped it was Matt apologizing for cutting her off earlier. Or perhaps he'd lost signal again. But when she looked at her phone laying on the bed, her heart jumped. It wasn't from Matt. It was from Jack.

Only one word, but that was all that was needed to say everything.

Jack: **Dinner?**

Oh, I shouldn't, said her good girl voice.

And why not? asked her bad girl voice.

Because she knew better than to meet her doctor for dinner.

Her fingers hovered over the phone as she chewed her lip. Typing quickly, she hit send before she could stop herself.

Sure, where and what time? Her heartbeat rapidly as she waited for a response. A volcano eruption rose inside her, its heat flowing through every inch of her body.

Jack: **Toni's across the bay, 8:00, tonight?**

Emma hesitated for more than just a beat. She'd already agreed to meet him, what was she thinking. Jack asked her out on a date. Did he see it as a date or was she exaggerating all this in her mind? He just wanted to see her, be sure she's okay while Matt was away.

Jack: **Emma?**

Okay, see you soon. Emma sent back. She gave in to her desires, her wants, her needs. She wanted to see Jack, be with him. She didn't want to tamp down her emotions for him any longer. The restaurant Jack chose was across the bay, far enough away so no one would recognize them or think it odd she was with a much younger man.

She tried all she could to convince Matt to come home to her. It was one crisis after the other and Emma was over it. Her life on hold was done. She was going to see whoever she wanted, be with whoever she wanted.

Emma waited for the Uber to pick her up at home. She paced around the kitchen until the text came, letting her know the car was out front. It was dark by the time she was to have dinner with Jack. She didn't worry about her neighbors seeing her, she'd make an excuse if anyone asked.

On the forty-five-minute ride across the bridge to Toni's, Emma's heart raced, fluttered, pounded. Her palms were sweaty, she opened her small purse and brought out some tissues to dry her hands. She watched out the car window, trying to calm her nerves. Was she going on a date with Jack? They're married to other people; it couldn't be a date, especially not the first date.

She brought out a lighted compact mirror and checked her makeup, her hair, her dress. She wanted to look her best for Jack. For their dinner together. She touched up her cherry red lipstick just as the Uber arrived at Toni's.

***

"May I help you, ma'am?" A young man asked, looking like he was still in high school. *Ugh.* She disliked being called, ma'am. It made her feel old.

"I'm meeting someone for dinner. He's tall, brown hair, blue eyes."

"Are you Emma?" he asked.

"Yes."

"Follow me. Your date is waiting."

Her date is waiting. Laughing quietly, she followed the young man. No, she was meeting Jack for dinner. Her stomach tumbled like a gymnast doing a floor routine. Her nerves tingled as though it was a first real date. What was she thinking? She hugged herself, as she felt her adrenaline rising. She took in several deep calming breaths as she glanced around at the dimly lit restaurant. Releasing them when she didn't recognize anyone. The aromas coming from the kitchen settled her nerves.

He led Emma to a table for two in a secluded area of the restaurant. *Oh my God, it is a date.* She gulped, as butterflies flew inside her stomach. Grabbing the door frame, she steadied herself when her knees went weak.

Moving to the side, he allowed Emma to pass by.

"Thank you." Emma smiled at the young man.

"You're welcome. You two enjoy dinner." Turning, he left as Jack rose to help Emma with her chair. Her heart smiled.

His full lips curved upward; his eyes shone like diamonds. "Hello, Emma, you look stunning," Jack's voice oozed charm and sensuality.

"Thank you, Jack." She'd dressed in a beaded black cocktail dress and five-inch black heels.

He helped her as she scooted her chair into the table.

Her body tingling fiercely. She reached for her cloth napkin as Jack reached for his. Their hands brushed lightly. She quickly flicked open the napkin, covered her lap, and clasped her hands together.

Emma kept her eyes on her hands as she twisted her fingers around in circles, then she peeked through her loose hair strands to see if Jack was waiting for her to look at him.

He appeared relaxed, sitting back in the chair with his right calf resting on his left knee. His arm laying on the table, she could see his gaze taking all of her in.

Emma wiggled in her chair and sat straight, crossing her legs. She slowly turned to look at Jack. She knew once their eyes met, she'd be caught. She began to breathe deep when his scent entered her nose; she felt instant wetness between her legs. Her heart pounding and warmth spreading all through her.

Emma swiped her hair from her face and grabbed Jack's intoxicating blue eyes. Fluttering butterfly wings filled her stomach again as Jack's eyes penetrated her soul. They held their gaze in complete silence.

Jack rested his soft hand on her shoulder, she leaned her head down as his hand came to her cheek. The warmth of his skin sent shock bullets to her core.

She slid her hand down her thigh ready to touch Jack's knee when a server appeared.

"May I interest you in a glass of wine?" he asked.

"No, thanks. I'll have a whiskey, please," Emma answered.

"I'll have the same," Jack said.

"If it's a whiskey you both enjoy, we have a sampler that may interest you. Would you like to try that?"

"Sure," Jack answered, and the server walked away.

The whiskey flight was brought over, and they ordered dinner.

"Cheers, Emma." Jack's eyes sparkled as he spoke.

"Cheers, Jack." Emma clanked her glass to his and they each shot back the whiskey. That particular brand sent heat down her throat to her belly. She shook her head from side to side.

"How have you been since I saw you at your last appointment?" Jack asked as he placed the glass down.

"I'm fine, Jack. Ready to be discharged." Emma smiled and blinked slowly. She sipped on another whiskey.

"Only a few more months. Maybe we can celebrate with another date when you're free of me." He threw her his sweet grin, wetting his lips.

A couple of servers came in with their dinner before Emma could correct Jack's 'date' statement. They each picked at their dinner.

Emma peeked at Jack, watching him lick his lips. Seeing his tongue, she longed for it on her body.

When they finished dinner and the plates were cleared, Emma broke the silence. "Brandi and I are planning another exhibition right before I'm to be discharged. I hope you'll be there." She chewed her lip, waiting for him to assure her he'd be there for her.

"Always. I'll move heaven and earth to be at your exhibitions, Emma. I promise." He placed his hand on hers. Grasping her fingers, he picked her hand up and pulled it across the table.

She sat dazed as she watched him control her. She couldn't move from her trance. "Jack—"

Drawing her toward him, he lightly grazed her lips with his. Brushing against her earlobe with his soft full lips, he whispered, "Don't talk, Emma, don't talk."

Jack trailed his mouth along her cheek, sending incredible amounts of lightning heat bolts to her core. Making her quiver incessantly.

His lips met hers. He kissed her deeply. His tongue pushed through her pursed lips. His hand held her at the nape of her neck. His touch made her feel safe.

She knew she had feelings for Jack.

He filled the crater that formed when Matt went to Maine. Jack touched Emma like she longed to be touched. He kissed her like she wanted to be kissed. He held her as if he loved her.

Emma knew she was falling deeper in love with her doctor, the one man in her life who was forbidden to her, he was who she wanted to be with every waking second.

CHAPTER 28

"We're ready to hold another event. Can we get on your schedule for August?" Brandi asked Jenna as she and Emma were wanting to hold another exhibition sooner rather than later.

"No, sorry ladies, we're booked solid until early fall," Jenna answered reluctantly.

"Wow, I'm happy you're busy," Brandi said.

"We knew your business would take off," Emma chimed in. "Let us know if there's a cancellation." Then Emma thought, maybe working with Jenna wasn't a good idea. Or maybe it was, if she insisted on a new caterer, that would send up a red flag, she couldn't have Brandi any more aware of her and Jack than she was. She'd been able to keep Brandi under control.

"I can do that," Jenna said.

"We'd like to do a weekend event. Friday and Saturday nights. Is that something y'all can do?" Brandi asked.

"Yes, we can do as many nights as you want. A two-night event sounds fun. You can pick two of those themes we gave you. It'll be like two different parties. A two-night reservation will need to be even later in the year."

"How much later?" Emma asked thinking maybe Jenna saw a text she'd sent Jack or saw them together somehow. She needed to talk to Jack. Ask him if he still attends Jenna's events to help her.

"Probably in mid fall Emma. My team and I have a lot of weddings and family reunions. I'll get back to you as soon as I can." Jenna sounded anxious to end their call. "Brandi, I almost forgot, Jack and I need to postpone our photoshoot. His schedule got switched around and he can't make it next week."

"No problem, Jenna. Call me when you and Jack find a new date. I'll fit you in," Brandi said and ended the call.

Emma glared at Brandi when she heard the conversation about the photoshoot. She released a breath when it was canceled, and balled her fist when Brandi said she'd fit them in. She never offered that to anyone else. She was strict with her photoshoot schedule.

"You'll fit them in. Since when do you fit anyone into your schedule?" Emma's voice rose.

"Well, Jenna is a business associate and I'm trying to accommodate their busy schedules," Brandi explained as she put her phone in her bag.

"So, we are Jenna's business associates and she said 'no' to us. She didn't accommodate us," Emma pushed on.

"I think it's a bit different, Em. I'm one person, I can make changes easily. Jenna can't just move things around for us. And besides, the fall will be better."

"Summer, fall, what does it matter? We're ready when we're ready." Emma crossed her arms and puffed out a breath.

"We'll be better prepared in October. You know that. This isn't about accommodating anyone. This is about the Bryant's having a photoshoot and most likely a romantic or sensual one. It bothers you, Em. I can read your face." Brandi leaned on the table, drumming her fingers, staring at Emma.

"What?" Feigning surprise, she sat with her phone in her lap, open to Jack's number. Thinking of what to say to him. Being in the same place with Jenna and Jack; would be uncomfortable. She'd have to hide her jealousy if she saw Jack kiss Jenna or hold her hand. This wasn't a good idea.

Emma thought she'd heard something off in Jenna's voice. She wasn't as bubbly and friendly as she'd always been with them. *Or maybe she's having a bad morning and you're overthinking it all.* She typed a text to Jack. **We should talk, soon.** She read and reread it, then finally hit send.

"The Bryant's canceling their photoshoot, I know it bothered you. I know you, Emma." Brandi leaned back in her seat, staring at Emma.

"They're postponing it, not canceling it. I'm sure Jack will be available soon." Emma shrugged off Brandi's allegation.

"Okay. Keep telling yourself you're fine with them having a romantic photoshoot and you may be asked to paint a portrait of them in a sensual position. I know it'll bother you," Brandi stated.

"If they ask. Maybe they won't." Emma played it down. Her chest tightened at the thought of having to paint Jack holding Jenna, clothed or naked.

"I'm sure Jenna will ask."

Emma stood and stated confidently, "I look forward to her asking." She patted Brandi's shoulder and headed to her office. She tossed her hair as she passed by Brandi. When she got to the hallway, she turned and said, "It doesn't bother me."

"Okay, Em. Whatever you say," Brandi's voice trailed off as Emma walked to her office.

She'd felt her phone vibrate in her pocket and hoped it was Jack answering her text.

Pulling out her phone, she kicked her feet up on her desk, sat back in her chair, and opened her phone. She smiled when she saw Jack's text in her previews. She flicked to her messages and read his text, **okay, Can I call you tomorrow? I'm just finishing up.**

Emma thought about her words before responding to Jack. She'd rather see him face to face, but a call would be okay. Matt wasn't home and even if he were, she could play it off as Jack calling to check on her. **Sure, I'm available whenever you are.** She sent back.

***

Lying in bed, Emma's phone rang with Jack's tone. Instant heat flowed like lava to her core. Smiling, she answered, "Good morning," her voice was light and bubbly.

"Good morning, Emma." Jack's smooth chords made her senses tingle. "Are you okay? What did you want to talk with me about?"

Clearing her throat, she said, "Um, yes, I'm fine but I'm worried about working with Jenna on our next exhibition."

"Why?"

"When Brandi and I last spoke with Jenna, she seemed distant. Not her bubbly, happy self. She hasn't said anything to you about…"

Emma paused, not sure how to ask Jack about them if he thought of them as an 'us.' "About us, has she?"

"No. Emma, if Jenna saw anything, she'd say something to me. She knows I'm a flirt and gives me a long rope to play with."

Waiting for a beat to respond, Emma felt a pain in her chest. Like a knife slicing her. "So, you're flirting with me?" her voice rose and her face warmed.

"When we first met, of course. That night at Matt's office party, when I saw you all alone, I made my move to see if you'd be willing to play along. And you did. Something about you, Emma, changed me. I'm not flirting with you anymore."

"I played along?" her voice rose again.

"You did, it was fun. Then when the party ended and I watched you as you were leaving; you turned, you knew I was watching you, didn't you?" Jack asked.

"I felt someone's eyes on me. That's why I turned." Emma tried to explain it away. She felt her body heating up.

"You knew it was me watching you and that's why you turned around," Jack stated, confidence oozing through the phone.

"Okay, maybe," Emma confessed, smiling.

"I know you're smiling right now; I can tell," Jack said.

"You know me so well." Emma laughed softly.

"Of course, I do, I'm your doctor."

And just like that, Jack drew the invisible line between them. Their cat and mouse game was fun, but she knew how much he could lose, how much they both would lose if either were caught.

"Yes, you are. Thanks for calling. I should go." Emma turned her voice from seductive to businesslike.

"Okay, Emma. Have a good day," Jack said sweetly.

"You too. See you around." Emma ended the call and got ready for her day alone.

CHAPTER 29

Spending the last several months painting, drawing, hoping to save her marriage and have Jack in her life, Emma stepped back from her last painting for the Pictures to Paintings exhibition. This last portrait featured a baby boy, with curly sandy blond hair, it reminded her of Matt's when they first met. Her mouth turned upward thinking of him. He still meant something to her, she didn't know exactly what anymore.

Her marriage slipped away right before her eyes. And for all she knew, Matt had no idea there was something wrong. He had no clue she'd fallen in love with another man and out of love with him.

Shaking her head to clear her thoughts, she picked up her paintbrush and began with long strokes of green for the yard the boy was laying on. The sky in the photo was a soft blue; *there's Jack's eyes.* Her heart warmed as Jack appeared in her mind. His tall firm body and strong arms, inviting her to come to him. *No, I have to get this done. Ugh.*

Emma stepped out for a while and drove to the coffee shop. Entering, she heard Claire's familiar sweet voice, "Hi Mrs. Taylor, it's been a bit, how are you?"

"Hi, Claire. Yeah, I'm good and busy. I've been in, I guess I come in when you're off."

"Probably, I don't work as many shifts as I did. Can I get you your usual?" Claire asked pointing to the fresh pot of black coffee.

"Yes, please. I need to clear my head. Thank you." Emma found a cushioned chair and plopped down waiting for her coffee.

"Here you go, Mrs. Taylor." Claire handed Emma the mug.

"Thanks." Emma's eyes bounced as she inhaled the aroma of her hot black coffee. Leaning back, her phone rang. She didn't recognize the number, but she took a chance and answered it. "Hello, this is Emma."

"Hi, baby," Matt's voice came through.

"Matt? Why are you calling me from a strange number?" Emma frowned and her brain began overthinking.

"I dropped my phone, it's destroyed. Miranda was nice enough to let me borrow hers." Matt mumbled something Emma couldn't make out, she assumed he said something to Miranda.

"That's nice of her," Emma sighed, rolling her eyes. Good thing he didn't video call her.

"I'll get it replaced later and call you. It's been crazy here and I'm sorry for not calling more often. Every time I get settled in to call, it's so late." He mumbled again.

"You know you can call me whenever, Matt." She heard his hand cover the speaker, there was a crunchy noise, like static. "Matt, what are you saying? Are you talking to me or someone there?" She pinched her face and waited. Hearing Matt talking with who she assumed was Miranda, she puffed out a breath and waited for him to answer.

"Sorry Em. As I said, it's crazy here, but I wanted to call and check-in. I love you."

"Whatever Matt. I need to get back to the gallery..." Their call dropped. She stared at her phone, willing it to ring. Finding the unknown number, she called it back. It went to voicemail with Miranda's upbeat greeting. Emma shoved her phone into her purse.

Matt had finally said, I love you to her. It'd been way too long and now too late. She wondered if he even realized that she didn't return his I love you with one of her own. She rubbed her face, raked her fingers through her hair, and stood to leave. Her mind so far gone, she drove back to the gallery and finished her last piece.

***

With only a few days before the exhibition, Emma, and Brandi doubled and tripled-checked their pieces. Checking details from their list, Emma called Jenna while Brandi finished with Ben and his marketing strategy.

Sitting at her desk, she listened to the rings. "Jenna Bryant, how can I help you?" her voice was businesslike.

"Hey Jenna, it's Emma."

"Oh, hi. What do you need?"

Emma shivered when Jenna sounded cold. "It's just our call to double-check with you…"

"No, not that, dammit," Jenna yelled, but not to Emma. "I need to go, we've got everything for the events, don't worry." Emma's phone went blank.

Glaring at her cell phone, wondering if Jenna knew something. If Jack confessed or someone told Jenna, they saw them together.

"Knock, knock." Brandi startled her as she walked into Emma's office and sat in the chair across from her. "Did you speak with Jenna?"

"Well, sort of. She was either super busy or didn't want to talk to me." Emma shrugged, still looking at her phone.

"I'll go with super busy. Are they all ready for the exhibition? That's all that matters." Brandi leaned forward and placed her hands on Emma's desk.

"Yes, she said they were, but I think we, or maybe you should call her later." She fiddled with a pencil. Rolling it through her fingers, worrying about what the fuck Jenna knew.

"We can try again after hours. She's probably just busy. You know how things can get when you're on a deadline." Brandi seemed to always make excuses for Jenna and maybe that was all it was. But Emma felt something wrong with Jenna. Her voice was snappy, not her usual sweet and cheerful voice.

Emma worried Jenna had found out about her and Jack's much more than just flirting. She worried Jenna would make a scene at their event, but then Emma thought if she did, she'd ruin Jack's career too and she hoped Jenna wouldn't do that.

"I want to be on the call too," Emma said as she twisted a wild strand of her hair.

"Okay. Let's call her around six tonight," Brandi suggested.

"Sounds good."

***

At a minute before six, Emma entered Brandi's office and pulled up a chair. "Ready?" she asked clasping her hands together.

"Sure, Em. Let me get my phone." Brandi found her phone on the shelf behind her desk. She tapped it awake and called Jenna.

"Hey, Brandi, what's up? Didn't Emma call this morning?" Jenna asked, her tone sharp.

"Yeah, she did but we wanted to double-check to be sure you're good for the event. You're on speaker," Brandi announced.

"Of course, I'll be ready. There's no need to double-check with me. We'll be there and have everything you've chosen. Let me do that," Jenna's voice rose.

Emma and Brandi looked at each other, shrugging their shoulders. "Jenna is every—" Emma began before Jenna's voice bellowed over the speakerphone.

"Dammit, I said I'll do that." The phone went black.

"Somethings wrong." Emma nodded her head up and down. She knew something was up with Jenna. She'd never held a sharp tone with her or Brandi before.

"She's probably busy with our orders. We do have a big exhibition in two days. We caught her on a difficult day. We all have them." Brandi shrugged off Jenna's unusual mood. "I'll call her tomorrow morning and ask her about it. Don't worry Em. That is if there's nothing to worry about, is there?" Brandi questioned her.

"No, there's nothing for you or Jenna to be worried about. Ugh, please stop with the accusatory looks. I pinky promised I wouldn't do what you did and I'm not." Emma huffed as her eyes flicked upward. She crossed her legs and scrunched her nose.

***

Walking toward what Emma knew was Matt on the phone with Miranda, working again, she knocked on the office door and waited for him.

"Come on in Em," Matt said.

"Are you ever—" He hushed her with a finger on his mouth. She hated being hushed as much as she hated forehead kisses. She clenched her jaw, sat on the twin bed, crossed her arms, and waited.

"Yeah, I know, but I can't tomorrow. My wife's exhibition opens at seven. Miranda, you can go, you can manage it." Silence from Matt as Emma knew Miranda was trying to convince him to go with her to wherever the problem was. She glared at Matt and shook her head from side to side. He promised he'd always be at her events.

"I can't Miranda, that's final." Matt ended the call and turned to Emma. His face drawn, he rubbed his scruffy jaw and puffed out a long breath. "Emma…" he began.

"No, no, no, no, Matt," Emma insisted. She didn't have to say anything else; he knew.

"Fuck, this damn Jacksonville crew. Em, I might—"

Interrupting him again, Emma's voice rose, "No fucking way, Matt. You're not breaking this promise. No!" She stood and stomped out of his office. Slamming the bedroom door, she fell onto their bed, her heart tightening, she rubbed her eyes to keep the tears from falling.

Hoping Matt would come to her and promise to be with her, she lay staring at the bedroom door. Nothing. She stewed in her anger all day while Matt worked, she assumed he worked.

When night came, she opened her phone to Jack's number. Touched the 'message' icon and wrote him a text.

Can't wait to see you tomorrow night.

CHAPTER 30

Matt and Emma entered BE Unique on night one of Pictures to Paintings. He wore a tan suit, and she had on a cream mini dress with sparkling four-inch heels carrying a small jewel-covered clutch.

Brandi and Ben met Emma and Matt in the center of the main room. Ben wore a grey sport coat and slacks; Brandi wore a charcoal fringe dress and wedge-style sandals.

The gallery was dressed up as well. They chose maroon tablecloths and silver runners to layer each table. The drapes were silver with sequins and sparkled when the lights hit them exactly right.

Emma hugged Brandi, she swallowed down the anger she still felt toward Matt. He'd worked well into the early morning hours, then was up and in his office again this morning. She pasted on her sweet smile and pretended all was well.

"There's a lot of guests waiting to come in already. I wasn't sure if we'd get this many again. It's been less than a year since our last exhibit." Emma noticed the crowd outside.

"Yeah, I'm happily surprised too. We should welcome them in and mingle with everyone, okay?" Brandi squeezed Emma's hand as she turned to Ben and clasped his.

The foursome went to the front entryway and opened the gallery for "Pictures to Paintings, night one."

Greeting their guests as they came in, Emma smiled at each as she shook hands or gave a quick hug to those she knew personally.

When their guests were all inside, taking in the exhibition, Emma turned to Brandi and said, "I'm going to grab a water. C'mon

Matt. Let's say hello to Kaitlyn." Emma grabbed Matt's hand and led him away from Brandi and Ben. She yanked on Matt's arm.

"What the hell, Em." He had his phone in his hand, thumbing the screen.

"Please put your phone away. This is my night, not yours." Emma stood with her hands planted on her hips. Her lips forming a thin line.

"I can't do that, and you know it. Dammit, Emma. I need to take this, it's Miranda." He turned and headed to a corner of the gallery away from her.

Well, fuck you then. Scanning the room for Jack, she spotted him with Jenna. A pout formed on her face as her body tightened. She walked to the bar and took a seat on the stool. "Hi, Kaitlyn."

"Oh, hi Emma. What'll it be? Whiskey?" Kaitlyn asked grabbing Emma's usual.

"No, not tonight. Water is all, thanks." Emma's jaw hurt from clenching her teeth. Her smile turned flat as she avoided watching Jack with Jenna.

"Taking it easy tonight?" Kaitlyn placed the ice water by her.

"Yeah, for now. Maybe I'll have a drink later." Emma lifted the glass and nodded toward Kaitlyn. She spun the stool and sipped the water. *Fuck, I need a whiskey.* Knowing she was working; water was her drink for the evening.

Scanning the gallery's main room again, Emma found Jack closer to her and away from Jenna. She poked her arm up to get his attention. Waving to him, her fingers rolled into her palm, her lips slipping into a sinful grin.

Emma made a quick check of Matt, still deep in conversation on his phone. His free arm making exaggerated movements. She meandered toward the hallway that led to hers and Brandi's offices, the storage rooms, and the bathrooms. Her head turned a tad to check on Jack, she noticed him stealing further away from Jenna and coming toward the hallway.

Halfway to her office, she took one more look in Matt's direction.

He paced as he spoke into his phone.

She puffed a breath and kept going. Her hand on the doorknob of her office, she waited. Her body warming at the thought of touching Jack, and more.

"Let me in." Jack breathed upon her shoulder as he placed his soft lips on her skin.

She shuddered and spun to face him.

His smile filled with mischief.

She reached up and ran her hand through his soft brown hair, resting it on the nape of his neck, pulling him to her. Their lips met; tongues hungry for each other.

His hands grasped her slim waist as she turned and opened the office door. They stumbled inside.

"Damn Emma, you smell delicious." Jack drew in a deep breath as his nose touched her bare neck.

Her body quivered, she giggled and rotated to face him once again.

"Jack, you feel incredible." A mischievous grin formed as she dragged her hand across his hard cock beneath his suit pants. She held his manhood and moved her hand up, then down slowly. Her folds dripped, her panties wet. She backed them up and hopped onto the desk once she felt it against her backside. She glanced around Jack and noticed her office door still open. A sudden fear and excitement jolt ran through her. She wanted to leave the door open. *Let them catch us.* "We should close the door, maybe lock it?" Emma asked Jack.

"Probably." He shrugged and grinned, then walked over and closed the door. His fingers were on the small lock as he threw Emma a dangerous grin.

She nodded yes for him to lock the office door.

He did and came back to her waiting arms.

Jack scooped Emma from the desk.

She wrapped herself around him. Cupped his face in her palms. Staring deep into Jack's beautiful blue eyes, recognizing his undying love for her, she held his gaze as she had at all her appointments. Memories of those days floated through her mind. She loved flirting with him, playing with him, and the risks they took.

Her body ached for him inside her. She'd dream of him licking her clit, his soft brown hair tickling her inner thighs as she'd squeal his name.

His cock penetrating deep into her center. Plunging as her core walls contracted around his throbbing shaft.

Her dream was seconds away from coming true.

"I want you to fuck me, Jack. Tonight, here in my office as everyone is mingling around the gallery, Fuck me, Jack!" Emma held his gaze as she spoke to him.

He gently placed her ass on the desk.

She spread her legs as his hands crept under her dress.

His fingers slipped around the lace edges of her panties. He slowly dragged them down her legs, holding eye contact with Emma, grinning sinfully.

"I want you so damn much." Tossing her panties, he leveled her body on the desk with his. He covered her mouth with his. Sliding his tongue across hers.

She dug her fingernails into his suit jacket, tugging on it, wanting him to take it off.

He stood and tore off his jacket, she untied his tie, then grabbed his white dress shirt.

Grinning, she ripped at his shirt and the buttons flew in all directions. Pushing his shirt down his arms, slowly caressing his firm ripples, she crawled her fingertips over his delicious pecs. Her eyes rolled across him as she admired his physique. Placing her hands upon his hips, she moaned as she drew him to her and lightly brushed her lips across his nipples. Her tongue circling, her teeth nibbling.

"Oh God, Emma," Jack moaned as he fisted her hair, gently holding her face against his chest.

Her lips dragged down his abs. Kissing each firm ripple, tasting his delectable skin, finding his trail that led to her prize. She began to unbuckle his belt when a knock on the door startled them.

"Emma, are you in there?"

"Oh shit. It's Matt," Emma whispered with eyes the size of the moon. Her voice cracked as she quickly answered, "I'm coming, Matt."

"Why is your door locked? What's going on in there?" Emma heard Matt trying to force the door open. Her body froze.

"I must have accidentally locked it, sorry. Hold on. I was looking for my inventory list. I'll be out in a second." She and Jack hastily put themselves back together.

Jack went and hid in the closet in her office.

Emma straightened her dress, her hair and unlocked the door, smiling brightly as she faced Matt, "Hi honey, so sorry about the door. I'll have that checked this week. Let's go and grab a drink," she spoke rapidly in a high-pitched tone and hooked her arm through his. She tugged him out the door and started toward the main room of the gallery. Peeking back over her shoulder, seeing Jack steal away into the men's bathroom, she let out a breath.

Matt suddenly stopped. "Emma, what's going on? No, what were you doing in your office, where's your list?"

"Nothing's going on Matt. I said I was looking for my inventory list. I didn't find it. It's no big deal, I'll look after the exhibition is over. Now c'mon babe. Let's get that drink and mingle." She tried to coax Matt, but he wasn't moving.

"I can't. I have to leave and meet Miranda at the office…"

"Wait, what? Now, tonight?" Emma turned toward Matt with her hands on her hips, her face heating up.

"Yes. She was the call I had to take. The job in Jacksonville has a huge problem and we both need to go. I'm going home to pack an overnight bag. I hope it's only one night—"

"Stop, just stop right there, Matt. I don't want to hear any more about any damn problems with your work. You promised to be here for this. You promised never to miss one of my exhibitions. Didn't you train this woman to oversee this fucking shit?" Emma's arms flailing as she spoke, her face red.

"Emma don't be like this. Please. I'll do my best to get back tomorrow, but I wanted to warn you that I might not. If we leave tonight, it gives me a better chance to be back for you tomorrow night."

"Fuck that shit," her voice raising. "I'm done with all your traveling. You hired Miranda to do the out-of-town work. You promised it would end once you were promoted. You—"

Matt cupped his hand over her mouth.

She slapped it away and stared angrily at him.

"I haven't been promoted yet, Em."

She held her hand up in his face and shook her head from side to side.

"Whatever. Just go. I'm over it." Emma began to walk away from Matt, but he grabbed her arm.

"Don't be mad, baby. I'll try to be back for you tomorrow. I promise." He leaned in to kiss her lips, but she turned her head. His lips barely grazed her cheek.

"It's too late for that Matt." She stood with folded arms and watched him walk out of her gallery. She thought about going back to her office, back to Jack, but she didn't. She walked to the bar.

"Hey Kaitlyn, whiskey please." Emma leaned against the bar, watching the hallway for Jack to return to the gathering.

"Sure Emma. Nice exhibition you're having tonight." Kaitlyn slid the tumbler with the amber liquid in it to Emma.

"Yeah, thanks." She slugged the drink, slid the glass back to Kaitlyn. "Another." She didn't care that she was working. She looked up when she heard Jack clear his throat.

"Hey, Emma, nice crowd tonight." Jack put up his index finger to Kaitlyn.

"Thanks, Jack. Happy to see you again." She caught the tumbler Kaitlyn slid to her and slugged the drink down once more. "One more." She slid the glass back one last time.

Kaitlyn threw Jack a look of concern. Emma watched her and Jack communicate without words about her.

He nodded and Kaitlyn filled Emma's glass. She handed them each their drinks. "Y'all enjoy the rest of the night."

"Thanks, Kait." Jack put his arm around Emma and escorted her to a seating area. "Sit here while I get you some food."

Emma plopped into a big chair and sipped on her third whiskey. "Thank you, Jack. At least you know how to take care of a woman." Emma licked her lips and smiled sinfully.

He grazed her hand and walked toward the food tables.

I almost had him. I was so close to fucking Jack. Will there ever be another chance?

She glanced around the room. Watching her patrons taking in all her and Brandi's hard work. Their artistry blended so beautifully and made the gallery what it was.

Jenna suddenly walked into Emma's line of sight. Trying to loosen the thickness she felt in her throat, she massaged her neck. She felt heat rising to her cheeks. *Oh shit, what did I— we— what did we just do?* Her breath hitched; she covered her mouth as she let out a shameful cry. She loved Jack, yet she hated hurting Jenna. How could she have both? Her happiness meant Jenna would be in pain, and heartbroken, while Emma's heart would be filled with joy. *How can I do this?* She pinched her eyes tight, waiting for Jenna to clear her sight path.

"Emma." Opening her eyes, she saw Jack before her. "Here, eat some of this to soak up that whiskey." He handed Emma a plate with bread and pasta.

"Thanks. I'm okay, Jack. You don't need to babysit me. Go enjoy the exhibits, find your wife. We can talk later." Emma placed the small plate in her lap. She saw Brandi walking toward her and wanted to move Jack along.

"Okay. I'm going to check on you later. No more booze tonight." Jack smiled and walked toward where Jenna stood serving a tray of champagne.

"Hey, Emma. Are you okay? Where's Matt?" Brandi took a seat by her in a matching big chair.

"I'm fine. Miranda called and he left. Some fucking job issue again. I don't care anymore." She shot the whiskey down her throat.

"I think that's enough of that for tonight." Brandi took the glass. She grabbed Emma's hands and held them to get her attention. "Em, I'm sure it's really important if he left tonight. He'll be back for tomorrow night's show. He won't miss it." She patted Emma's hand.

"No, he won't be back. He's packing an overnight bag. He's going to miss our show. And I don't give a fuck anymore." Emma pulled her hands free of Brandi's grip and sat forward. She looked around the gallery.

"Don't say that Em. He could make it back." Brandi tried to reassure her. She scooted closer to Emma and spoke softly, "stop looking for Jack."

Emma shot Brandi a nasty look. "I'm not. I was looking around at all our loyal patrons. Being grateful for their support. Why do you always assume I'm looking for Jack? And so, fucking what if I am."

"Because I know that look in your eye. I know how you look when you are trying to find Jack. Jesus Emma. We've talked and talked about this. Please don't do this," Brandi kept her voice low so no one would hear her but Emma.

"I wasn't looking for Jack," Emma bit at Brandi and glanced at her iWatch. "It's almost time to end this. Let's go and thank everyone for coming." She laid the empty plate on the side table.

"Okay, let me find Ben and we'll wrap the night up." Brandi walked away.

Emma spotted Jack with Jenna as she and her staff were gathering up plates and cups, beginning their cleanup process. Clenching her jaw, she folded her arms under her breasts and began to walk toward them. When she caught Jack's gaze, she cocked her head, motioning toward the hallway.

Meeting him at her office door again, she gazed up into his lustful eyes and asked, "Will you be here tomorrow night?" She drew her fingers through his soft chest hair, her smile full of sin.

"I wouldn't miss it." He touched her chin tenderly as his lips met hers, he brought her close as their kiss deepened.

"I have to go now. It's time to close the exhibition tonight. See you soon." She trailed her hand down his arm, their fingers locked, their eyes locked. Their lips locked.

Emma met Brandi in the center of the gallery as they thanked everyone for being there and invited them back for the second evening.

Scanning the gallery before leaving, she found Jack helping Jenna and her team with the final cleanup. Her emotions ran wild. Her heart drummed heavily, while she followed Jack's movements. Jenna came up and hugged him from behind. Emma began walking to them, stopping herself as she realized what she wanted to do would've ruined everything she and Jack had, although what they had was unclear to her. She spun and ran out the back of the gallery.

CHAPTER 31

"Hello, Matt Taylor's phone," a woman answered.

Emma's mouth fell open. She waited for a beat, took in a breath then replied, "Hello… this is Matt Taylor's wife. Where the hell is my husband?" A light pain shot through her, she sucked in a quick breath. *What the fuck?* Her fingers felt numb holding her cell phone, she pushed the speaker icon and laid it on the bedside table. She pressed her hands to her ears, hoping she didn't just hear a woman answer Matt's phone.

"Oh." Silence for a second or more. "Hi, Emma, how are you?" the woman's voice was upbeat and confident.

Emma rubbed her forehead, tears filling her eyes, she plopped down onto her bed. "Where's Matt? Is this Miranda?"

"Um, yes, hold on, I'll get him. He went to shower," Miranda spoke quickly.

"Shower?" Emma raised her voice. Her body numbing, she felt dizzy and laid back against the pillows. The pillows became wet as her tears stung her cheeks. Maybe Matt did see something at the gallery last night when he nearly caught her and Jack in her office. Her thoughts ran amok, was he retaliating for Jack with Miranda? This soon? Were they already fucking around, and she never suspected because she was so in love with Jack, blinded by Jack's love?

"Uh… I'll have him call you." The phone went dead.

"Fuck!" Emma screamed into her pillows. She clasped her hands tightly to stop the trembling. She let out several screams to remove the rage that ran in her blood.

After a while, Emma picked herself up and got ready for her day at the gallery.

***

"Hey, Emma," Brandi greeted her when she arrived.

"Hi." She walked in with her head lowered, her voice sullen. She went straight to her office. Shoving open the door, it slammed against the wall making a loud bang. She plopped into her chair and slid open the bottom left desk drawer. Pulling out the new bottle of whiskey, she had a glass on the shelf behind her desk. She poured a small amount in and shot it down. She shook her head from side to side, poured more of the amber liquid into her glass, and started to shoot it when she heard Brandi.

"Em, really? It's only ten a.m." She walked over to Emma and grabbed the glass from her hand.

"It's five o'clock somewhere," Emma threw back. "Give me my glass." She pinched her lips together and held out her hand.

"Talk to me, girl." She gave her the glass. "Give me your keys. You're not driving today." Brandi held her hand out while Emma dug in her purse and tossed her keys across her desk.

"Matt's still in Jacksonville. Miranda will have him call me–" She stopped and sucked down another shot. Her eyes were wide, cheeks hot.

"Alright, you knew she went with him, so what's wrong?"

"–When he gets out of the fucking shower!" Emma finished as she pinched her entire face, her pulse racing.

"Oh, crap." Brandi's gaze fell to the floor.

"How does Miranda know Matt is taking a goddamn shower?" Emma's body shook, her eyes were an even darker shade of blue. She clenched her fists on her desk.

"I don't know. Maybe she heard the water?" Brandi tried to make excuses that made some sense.

"Why is Miranda answering my husband's fucking phone?" Emma's eyes bulged as she stared at Brandi and took a long gulp of the whiskey, slamming the glass on her desk, then shaking off the sting of it winding down her throat.

"Em, calm down. I'm sure there's a good excuse for all this." Brandi tried to settle Emma.

"No, there's never a valid reason for a woman who's not his wife to be in his hotel room," Emma's voice hit an octave above yelling. Her heartbeat thumped hard. But why did she care who answered Matt's phone if she wanted to fuck Jack? Why was she so damn mad Miranda answered Matt's phone? She couldn't help herself. She kept trying to hold onto Matt, knowing deep inside she wanted Jack. She pulled at her hair and screamed, "Fuck me, I can't anymore."

"Emma, what the hell? What are you going on about?" Brandi asked.

"Nothing, it's nothing. Forget about it. I'll confront Matt when he gets back." Emma poured another shot and tipped the bottle toward Brandi, offering her one.

"I'm sure there's a reason for all of this. And no thanks. You know I won't touch that shit."

"Fine, more for me, and I'll play. Give me one valid reason, just one." Emma sat forward, her eyes penetrating Brandi.

"They have adjoined rooms and the door between was open." Brandi shrugged.

"No, there's no reason for adjoining rooms with co-workers. Families, sure. Not co-workers of the opposite sex." Emma smirked.

"Alright, then Matt's door was ajar, and Miranda heard his phone ringing and went in to answer it for him to be nice," Brandi offered.

"Matt would never leave his room door ajar. Nope, do you want to try for strike three?" Emma folded her hands neatly and relaxed her shoulders, waiting.

"Miranda was already in his room when he told her to wait while he showered. It was a completely innocent incident." Brandi went for strike three. She held her hands in the air.

"Extremely inappropriate for Matt to ask a much younger female subordinate to wait in his room while he showers. Strike three, Brandi." Emma pointed her finger across the desk and shook her head slowly from side to side.

"Okay, Em. I'm not sure what to say but I know Matt won't cheat on you. That's not who he is. C'mon, you know that too." Brandi reached for Emma's hand. She pulled it away.

"I don't know anything anymore." Emma slipped her hands into her lap and lowered her head.

She felt Brandi's hand on her shoulder, Jack's shoulder. She didn't know what to do next. Was Jack her future or was he just a fun affair. Could she even sustain an affair? Did she want to have an affair with Jack, or did she want more?

Emma tossed her hair back and said, "I have paintings to do. I'll deal with Matt later, whenever he decides I matter to him again." She pushed her chair back and stood next to Brandi.

"Hey, if you need to take some time that's fine. With the exhibition going on, your orders can wait a few days. Call an Uber and go home, relax in the spa, dream about what you'll do with Matt when he comes home. He will come home to you. He always has." Brandi pulled Emma in for a tight hug.

"You're right. I'm going to go home and relax until it's time to be back here for night two. See you later." Emma left the gallery when her ride arrived.

***

Relaxing in the spa with a coffee and some lunch, Emma closed her eyes and let the hot water take her away.

Her phone rang with Matt's tone, she thought about ignoring him, then answered.

"Hello," Her voice was low and quiet.

"Hi, Emma. Miranda said you called. I'm sorry I didn't call back sooner," Matt's voice shook.

"Whatever. Will you be home for my exhibition tonight?" Her voice calming. She knew his answer before he told her.

"I won't make it back. I won't be back for a few days." She heard him mumbling to someone.

"I don't want to fight or argue with you over the phone, but I have to know why Miranda answered your cellphone this morning... while you were in the shower, Matt?"

"She happened to come to my room at just that moment. Nothing is going on. She could be my daughter. C'mon, Em, be real."

"I am being real." Emma clenched her fists and pushed them under the water.

"No, you're being jealous of nothing."

"I'm not jealous. A young woman answered your phone in your room while you showered. Think about that. If it were me in a room and a young man answered my phone, how would you react? Be honest Matt." *Or me in my office with Jack?*

"Okay, I get it. I swear, it was just bad timing. Nothing's going on."

Emma puffed a breath as Matt was clearly distracted mumbling to that person again.

"Matt!" she raised her voice.

"Yes, Em. I need to go. Call me when the exhibition closes."

"I—" Her cellphone went black. Matt had ended their call and again no I love you.

Her eyes were dry, she held no emotions for Matt. He made work the priority and she was an afterthought. She thought about pouring a shot but decided against it. She couldn't be drunk at the exhibition in a few hours.

Jack would never treat her second to his career if they were together. He's almost admitted it to her. A tightness ran through her chest as she wondered how in the hell her marriage disintegrated in less than a year.

She loves Jack, it's that simple for her. Does Matt love Miranda? Maybe so, he did choose her over Emma much too often. Did Matt have it in him to cheat on her?

Emma never thought she'd be attracted to another man, let alone fall in love with one. At one time she loved them both, but Jack took over her heart. He moved in and claimed his spot in her life and heart forever.

CHAPTER 32

All eyes turned to Emma when she arrived at the gallery in a white lace camisole dress, above mid-thigh in length. Her matching thigh-high boots with five-inch platforms gave her a bit of height.

Brandi's jaw dropped as she stood by Ben's side in a tight navy-blue mini dress with five-inch heels.

Walking over to her, Brandi grabbed Emma's arm and dragged her to a quiet space. "Jesus, Emma, what the hell?" She waved her hands up and down Emma's body.

"What?" Emma asked innocently.

"Um, you're a bit overdressed."

"It's Greek night. Greek's love it when a woman dresses sexy." Her chin up, Emma walked away from Brandi and to the bar.

"Evening, Kait."

"Hey, Emma," the young woman said with a smile. "You look fabulous. Where's Matt?"

"At work. Can I get a glass of water?"

"Sure."

"Thanks, see you later." Emma picked up her glass and strolled around the gallery. While speaking with an older couple, her phone rang with Matt's ringtone.

"Please excuse me, my husband is calling." Digging her phone from her small clutch, she went down the hallway. Frowning she answered her phone, "Hi Matt."

"Hi Em, how's your exhibition going?"

"You'd know if you were here," she bit back.

"Baby, I am sorry. I won't miss another one, I promise," Matt pleaded. "What, what did you say, hey…"

"Who are you talking to? Me, or Miranda?" Emma wanted to scream but kept her voice low. She paced past her office door.

"Em, I have to go." Her phone went black. She slumped against the wall. Her lips tight, her face hot. She wanted a drink but knew she couldn't. Not while she was this mad and she was working, so she paced up and down the hallway, counting to herself, calming down, releasing her anger.

Brandi met her as she entered the main gallery room. "Em, talk to me." Brandi took Emma by the arm. "Is Matt on his way?"

"I'm fine. He can't make it back, whatever." Emma gazed around Brandi, looking for Jack.

"Stop searching for him, dammit. Look at me. Don't do anything stupid. Matt loves you. How many times do I have to tell you that? If it weren't important, he wouldn't miss this. He was here last night, so he really didn't miss our exhibition, Emma," Brandi raised her voice as Emma kept looking around the gallery.

"If you say so. I need a drink. Want one?" She purposely ignored all that Brandi had said.

"No, Em. I don't want a drink. I want you to listen to me. Don't spend all night talking with Jack. You'll mess all this up. You need to mingle with our guests. Look. At. Me." Brandi took Emma's face in her hands and held it tight.

"Let me go. I'll do what I want." Emma shook free and walked toward the bar. She glanced back at Brandi and wrinkled her nose and squinted.

"Hi, Sherry. Where'd Kaitlyn go?" Emma asked as she approached the bar area.

"She wanted to help serve the floor, so we switched. Can I get you something?"

"Another water please and thanks." Emma turned and leaned against the bar, taking in the room again. Not finding Jack, her heart sank. *He promised to be here, where is he?* "Dammit."

"What's that, Emma?" Sherry handed her the water and wiped down the bar's surface. She refilled the small bowls of peanuts and pretzels.

"Oh, thanks. Nothing, I was thinking out loud. Are Jenna and Jack here yet?" She knew asking for Jenna first would cover her ass and find out what she wanted.

"Jenna texted me and said they were running late. Oh, there they are." Sherry pointed to the gallery door just as Jenna and Jack entered.

Emma's pulse quickened. Her face heated, her knees went weak. She grasped the bar to steady herself. A grin slowly formed as Jack's eyes met hers. Her panties became wet when Jack left Jenna's side and approached her. Emma watched Jenna head to the serving table, grab a tray and begin mingling around the gallery. Jack was hers for the evening and she couldn't wait to get him alone.

Her smile grew as Jack came up beside her. His soft hand slid against her bare thigh, teasing her.

"Hey, Jack. What'll it be?" Sherry asked and broke the spell Jack had on Emma. She spun around to face her.

"Whiskey, thanks. Only water tonight, Emma?"

"Yes, technically I'm working." Emma smiled and blinked slowly. She moved closer to him, sliding her hand across the front of his suit pants. She felt his hard cock under the fabric and let out a sigh.

"Here ya go, Jack. Enjoy the exhibition." Sherry placed the tumbler on the bar and went to serve the other guests.

"Where to, Emma?" Jack placed his hand on her lower back, she shivered, not with cold, but heat traveling through her entire body.

She walked ahead of Jack toward a group of chairs in a corner of the gallery. In her mind, she sat on his lap, grinding on him, but in reality, she took a seat across from him. She checked on Jenna and saw her across the room serving a group of couples. A guilt thought ran through Emma, and she shoved it out. She leaned forward and shifted herself to face Jack.

"I didn't see you when I arrived. I thought you forgot about me." Emma threw Jack a pouty grin. She reached for his hand, fluttering her fingers.

"I promised I'd be here. Jenna took a last-minute call for a potential client. She called Kaitlyn and told her we'd be late. I'm assuming Kait didn't mention that to you or Brandi?" Jack laid his palm upward as Emma walked her fingers into it.

"She didn't tell me, but I was late myself. Maybe she told Brandi, and it wasn't passed on to me. Doesn't matter now. You're here." She squeezed his hand.

Emma and Jack released their hands when they heard Brandi's voice say, "Hey Jack."

"Oh, hi Brandi, Ben." Jack rose to greet them. He shook Ben's hand and kissed Brandi's cheek.

"I'm glad you both are here now, we missed Jenna at the start of the evening." Brandi stood between Emma and Jack.

"Sometimes Jenna just can't say no to the next client. Sorry if it caused any issues." Jack pointed to Jenna moving through the crowd of people with a large tray of champagne flutes.

"No worries. Kaitlyn had told me, and the rest of the team had things under control. It's all good."

"Brandi, do you need something?" Emma rolled her eyes.

"Yes, come with me. We have some customers asking about a piece of yours. Ben will keep Jack company." Brandi nodded at Ben, and he acknowledged her with a wink.

Emma looked at Jack, apologetically. "Lead the way, Brandi. Talk to you later, Jack." Emma followed Brandi to a couple standing by her painting of the downtown skyline with the river cutting through the center. It was one of a handful of single paintings on display.

"Mr. and Mrs. Sutter, this is Emma Taylor," Brandi introduced Emma. "She can tell you where she painted this."

"Nice to meet you both." Emma extended her hand to them.

"You too," Mrs. Sutter returned. "We love this piece you painted, Mrs. Taylor. It's our favorite. Is this the city here or another location?"

"Oh, please call me Emma, and yes this is our beautiful city. It's downtown just before sunset. I'm happy you like it, Mrs. Sutter."

"Then please call me Cara."

"Cara it is and…" Emma gestured toward Mr. Sutter.

"I'm Charles. Nice to meet you Emma, is there a Mr. Taylor here tonight?"

Her heart hurt. "Matt had an emergency at work and couldn't come tonight. He's usually here." Emma's gaze fell to the floor. She pulled in a deep breath and raised her chin to see her guests.

"We'd like to purchase this," Cara informed Emma and Brandi.

"No problem, we'll mark it sold and take care of the sale when you're ready to leave this evening. Thank you. I hope you enjoy the rest of your night." Emma shook their hands again and the Sutters made their way around the gallery.

Turning to Brandi, Emma spat out, "You didn't need me to tell them where I painted this piece. You know the location very well. You pulled me away from Jack on purpose. We were just chatting. And about Jenna."

"Like hell you were. I watched you and Jack at the bar and then walking to the chairs in the corner. You're playing with dangerous fire Emma. Please hear me when I tell you, do not do this." Brandi held Emma's arm to keep her from walking away.

"Let go, dammit." Emma shook her arm free. "I'll talk to whomever I want. Jack happened to come to the bar when I was there. It's not any plan, Brandi. I was being polite."

"Christ, Em." Shaking her head, Brandi turned and walked away.

***

Emma made her way to the table of food and made a small plate. Everything smelled and looked delicious.

"Emma, you look hot tonight," Jenna said, coming up beside her.

"Thanks, Jen. Have to try and stay young, you girls make it hard on us older women."

Standing next to Jenna, Emma's hands balled up and fell open. The hair on the back of her neck lifted. She peered up at Jenna and gave her a quick smile, then turned and scanned the room.

"Emma, are you okay?" Jenna touched Emma's shoulder.

She jumped away. "Yes, I'm great, I need to mingle. Thanks for all the great work you and your team have done," Emma spoke rapidly and walked away, leaving her plate of food. She had to get away from Jenna Bryant. She was just too nice to Emma.

Emma's desires for Jack remained fierce. Her heart pounded with both the need to be with Jack and the guilt for hurting Jenna. Emma wasn't a selfish person; she gave of herself all the time.

What the fuck am I thinking, God, I want Jack more than anyone I've ever met. I'm sorry Jen but I love him, I need him.

Shaking off the anxiousness trying to overcome her, and lifting her chin, she roamed around the gallery; welcoming and speaking with many of their guests. She glanced around to locate Brandi, then headed toward the bar. She noticed Jack with a group of men his age looking at several of the more sexual displays. She gave him a nod toward the hallway and watched him excuse himself from the group.

"Hey Sherry, can I get a bottle of whiskey please?" Emma asked.

"Of course, glasses?" Sherry placed the fifth on the bar.

"Nope. Thanks a lot." Emma grabbed the bottle by the neck and turned toward the hall. She glanced around checking on Brandi again and saw she was deep in conversation with several patrons.

Jenna passed by Brandi, and they shared smiles.

Jesus, what am I doing? Emma stopped. She fumbled with the whiskey bottle and bit her lip. Catching sight of Jack heading into the hall she moved that way too, then hesitated for a beat again. Thinking about what may happen if she and Jack hook up. Thinking about leaving the gallery and waiting for Matt at home. Thinking about Jenna and how nice she always was and… *Fuck all that, go get him, now!*

Her feet strolled down the hallway. "Oh, damn." Looking up, she felt hands pulling her into the storage room. Before she could say more, his lips covered hers. His tongue diving into her mouth, lapping hers.

Placing her hand on Jack's chest, holding him at arm's length, she tilted a fifth of whiskey back and forth in the dimness of the small nightlights. "I brought us a bottle to enjoy in private, want some?"

"No, Emma. I want you. Just you." Jack took the whiskey bottle and sat it on a nearby shelf. He drew her into him. Pressing his body tight against her. "I can't wait any longer to have you." His mouth covered hers again before she could respond.

Fierce passion took over as they groped one another. Her hands were hungry to touch his soft skin. She pushed his suit coat off his broad shoulders, tugged it down his long arms, and tossed it into the shadows of the room. Emma's fingers worked fast and untied his tie. Their kisses were hot and wet as they continued to undress the other.

Jack unzipped her dress, she raised her arms as he ripped it from her tiny body, it disappeared. He unhooked her bra and skimmed his fingers along her arms as he removed it, sending sweet chills across her.

His mouth took in each of her breasts, tickling her nipples with his velvet tongue. "Oh Jack," she moaned as his fingers crawled into her lace panties and between her slick folds. "Baby, I need you; I want you inside me. Oh, Jack, take me. Fuck me!" she begged as she ripped his shirt for the second night in a row, the buttons flying.

"Damn Emma, you're so wet. I want you, love," he breathed into her neck.

Emma knew there was a small table in the back of the storage room. Leading Jack there, she hopped onto it and raised her legs for him to slide her boots off, one then the other. Her tongue traveled around her lips, her chest rising with each deep breath she took.

He slid her panties off.

She sat forward; legs spread for Jack to see all of her.

His eyes danced in the faint light of the nightlights. He quickly removed his suit pants and boxers.

She chewed her lip when he revealed his manhood. *My God.* Emma's pulse beat rapidly, her body trembling, her folds dripping, wanting him inside her, fucking her senseless.

She held her arms out straight, wriggling her fingers, inviting Jack into her body. "Baby, fuck me," she demanded, pulling him onto her. Her ass sitting on the edge of the small table as he slowly entered her hot, wet pussy. "Jesus, Jack. Oh, dear God." Wrapping her legs around his tight, peach-shaped ass and leaning back on the small table, she arched her back. "You feel so good. Go slow, I want to enjoy you for a while, baby."

Jack went in slowly, his cock filling her core and throbbing inside her. His hips moved back and forth in a methodically slow motion, giving Emma exactly what she wanted.

"I've waited so long for this, for you. You feel so damn good. I want to make love to you all night long." Jack plunged deep into Emma, leaning down, and grazing his lips on her breasts. He held her tight around her slim waist, pulling her to him as he penetrated her core over and over.

Her legs clutched his ass tighter as their bodies smacked together in a beautiful, sensual rhythm. She grasped his forearms and lifted herself to him. She locked her fingers around his neck.

Jack slid his hands under her ass, raising her from the table. His cock went deeper into her as they switched places and Jack leaned against the table.

Bouncing on him, and riding him to her bliss, she brought him along to his.

They kissed deeply, tasting all of each other. Her hands threaded through his perfectly quaffed hair.

His grip tightened around Emma.

Her center walls clenched around his stiff shaft. "Oh fuck, Jack!" Screaming quietly against his firm chest.

"Emma, baby. Oh God, Emma." His entire body stiffened as she sensed his cum spraying inside her.

She climaxed, letting out a sigh, holding him tight. She laid her head on his shoulder, breathing quickly, sweat trickling from both their bodies.

Jack's hands glided down her back and up to her slick neck. Holding her, he kissed her deeply, their tongues playing tag.

Their eyes met in the dim light; her lips softly grazed his. She cupped his soft, clean-shaven face. Emma ran her fingers through Jack's hair to try and straighten it for him. Smiling sweetly, she kissed each of his cheeks.

"You're amazing, Jack. Better than any dream I've had of you." Wiggling her ass against his groin, she knew he could fuck her again; she felt his stiffness inside her drenched pussy.

"So, you've been dreaming about me?" He teased Emma and thrust his hips upward, letting her know he was ready for more.

"Oh, yes, and, baby, you outshined all of them." Emma planted her lips on his, pushing her tongue inside his warm delicious mouth and letting out a moan as she sensed his cock throb. "Again," she groaned into his mouth.

Standing and holding Emma, he turned and gently laid her onto the table, placing her ass at the edge.

She braced herself on her forearms, trying to grasp the flat surface.

"All night long love, all night long." He grinned and thrust hard into her. His hands were on her knees, spreading her wider, allowing him to go deeper into her hot core.

"Jack, dear God, Jack, don't stop, please don't stop." Emma let out with each plunge inside her. She found the table's edges and held on tight as Jack pounded her body. "Yes, oh damn, yes, baby, harder," she commanded.

Jack drew his rock-hard shaft out to her rim, then pushed harder each time into her. He circled her clit with his thumb as her pussy clenched his cock. "Emma, oh my God, Em." He slammed his rod into her with a fierceness she's never felt. His hot semen spread inside her again. His thumb still rubbed her mound, her body moving beneath him as she reached another fabulous orgasm.

"Jackson, oh fuck," she softly squealed as her thighs quivered around him.

Pulling out gently, he stood before her. His physique glistened in the dimness.

She admired his perfect body, licking her lips as she grazed her hand across his abs. "You are so beautiful, so perfect, Jack."

She glanced down at her wrist as her iWatch vibrated. Her eyes were the size of saucers as she looked back at Jack. "Shit, it's Matt calling. Where's my phone, my purse?" A panic look appeared on her drenched face. She looked around the shadowy room, no sign of her purse. She must have left it in the gallery.

Jack found their clothes. They dressed and tried to straighten themselves up before going back to the exhibition. He leaned down and kissed her deeply. "I'm going to head out. See you later?" he asked.

"Okay. Um, definitely." She patted his sweet peach ass as they walked to the storage room door. Emma opened the door slowly and peered out to be sure no one was near the hallway at the gallery end. The coast was clear and after a quick kiss, Jack walked to the men's room.

Emma waited a few seconds and went into the ladies' room to check on her appearance. When she saw her reflection, she laughed aloud. *Oh fuck, yes it was a fabulous fuck.*

She began to fix her makeup and her hair with her fingers when the restroom door swung open, startling her. Brandi grabbed her by the arm. "Emma. Where the fuck have you been? A guest gave me your purse. They said they heard the phone ringing and ringing. They asked Sherry whose it was, and she told them it was yours. They said they looked for you and when they didn't find you, they gave it to me." She yanked angrily on Emma's arm.

"Ow. I was in the storage room looking for something. No big deal, so I left my purse lay. My watch only rang once. I know it was

Matt and I don't want to talk to him, so I ignored him." She tried to free herself from Brandi's grip to no avail.

"Bullshit, Emma. Where's Jack?"

"I don't know, ask his wife. I'm not his keeper." Emma finally freed herself. "Are you trying to break my arm?"

"If I find out you and Jack messed around right under Jenna's nose tonight—"

"What? What the fuck will you do? This is half my gallery too. I was looking for something, that's all," Emma insisted and folded her arms across her chest.

Brandi threw Emma's purse onto the vanity in disgust. "Fix your makeup." Brandi drew a circle in the air around Emma's face. "It's time to close the exhibition. We'll finish this discussion another day. I'm not done talking to you about staying the fuck away from Jack Bryant." She turned and left Emma in a huff.

CHAPTER 33

"Emma?" a young woman called out.
"That's me." Emma walked over to her.
"Hi, I'm Celeste. Follow me, please."
Following the nurse, Emma went by Jack at his computer. Their eyes met and heat erupted within her. Smiling at him, she continued into exam room two.

***

Waiting alone in the exam room, Emma thought about their secret meeting at her gallery. Smiling, she wished she were back there, kissing Jack, holding Jack, fucking Jack. She reminisced about that night often, hoping for more, hoping he wanted the same.

A soft knock brought her back as she sat upright and crossed her legs.

"Hi, Dr. Bryant," Emma greeted Jack, not sure if Celeste followed him.

"Hey, Emma. No need for formalities, we're alone today," he said, sliding into her personal space and touching her bare knee.

She shivered and smiled wide. "Okay, Jack. I'm happy we're alone." She placed her hand on his and uncrossed her legs.

He caught her gaze then went straight into doctor mode. "Emma, this is it. Your last appointment. You're finally getting rid of me. Let's check your range of motion one last time." Jack held his hands up as he'd done before.

She reached up and clasped his fingers.

He squeezed them before letting go.

"I feel great. Better than new. Especially after the other night. Jack..." Emma stopped herself from admitting her real feelings for Jack. She remembered the gift she'd brought and leaned to her side to retrieve it. She caught his gaze when she sat upright again. His fuck me eyes danced before her. She wanted to tell him she loved him. But the exam room of his office wasn't the place. Besides, there was something she had to ask him, so she bit her tongue and held the gift bag for Jack.

"What's this?" he asked, taking the gift bag from her.

"It's a thank you gift for repairing me and being the best doctor ever." She smiled as he pulled the bottle of bourbon from the bag.

"Thank you." Jack grinned and replaced the bottle in the bag. He rolled close to Emma.

"I hope you enjoy it." *As much as I enjoyed fucking you.*

"I know I will." Jack rolled the stool even closer to Emma.

Emma placed her hands on Jack's chest, holding him at arm's length. "I need to ask you something."

"Anything, ask away." He took her hands in his and gazed deep into her soul.

She thought for a moment. She needed to know if he was going to do the photoshoot with Jenna. She sucked in a deep breath, then asked, "Brandi told me you and Jenna have rescheduled your session with her. Are you going to do this with Jenna?" Her eyes pulled together; her lips narrowed. She'd be crushed if she saw him with Jenna like that. She knew how Brandi ran her photoshoots, especially the romantic ones.

"Emma, I don't want to, but I have to. I wish it were you and me." Jack kissed her hands and scooted still closer to her.

Sitting back in her chair, she pushed back. "Find an excuse. Use a patient, Get out of it, Jack, please." Her chin trembled as her eyes were glassy. She lowered her head to her chest, waiting for Jack to respond.

"I'll do what I can. I promise. I'll try." He lifted her face and planted his mouth on hers, kissing her deeply. "I'll try," he said again, holding her gaze for several minutes.

"Please, I don't think I could stand to see you with Jenna like that." Her heart ached.

"I will, Emma. Now let me make your discharge official." Jack filled out something on her chart and stood before her. Extending his hand to her, Emma smiled and laid her hand in his. He pulled her into him, embracing her, stroking her back up, then down.

She hugged him tightly, not wanting to let go. She tilted her head up as Jack leaned down, they kissed passionately for the final time in the exam room.

***

With Emma's discharge from her surgery final, she and Matt met Brandi and Ben at the casino once Matt got home from another trip away.

Waving to the server for a drink, Emma scooted into the booth, while Matt slid in next to her, she placed her purse between them. Something she'd never done before. She waved when she noticed Brandi and Ben at the host's desk.

"Over here guys," Emma shouted over the loudness of the casino restaurant.

"Hey, Matt, where the hell have you been?" Ben teased as they fist-bumped.

"It's called work, man," Matt said sharply.

She winced and slowly shook her head from side to side when she saw Brandi's surprised look.

"It can be a bitch sometimes, but I'm glad you're back." Ben shook off Matt's sharpness and waved his arm for Brandi to slide into the booth.

"What'll it be for everyone tonight? Drinks? Appetizers? Oh yeah, I'm Kurt. I'll be taking care of you tonight."

"A whiskey neat for me, thanks Kurt," Emma answered first.

"A Michelob lite, bottle," Matt went next.

"Diet Coke, thanks," Brandi said.

"Budweiser, draft," Ben was last.

"Will it be twelve or twenty-four ounces, sir?" Kurt looked at Ben.

"Twenty-four."

"Be right back with your drinks and to get your food orders." Kurt spun on his heels and left the table.

"So, Em, are you all done with Dr. Bryant?" Brandi asked.

"Yes, it was a long year. Too long for me. I'm good as new." Emma whipped her left arm over her head, waving it back and forth.

"He's a good surgeon." She added lifting her eyebrows and smiling sinfully. She glared across the table at her bestie when she felt a kick to her shin. Scowling, Emma went on, "I think I'll send him a thank you note."

"I'm glad you're good as new, babe. I'm sorry I wasn't there for you like I promised." Matt draped his arm on Emma's shoulder.

She froze, not wanting to make a scene in public or around their best friends, but she cringed inside.

Matt had broken too many promises this past year. He wasn't there for her as a husband should've been.

Her heart lay heavy inside her chest.

When the band began playing, Emma's eyes lit up. "C'mon, Brandi. Let's go dance before dinner." She gave Matt a weak smile before shrugging his arm from her and sliding out of the booth.

While dancing, Emma said, "Don't worry about me, I'm going to be fine. I'm used to Matt being gone now. We'll be fine."

"Girl, I told you he'd come home to you. Why don't you listen to me?" Brandi poked Emma in the arm.

"Oh no, I think you broke my arm, I need to call Jack." Seeing Brandi's face turn red and her nostrils flaring, Emma began laughing hysterically. "Jesus, Brandi, I'm kidding. I never want to be Jack's patient again." Emma smiled. *I can't play with Jack if I'm his patient, and I want to play with him.*

"You better be because I like our foursome. Even when Matt gets busy, I know we can all hang out and have fun when he's home." Brandi pulled Emma in.

Her heart ached to hear her best friend go on about the four of them and how much fun they had together. She knew Brandi was right.

"It's all good, I promise," Emma said in Brandi's ear as the music volume rose.

Emma broke loose and shook her head wildly to the fast-paced music. She needed to clear her thoughts and concentrate on dinner with Matt, Brandi, and Ben.

"Jesus, you worked me out good. I haven't done that in years," Brandi said as they got back to their table.

"You must be out of shape then," Emma teased. "I'm ready to dance some more."

Kurt came up behind Emma with everyone's meals.

She scooted into the booth and placed her purse between her and Matt again.

"Guess dancing will have to wait," Matt said dryly.

Emma noticed Matt's phone laying on the table. "Please put that thing away. No work tonight." She glared at him, her lips tight.

"Whatever, Em." Matt slid his phone into his back pocket.

Halfway through dinner, Matt excused himself and walked toward the restrooms. Her eyes trailing him, Emma noticed him pull his phone from his pocket.

"Goddammit," she huffed and smacked the table.

"What's wrong?" Brandi jumped in her seat.

"Matt isn't going to use the restroom."

"Now how do you know he isn't?" Brandi scrunched her eyes together and shrugged.

"Because I can see he's on his damn phone. I bet you, he'll come back here, apologize profusely then leave and go to Miranda. Bet me." Emma shoved her hand across the table at Brandi. Her eyes seething.

"No, Emma. I'm not going to bet you. Let's just wait till Matt gets back from the restroom." Brandi swatted Emma's hand away.

"Okay." Emma flopped back against the booth and dug for her phone in her purse. She opened it to Jack's number, thinking of what to say to him. She knew she'd be alone soon, so why not go and play?

A few minutes passed when Matt returned. He stood at the end of the table and cleared his throat. "Emma, I…"

She waved her hand and shook her head. "Go, just go Matt. I'll Uber home." She smirked Brandi's way.

"Sorry guys, but it's an emergency and my assistant can't manage it—"

"She never can," Emma said aloud and threw Matt a fiery stare.

"I'll make it up to y'all when I can." Matt leaned into the booth and tried to kiss Emma, she turned her face and looked into her lap, his kiss skimmed her cheek. A tear dripped from her eye, she swiped it away and pulled in a deep breath.

Awkward silence floated over the table as Emma fiddled with her hands. She finally flipped her hair and smiled wide when she looked at Brandi and Ben.

"So, what do you two want to do?" Her eyes glazed; her face drawn. She put on a fake smile and pulled herself together.

"We'll drive you home, Em. Let's go." Ben waved for Kurt and paid the check. Brandi put her arm around Emma as they walked to the car.

"He'll come home to you; he always does," Brandi whispered in Emma's ear.

She turned and laid her head on Brandi's shoulder, tired, beaten. She wasn't sure what was next.

CHAPTER 34

Lying across her bed after waking up alone, Emma's thoughts took her back to when she first encountered Jack. She remembered his sweet velvety voice when he answered her question; not meant for him, but it led her to where her life is now.

How different her life would be had he not come up to her that evening. His first flirt with her. A warm feeling floated across her, a smile formed. That was his first move on her.

She would've still gotten injured, she's sure of that. Getting those sunrise paintings had become a necessity, almost an obsession for her. She would've met Dr. Jackson Bryant eventually, but would he have flirted with her had she been his patient first and not someone he'd met at a party? She'd never know.

While these happy thoughts of Jack and her made her giddy with excitement, her heart ached for what she'd done to her marriage, to Matt when she cheated on him with Jack.

What the fuck have I done? How could I have cheated on Matt? Oh my God. Her hand covered her mouth, her cheeks flushed, and tears trekked down her face. She curled into a ball and hugged herself.

Their marriage was great. Everything about their life was coming to the pentacle. Matt was about to be promoted to the position he'd been working for. Emma's partnership with Brandi at the gallery was perfect. Nothing was out of place, but something was amiss. Something was missing that Jack filled.

She had realized she'd not only cheated on Matt, but also Jenna, her business associate and someone Emma considered a friend, not a close one, but a friend. *I must've lost my mind.*

Emma considered calling Shea, spilling as much as she felt comfortable telling her sister. She knew Shea would be on her side, that's what sisters are for. Emma knew she'd always have Shea's back, no matter what.

She'd go to South Carolina to free herself from Matt and Jack. To try and clear her mind, regain control of herself. Figure her life out. She'd leave Matt a note, send Jack a text, and go. Emma would tell both men she wanted to get some sister time, just her and Shea. That would work.

Did she want to stay with Matt, confess to him, and ask for forgiveness? Promise to never stray again, love him and only him till death do they part. *Shit, that won't work, I already broke that vow, why would he trust me ever again?* She squeezed her body tighter, trying to push the pain of what she'd done out. She pumped her arms and blew out a breath, releasing the heartache.

She knew Shea would try to talk her into staying with Matt, just like Brandi. And Emma knew deep down, they were probably both right, but neither knew exactly how much Matt had let her down. How many promises Matt had broken? How many calls were dropped and never returned? How many calls cut short, how many times did he leave her for work?

She stretched and let out a scream, "Fuck!" She searched her heart and soul for the love she once had for Matt, sadly it was gone. She'd hope the night at the casino would've given her a chance to rekindle something, there had to be love in her for Matt, she needed to dig deeper. Then work called and he left, as did the last tiny particle of love. She watched it float off as Matt walked away from her that night at the casino.

Why was she in such pain then? Confused over cheating on Matt, she knew their marriage was over. She dragged her fingers through her hair, yanking on it, causing herself physical pain to try and stop her emotional pain from running through her heart and mind.

Emma believed Jack was just flirting with her that first night they met. Jenna admitted he was a flirt; it was who he was and what she found attractive about him. Emma could not have agreed more. Jack's flirty glances, his smile, his soft blue eyes. She'd drowned in those pools many times.

Jack's flirting became more seductive. His touches lingered and made her tingle all over. Their first kiss in the hallway of KCs, she knew then it was more than just flirting but she didn't know how much more.

When Jack kissed her in the exam room at one of her appointments, she was sure he wanted her. It was in the way he kissed her, so full of risk. Anyone could've opened that exam room door. He embraced her and caressed her gently. His touch changed; his glances held longer.

They were almost caught in the act by Matt, but he was too preoccupied with work and leaving again, Emma made up a lie and he accepted it. The knot in her stomach from that near miss came rushing back to her. She curled up again and hugged herself tightly. Rolling back and forth on her bed to quell the pain, the anxiety, her sadness for what may be the end of her marriage. But it meant the possibility of a new adventure with Jack.

Would she stay married to Matt? Keep cheating on him with Jack? How would she avoid making love to her husband, what excuses would she have to use? Now that she and Jack had sex, she knew she loved him and didn't want to cheat on him.

And that sounds so shitty. I'll cheat on my husband of over thirty years, but not my lover of what? Less than a year. Fuck me!

Emma softly smacked her face then dragged her hair again and tugged hard, trying to yank some sense into her brain. She hung her legs off the side of the bed. Her toes didn't reach the floor as she swayed back and forth.

I've made a fabulous fucking mess of my life. Risking everything I've worked for, for what? A hot roll in the hay with a young stud? Jesus Christ. There's no way Jack will leave Jenna. Why should he? Their life is perfect, just like mine and Matt's was. Did Jack mess with me on purpose? I don't sense that. My intuition tells me he loves me, he wants me, we share the same feelings. But I have to break this off with Jack. I can fall back in love with Matt, I know I can. God, what a fucking mess I've made.

Emma fell back onto her bed and lay with her feet dangling. Tears streaked down the sides of her temples, wetting her hair, then the bed. Staring at the ceiling, she felt lost between two men. Trying to make any sense of her life, she rolled to her side and whispered aloud, "Where are you?"

Emma's phone sounded, she gasped when she heard it was Jack's ringtone. He always answered her question, how did he know? "Hi," she greeted him in a soft voice.

"Hi Emma, are you okay? You sound tired," Jack said.

"I'm fine." She rose from the bed and walked to the kitchen, "What can I do for you, Jack?"

"Will you meet me at the Hilton on Broad Street? Tuesday at noon."

"Is everything alright? You sound serious, Jack."

"Everything is fine. I want to talk to you in private."

"Okay, I'll be there." Thinking of what it could be Jack wanted privacy to talk to her about, her brow wrinkled, and she bit her lip.

"Meet me in room 1027. See you soon," Jack's voice was as smooth and soft as always.

She cleared her throat before she answered, "See you soon."

CHAPTER 35

At the hotel, Emma entered the elevator and pressed the button for the 10th floor. Her nerves escalated as she walked down the long hallway, glancing at each room number. The room was the one furthest from the elevator.

Her heart thumped. She took a few deep breaths and told herself there was no turning back once she walked through that door.

A sudden tightness came to her chest. She walked away from the room, twisting her fingers around themselves. Back at the elevator, she drew in a deep breath, pinched her eyes closed. The elevator dinged and an older man stepped out and held the door for Emma. "Um, no thanks." She quickly turned and went back to Jack's room. With her open hand, she fanned her face. In her purse, she found a small mirror and checked herself. Her cheeks were bright red. Another deep breath held and exhaled as she knocked on the door. When she didn't hear anything, her heart raced faster. Her shoulders grew tight, she looked down the hallway toward the bank of elevators. Thinking maybe she should leave before Jack opened the door.

The opening of a door caused her to flinch, but it wasn't Jack's. A young couple stumbled out into the hallway. They glanced at Emma, she nodded, and they quickly looked away.

The creak of a door's hinges drew her attention back to Jack's door. Standing in his green scrubs before her, she sucked in a breath. Her eyes blinked slowly, her pulse pounding in her throat.

He extended his hand and led her to the sofa. The lights were on low, and the curtains were closed. He brought her small hand to his full soft lips and placed a whisper of a kiss on it. The drums played fast and hard in her chest.

He leaned in close to her. She breathed him in. He smelled so damn good. Crisp, clean, masculine.

"I want you, Emma Taylor." She held her breath. "But you know that. What I want is for you and me to see each other every Tuesday at noon."

She blinked slowly. "Are you asking me to have an affair with you, Jack?"

"You can call it whatever you want. I want to be with you. I want to make love to you. I want you in my life, and not just when we run into one another at KCs. I want to see you every week. More, if possible," Jack said.

Jack told her everything she'd been dreaming of for months. Her heart fluttered as he spoke to her, it drummed harder when she realized they wanted the same. Knowing this, she wasn't going to break things off with him.

Emma felt her body float on his words, she held her breath for a beat, slowly allowing it to leave her. She thought she was in a dream, she and Jack were her ultimate fantasy, but her marriage; what would she do?

Emma shook her head, clearing all negative thoughts of her and Matt's failing marriage from her mind. She craved Jack, his soft touch, gentle kisses, his rock-hard cock. She was exactly where she wanted to be. But she still hesitated as a slight chill ran through her body.

She leaned closer to him, "Jack, I..." She stopped herself from saying what she knew down in the depths of her heart; she loved him, knew she wanted and needed him, but she had a small twinge in her heart gnawing at her.

Jack kissed Emma, he pulled back. Their eyes locked. "I don't want to talk anymore."

"I don't either." Emma blinked slowly. Her entire body tingled, her pussy throbbing, wanting Jack's cock inside her.

Standing, he held out his hand for her and drew her into him. She embraced his tall body tightly. Lifting her, he carried her to the foot of the bed a few steps away.

He tilted her chin up with his soft hands, and their eyes met, then their lips. He pulled back, his eyes sparkling. He pressed his mouth to hers with such raw passion and deep-seated wanting that her legs weakened.

She kissed him back with the same intense passion. Lying on the bed, she watched as Jack tugged off her clothes, then his own.

Bending her legs as Jack crept onto her slowly as though it were their first time, he nudged her legs wider apart.

"Oh, God," Emma moaned as he thrust into her slow and forceful.

His erection rubbed her hot center with the right amount of friction. It drove her crazy, the way her body would start to coil with pleasure and then recede when he pulled out. He slammed back into her, making her coil harder. Jack lifted Emma's leg and encouraged her to wrap her legs around his waist. The sensations changed, driving him in deeper.

"Christ, Emma, you feel so damn good."

She could barely respond. If she had any doubts about them being together, they all washed away that afternoon. No, it wasn't their first-time fucking, but it was their first-time making love to one another. The desire was as intense as it had been in the storage room of her gallery but this time, she sensed his love for her. He didn't say those three magical words, he didn't need to, she knew they were madly in love with one another.

Despite all the obstacles clearly in their way, Emma knew Jack would be hers. She had no plan, no clue how any of it would happen but she knew it would. Her intuition told her she and Jack were meant to be.

CHAPTER 36

"Troy has invited us to dinner. I'm sure he's promoting me tonight," Matt said when he arrived home from work.

"It's about damn time," Emma bit at Matt. She blamed Matt's work for their marriage crumbling. Marcus Construction and Troy Burns took Matt from her, she wouldn't forget that.

"C'mon, babe. It wasn't so bad, was it?" He shrugged his shoulders.

Emma clenched her jaw and bit the inside of her mouth, doing her best to keep how she felt inside. Matt deserved this night. She'd play the dutiful wife and wait and see if he kept his promises to her.

She slipped into a pastel purple knee-length dress with matching heels, whereas Matt dressed in a suit with a purple striped tie. She grabbed a small clutch purse to carry her phone.

"Are you ready?" Emma asked standing with folded arms, leaning against the kitchen counter. Not wanting or caring about going to this dinner.

"Yeah, let's go. Hopefully, we'll have some celebrating to do too." Matt patted Emma's hand and they walked to the garage and got in their BMW.

***

"Matt, Emma, thanks for coming. Sorry, this was short notice, but I've kept you wondering long enough. You've proven yourself invaluable to Marcus Construction, Matt. I'm happy to give you this well-deserved promotion," Troy said.

"Thank you, Troy. It means a lot that you've put your trust in me to take over for Joe. I'll give you all I've got to be the best."

Emma listened as Matt gushed over Troy, she saw how thrilled Matt was with his promotion.

"He's loyal to you, Emma and my company," Troy said.

Emma rolled her eyes as she stood stoically beside Matt. Too loyal in Emma's mind. Her eyes squinted when she forced a polite smile and bit the inside of her cheek.

"Emma, with you by his side; he's unstoppable," Marla added.

Emma felt a pain in the back of her throat as she swallowed hard. *Shit, if they only knew.*

"Thank you, Marla, but I'm the lucky one." Emma forced another weak smile and looked downward.

After enduring the long dinner with Troy and Marla Burns, going over how great of a job Matt had done the past months, taking over for Joe, and not missing a beat, Emma was ready to go home.

***

"Congratulations Matt," Emma said dryly, flicking the pages of her magazine as she laid on her stack of pillows.

"Thanks, babe. I wouldn't be where I am today without you. I love you." He walked over to where Emma laid across their bed. He sat beside her and touched her calf.

Emma looked at Matt as she moved her leg from his hand. Her lips drawn tight; her cheeks warm.

"Em, what's wrong?" Matt reached for her again, she moved away. "Emma." He frowned.

"So, I'm good enough for you when it's your work but you pass me off to my sister and my best friend when I need you." Glaring at Matt, she crossed her legs and held her arms tight by her sides.

"Baby, I thought you understood. I'm sorry, I love you." He ran his hand down her arm, she flinched. "C'mon Emma, please?" His eyes pleading with hers.

"When I needed you most, you gave me some of you. I needed and wanted all of you." She pinched her eyes shut to stop the tears from building up. She crossed her arms and bent forward; her insides felt like cement.

Matt petted her hair, she shot back upright, her eyes shooting bullets at him, her cheeks red.

"I took those first two weeks off and was here with you. Em, we talked about that, and you were fine with that arrangement. Weren't you?" Matt pinched his face; his gaze fell to his hands.

"I needed you more than those two fucking weeks, Matt. I had therapy for three goddamn months. Jesus Christ, do you even remember that I had major shoulder surgery?" Her voice rising, she shook her hands and felt her heart beating extremely rapidly. She clutched at her chest and drew in a deep breath, holding it for a beat, then slowly releasing it.

"But that's why I had Shea come and be with you. I knew Brandi and Ben would help. Emma, did you expect me to be here with you for your entire year of recovery?" Matt spoke quickly and raked his hand through his hair, sighing heavily.

"You still don't get it. I expected your ass to be here, as in this town. Not at home with me all the time but fuck, Matt, I needed you to be home. Working here or at the office, not in goddamn fucking Maine or Jacksonville or Bum Fuck Egypt." Emma smacked the mattress. She dragged her palm across her forehead, she stood and began pacing, shaking her head.

"Okay, I fucked up. I thought we had an understanding. I'm sorry." Matt came up to Emma. She abruptly stopped and glared at him, her eyes glassy, her breathing quick. "You've got all of me now. Can we please get past this?" He held his hands out to hug her.

She slapped his hands away and walked by him. Standing in the doorway of their bedroom, she said flatly, "No, Matt. I can't." She ran to her car and drove off.

Her phone connected to her car; Matt was calling. She pressed the red phone icon and turned the music up louder.

A text message came in a few minutes later. **Emma, I'm sorry. Baby, please don't be mad. Come home. I love you.**

Her car asked Emma if she wanted to send a text back to Matt, she said, "No," and kept driving.

CHAPTER 37

With both hands full, Emma peered through the glass of the gallery door and saw Brandi at the front counter. She tapped with her coffee cup to get her attention. Smiling when Brandi opened the door for her, she said, "Thanks, you're the best."

"No problem, Em. I didn't think you were coming in today," Brandi said and walked back to where she'd been sitting. Emma followed and pulled up a stool.

"I have some work to finish on a few portraits. They're easier to do here." Emma sipped on her coffee and placed her purse on the counter, her phone slid out. She glanced down and noticed a text from Jack, she quickly shoved her phone back into her purse. She avoided Brandi's glare, feeling her eyes boring holes in her.

"What does Jack want?" Brandi asked.

"I don't know, maybe just checking on me since I've been discharged from his care. You know doctor stuff." Emma peeked over the edge of her coffee cup, hoping Brandi accepted her lie.

"Bullshit. Whatever it is, you need to tell him you're fine. Matt is home and there's no need to text you."

"Okay, I'll do that."

"You do know the Bryant's have their photoshoot this afternoon at three. Jenna confirmed it when she called this morning."

"Yes, I know. So…" Emma shrugged, but inside her heart hurt.

"So, their shoot includes a topless session. I can text you when we are about to do that part so you can leave." Brandi touched Emma's arm.

"Why would I need to leave? They're a happily married couple doing what they do. I'm fine, Brandi," Emma lied through her teeth.

She twisted a wild strand of her hair around her finger, she felt her throat close. She sucked in a deep breath and let it out slowly.

"Em, I know you still have feelings for Jack. It's obvious. I don't want to see you in pain if you see Jenna and Jack in an embrace, especially when they are topless." Brandi stood from her seat and came around to Emma.

"Of course, I have feelings for Jack, he repaired part of my body. I'll always be grateful to him. That's all. I'll stay in my office working on my portraits I need to finish while the Bryant's are with you." Emma stepped back from Brandi, crossing her arms.

"I'm not getting into this with you now. I need to set up the scenes Jenna chose. But don't say I didn't warn you, Em." Brandi grabbed her planner and walked to her room.

Crinkling her nose, Emma flipped her hair, gathered her purse and coffee, and went to her office.

Sitting back in her chair, she opened her purse and brought out her phone. Tapping it awake, a warm sensation flowed through her when she saw Jack's text. **See you Tuesday**. Her heart filled with love, she grinned as she looked around her office, staring at the air.

Emma didn't respond. He'd know she read his text by the 'read' below his message when he'd check his phone.

***

After arranging the three portraits she needed to finish on easels and placing her paints on the side table along with the many brushes she'd need; she pulled her hair into a messy bun and slipped a smock over her clothes.

Waking her phone, she found her favorite music mix and turned it up loud to drown out any distractions.

Her first portrait was of a young newly married couple standing in front of their first home, expecting their first child. Emma needed to touch up the sky on the canvas.

Opening the blue and white paints, she swirled them together on her palette into the exact blue that matched Jack's eyes. With long strokes across the top of her canvas, she filled in the sky, then using a smaller brush she filled in the areas around the young couple and their home. While the sky dried, Emma mixed her bright white with a soft touch of black; soft like the way Jack touched her.

She used a medium-sized brush as she dotted the blue sky with the puffy clouds and feathered a thin line across the entire skyline. Stepping back, she touched her chin with her brush, tilted her head to the side, and finished as she always did, using a thin brush to sign the portrait on the bottom left corner, *EB Taylor*.

Standing back, she took in the one of a young male graduate from one of the local high schools. He asked if his portrait background could be a rainbow. Emma had asked if he wanted pastel or bright rainbow colors. He chose bright.

She glanced at the clock on the wall, it read two forty-five. Emma felt a chill shoot through her. Opening her office door and silencing her music, she strained to hear if Jack and Jenna had arrived. All she heard was Brandi moving things around.

Her last portrait was that of a baby girl. This one showed the little girl's first year of life. Her parents had Brandi photograph her at one week of age, three, six, nine, and twelve months. It was one of the gallery's most interesting displays. Emma and Brandi looked forward to exhibiting it at their next event. Emma only had done the pencil sketch of the baby across each age picture and knew this portrait would take her several hours.

For the newborn photo, there was a brilliant pink backdrop with wisps of whites and grays. Emma began with that photo.

The three-month photo shone light purple and gray, the six-month picture held a blue and purple mix with wisps of pinks, and the one-year photo popped with shades of red. This portrait was Emma's largest-ever commission.

Mixing the colors she needed for each stage of this beautiful baby's first year, she felt melancholy wondering what a little girl of her and Matt's would have looked like. Her heart tugged tight. She shook off those sad feelings and went about her work. Using each stroke to make this little girl shine. Gazing at the photo, Emma noticed the baby's blue eyes. They were the exact color of Jack's. She laughed because she knew the little girl wasn't Jack's; he and Jenna didn't have any children. But the amazing blue color of her eyes and Jacks were identical. Emma stared at the photo, then began mixing the blue and white paint. She added in a speck of silver. The little girl's eyes took Emma's breath away.

A knock on her office door startled her. She dropped her brush, then peered up and saw Brandi before her. "Hey," Emma said, flicking a stray hair from her face.

"Wow, Em. That's gorgeous. That little girl looks exactly like her daddy, she has his brown hair and stunning blue eyes. You're capturing the photos so well, wonderful job." Brandi walked closer to the portrait, looking closely at Emma's progress in each stage of the baby's life.

"Thank you. I appreciate that, Brandi. I hope they like it." Emma cleaned up the spot on the floor from the paintbrush. "This one is going to take me a while to finish."

Brandi glanced at her watch, then at Emma. "It's almost time for the Bryant's session. It's good you'll be busy."

"Yes, I'll stay in here, don't worry about me. It's all good. I promise." Emma tried to convince not just Brandi, but herself, that Jack and Jenna's photoshoot wouldn't bother her at all.

"I'll come back when they've left."

"Sounds great. See you later." Emma ushered Brandi out of her office so she could get back to her portrait.

The bell over the front door clanged. Emma heard Brandi greet Jack and Jenna as heat coursed through her. Leaving the door open, she went back to the easel.

Before resuming her work, she walked to her open door and listened again, she heard Brandi directing Jack and Jenna into position. Emma went back to her work, picking up the palette, she returned to painting. Every few minutes, she'd walk to the door and listen.

After twenty minutes Emma went to the door and heard Brandi's voice ask Jenna, "Do you still want me to take the topless photos?"

"Absolutely, right Jack?" Jenna said, her voice excited.

Emma strained to hear Jack's response, her heart slowing.

"Of course," he said.

"Okay, then you'll need to remove your tops and when you're both comfortable and ready we'll get started," Brandi said.

Her breath stopped. She stepped back and leaned on the door, holding her chest. Feeling tears filling her eyes.

Like in a trance, her feet moved her toward Brandi's room. She stopped just before the archway. Dizziness made her hold onto the arch's frame.

What the fuck am I doing? I don't want to see this.

Brandi began directing Jack, "Okay, Jack, I'd like you to embrace Jenna and look into her eyes, remember when you fell in love with her."

Emma nearly fainted. She braced herself against the wall.

"Jenna, place your hand on the back of Jack's neck, hold him and show us how much you love him."

Emma clenched her stomach and bent over. Her face was hot. She knew she shouldn't look, but she did. She slowly moved to see Jack and Jenna moving into the position Brandi had instructed them to do. When she saw Jack shirtless, her knees weakened and her pulse quickened, wishing it were her about to embrace Jack and not Jenna.

She covered her mouth to stifle her screams when she saw them coming together in an embrace. Jenna's smile beaming as she pressed her ample breasts against Jack's firm pecs. Jenna slid her hand right where Brandi told her to. She playfully flicked Jack's hair, tossed her head back, and laughed with glee. Clicking sounds were abundant as Brandi took their photos. Jenna gazed lovingly into Jack's eyes.

Tears fell from Emma's. Her breaths became short and fast. Her hands trembling. Her heart lay like tattered ribbons inside her chest. Emma stared and stared and stared.

Suddenly, Jack looked her way.

Her eyes met his, she swallowed hard, turned, ran to her office, and slammed the door. Emma sank into her chair, laying her head on her desk, silently crying, letting all her emotions out.

How could Jack do that to her? He said he wanted to be with her. Was it just an affair he wanted, or did he love her as she loved him?

Her mind ran in all directions, feeling betrayed by him. She grabbed her hair and pulled out the messy bun, throwing the hair tie toward the door. Emma wished it were a glass, she needed to break something.

She looked at the unfinished portrait of the little girl, with Jack's blue eyes. She knew she should gather herself and get back to work, but her mind wasn't in it. She gathered her purse and sweater and went out the back door of the gallery.

Sobbing, Emma sat in her car, gasping for air. Her heart ached from the deep betrayal she saw from Jack. She couldn't go home looking like she did, Matt would ask too many questions.

Emma waited for several more minutes before going back into the gallery. She stuck her head in and listened for Brandi's voice. Silence, so she went to her office and closed the door. She laid her head on her desk for what she thought was a few minutes.

Jumping when she felt a hand touch hers, she sat straight up. Rubbing her face and pushing her hair behind her ears, she blinked to clear her vision.

"Emma, my God, what's wrong, did something happen?" Brandi's eyebrows rose, along with her voice.

"No, I'm fine." Emma looked at her hands, clasping and unclasping them on her desk.

"That's a lie if I ever heard one. Talk to me." Brandi looked around and saw Emma's pieces on the easels. "You're not done; what happened?" she prodded Emma, reaching to hold her hand.

Emma pulled her hand and sat back in her chair. "I got distracted. I'll finish it next week." Emma stared at the wall, avoiding eye contact with Brandi.

Brandi gasped and dragged the chair around to sit beside Emma. "Dammit, Em. You saw them, didn't you?" She tried to hold Emma's hand, but she clasped them in her lap, bowing her head to her chin.

There was a deafening silence for several minutes, then Emma slowly raised her head and looked at Brandi. Her eyes red, cheeks stained, she brushed her face again and shook her head up and down. Tears beginning to fall again.

"Fuck, I told you to stay away from my room. You have serious feelings for that man, don't you?" Brandi pushed back her chair and stood in front of Emma with her hands on her hips.

"Dammit, Brandi. I don't know, maybe. I don't fucking know, alright?" Emma couldn't admit the full truth, she wasn't ready for Brandi's wrath.

"It's okay. It is. You can have feelings for Jack, just don't act on them. Hold them deep inside. Don't ever act on them," Brandi's voice softened, she brushed Emma's arm.

"Okay, yeah, sure, no problem. I can do that." Emma's eyes rolled as she sat forward and covered her face. She felt Brandi's hand on her shoulder.

"You can; and will. Matt loves you; you love him. Jack was a distraction when Matt traveled. That's done, and Matt is home now. Emma, Emma! You can't mess around with Jack, promise me." Brandi sat back down and took Emma's hands in hers.

Emma closed her eyes, she tried to speak but nothing came out, she slumped in her chair. She'd already messed around with Jack a couple of times and Brandi would kill her if she knew. She knew Brandi suspected something, but Emma had been able to convince her nothing had gone on between her and Jack.

"Jesus Em. You love him." Brandi confronted her.

"Okay, maybe, I love Jack. I don't know if I still love Matt. We had a huge fight a couple of nights ago. What the fuck? What's wrong with me?" Emma's eyes filled with tears as she stared at Brandi, hoping for answers.

"Nothing is wrong with you. It's possible to love them both. It happened to me. You helped me through my crisis and now, I'll help you. You have to put your love for Jack away and love him from afar. Matt's your life. It's one fight, have makeup sex with him, he's your real love."

"How do I know Matt is my real love and Jack isn't? How?" Emma locked eyes with Brandi, her voice cracking.

"Matt is. Look deep inside your heart. It's Matt in there and you know it. Jack's a fun toy, he's not your forever. Trust me, he's not," Brandi spoke in a low and steady voice as she moved closer to Emma. "It'll all be fine."

Emma buried her face into Brandi's shoulder and hugged her tight, hoping her best friend was right about all of it.

CHAPTER 38

Knocking on room 828, Emma's pulse raced but not for the same reasons it had the last time she met Jack in a hotel. He had some explaining to do. What she'd seen at that photoshoot, broke her. Crushed her soul. She wouldn't let Jack off easy. She wanted a complete and honest explanation of why he went through with the session, knowing it would hurt her.

The hotel room door opened; Jack stood on the other side with a single red rose. "I'm sorry. Please let me explain, love."

Ignoring the rose and walking past him, Emma took a seat in the desk chair. She placed her purse on the floor, crossing her legs and clasping her hands in her lap. "I'll listen." Her lips were drawn tight, but her heart ached. She hated being upset with him. She only wanted there to be love between them.

Jack knelt before her and laid the rose in her lap; she held the stem with only one finger. "I tried every excuse I could think of to avoid the photoshoot. I swear, Emma." Leaning his forehead against her bare knee, he ran his hands down her calf, sending heat pulses to her core.

"Stop trying to woo me, Jack. You didn't try hard enough to get out of the session." Emma uncrossed her legs and pinched them together.

Jack sat on the floor, looking up at her, his eyes glazed. He rubbed his jaw over and over, bowing his head. "When I saw you watching me and Jenna in that embrace, my heart shattered. I pretended every move Brandi told me to do. All of what you saw wasn't real for me. None of it was real. You, Emma. You are my reality; I only want to be with you."

"I don't know, Jack. How can I believe you?" She placed the rose on the desk. Staring at him as he sat with his face in his hands, his elbows on his knees, she wanted to reach out and caress him, but she didn't. She kept her hands, fingers locked together, laying in her lap; to keep them from shaking.

Coming back to his knees, Jack covered her hands with his. Hugging them tenderly, rubbing his thumb across hers, bowing his head, and kissing her hand. "Emma, please forgive me. I did try my best to not go."

Staring at him, she wanted to believe him, to trust him. But he hurt her. He promised to never hurt her, was he the same as all the men in the world? Or was he that perfect man she portrayed him as in her fantasies of him? Her body aching for him, she'd give him this one pass, for now.

"Dammit, Jack. I hate this. I hate that you go home to her. I want you to come home to me." She pulled her hands free and covered her mouth. Her eyes widened as she realized what she'd admitted. Was he ready to hear that from her? It was too late; she'd said it out loud. She drew in a breath, waiting for him to respond.

"I want the same, love. I only want you." Jack rose from his knees. Offering his hand to her, she peered up and caught his blue eyes. "Please, let me make love to you."

Wanting him more than ever, she tugged on the hem of Jack's top.

He pulled it up and off his body.

She rose from the chair and trailed her hand across his bare chest.

Grasping her hand, his lips touched her fingertips, creeping into her palm and onto her delicate wrist.

Her heart beating madly, her core pulsing, wanting Jack inside her. Emma's arm swept across the desk, knocking what few things sat on it to the floor. She tilted her head upward, smiling sinfully.

Jack drew her into him, pressing his hard cock against her, stripping her naked. He lifted Emma onto the wood desk, placing her ass on the edge. He leaned closer, kissed her shoulders, then her breasts, her soft lips brushed across his chest, she tickled his nipple with her tongue.

His cotton pants couldn't hold his full arousal as she pushed them down his hips. Jack's heated member was up and ready for Emma.

He kissed her as he entered her core with his hard rod.

She pushed her hips into him and moaned, "Oh, my God, baby." Tightening her thighs around Jack's waist, holding him deep inside her, she arched her back as her orgasm exploded.

Jack throbbed inside her when he came.

Breathing heavily, Emma kept her legs wrapped around Jack when she grabbed his biceps, pulling herself up to him.

Jack threaded his fingers through her hair, resting his hand on her neck. His eyes captured hers as he leaned in and kissed her softly.

She sensed he wanted to say something, his eyes prodded hers. "What is it, Jack?" She brushed his cheek and gave him a quick kiss.

"I love you," he blurted out, his eyes blinking wildly.

Emma's mouth fell open as she gasped for air. "I love you, too," she said quickly.

Jack drew Emma closer to him, wrapping her in his arms.

She snuggled into him, holding him as tight as she could. Her heart drummed rapidly, filling with complete love for Jack.

He loosened his embrace of her and touched her cheek. "Emma, I've loved you since I first saw you. I want us to be together. Somehow, I want to be with you." His eyes shining, holding her gaze. His lips gently touched hers.

"Oh, Jack, I've loved you since, I don't know when exactly. I want to be with you too. But how can we? We'll cause so much pain to others." She buried her face in his chest, tears beginning to fall.

"We'll make it happen. I can't live without you. I need to be with you all the time, not just once a week. All the time." Jack kissed Emma again, slipping his soft tongue between her lips, she took him in.

Moaning into his mouth, wanting to make love again. But there wasn't time for that.

They dressed and as she sat on the end of the bed, slipping her shoes on, she wanted to grab his hands and tell him, *"Let's fly away together. Start over far away from here."* But she didn't.

"God, I love you so much, my heart hurts," she said.

"I love you and my heart hurts too. Soon we won't be apart. I promise."

"I hope you're right. I do." Embracing Jack for as long as she could, she pressed her full lips to his, she devoured his delicious tongue with hers. Slipping her hand into his, she held on as they went to the door.

Jack touched her chin, tilted her face upward, and brushed away the tear trickling down her cheek. He kissed Emma one last time, knowing he must leave or be late. "See you soon. I love you." With her face in his hands, he gazed deeply into her blue eyes.

"Yes, see you soon. I love you so much."

Sitting at home at the breakfast table, Emma shook in her chair. She fiddled with her wedding rings, then took them off. She went to her bedroom and placed them in the jewelry box Matt had given her for a birthday gift years ago. Tears slipped down her cheeks. She quickly brushed them away and drew in a deep breath. Shaking her head, she tried to rid the fear of what she'd be doing to Matt. She could do this, she had to, her future with Jack depended on it.

CHAPTER 39

Her heart was breaking for her husband and for what she was going to do to him, to his life. But Matt deserved better. He was a good and faithful man. She'd cheated. She'd broken their vows.

Divorce was what she wanted. Her husband had done nothing wrong except being absent in their marriage for months; that wasn't a reason to leave, and yet, she wanted out. She knew he'd want to work it out between them, but she didn't.

Matt had chosen his work over her one time too many. He broke promise after promise. Whenever Miranda called, he went. Emma's calls and pleas for him to come home were pushed aside. She'd had enough of being chosen second. She wasn't so callous that she didn't ache for hurting Matt, but Jack was her love, her life, her everything. He didn't break promises as Matt did over and over.

***

Kicking back in his recliner, Matt stretched out and turned on the TV. He hadn't kissed Emma since coming in the door.

She hated how their love faded or was it complacency setting in? She paced in the kitchen, then into the bedroom. She'd packed her car, there was nothing else she needed to take with her. She shook her arms and flicked her fingers to free the anxiousness surrounding her.

Emma checked herself in the full-length mirror for what she knew was the last time. Drawing in deep breaths and blowing them out, she began to walk from her bedroom.

Staring at Matt from just outside their bedroom door, she pulled in one last courageous breath. She thought of Jack, how he promised to love her, be there for her every need, never hurt her. Yes, Jack is who she wanted, needed, and loved. Just Jack.

Picking up the remote, Emma muted the TV. "I have to talk to you about something," she said firmly.

"Yeah, what is it?" Matt asked, turning to her.

She saw his shoulders tighten; thinking he was bracing himself for what she was about to say. Her throat closing, she took a few seconds to swallow past the lump. The silence was deafening.

"First, I'm sorry for what I'm about to say and ask of you," she blurted. "It's not your fault; it's all mine, but I want out. I want a divorce," Emma spoke quickly. Her heart cracked when she told Matt what she wanted. That speck of love for him brought tears trickling down her face. She clutched her chest as she gasped for a breath.

He stared at her, eyes blank, his mouth drawn tight. The silence grew.

She started to fidget. "Did you—"

"I heard you. What the fuck, Emma?" He jumped to his feet.

She backed away.

"What do you mean you want out, a divorce? Why? What's going on? Where do you think you're going to go?" Matt dragged his hands through his hair over and over.

She took another step back, unable to stand so close beside him. "I just do. I can't say anymore. I don't share the same feelings with you. I need space and need to be with myself right now. I still care about you. Please don't fight me. I need to be free."

The pain on his face killed her, but he just wasn't the man that made her heart skip any longer, Jack did that. Jack made her body electric with each whisper of his lips on hers, with his soft touch, and simply walking into the same room. Jack's aura engulfed her and mesmerized her for eternity.

Somehow, she and Matt grew apart. The gap created by her needs from the accident, then the demands of his job, it all snowballed, and that crack became a canyon, one too wide, and too deep to fill.

"I don't understand. Why now? Where will you go? Is there another man? A woman? What did I do wrong?" Matt paced in their living room, scratching his chin, huffing out a breath.

"No, there's no one else," Emma lied. "I'm sorry. I have a place." She scratched her arm and pinched her wrist. She couldn't look Matt in the eyes, she kept her eyes low and shook her head slowly. Hating herself for hurting him, she knew Jack was waiting for her.

Matt slumped into his chair. The silence stretched for too long. His voice breaking, he said, "Okay, but I think I deserve a full explanation of what the fuck went wrong. When, where, and why it went wrong." His eyes grabbed hers, pleading as the tears rolled down his face. "You owe me that. You're throwing away the thirty years we built together. For what?? Nothing. Your freedom? I don't buy it! You're not telling me everything, but I'll let you go now. I'm not giving up on us yet. I can't. I'm hurting like shit, but I love you! I can't give up without a fight."

She sobbed, feeling the heat rising within her, Matt had no clue of what went wrong. She'd loved him once, absolutely loved him. He'd made her happy for over thirty years. She glanced around the room, realizing she's leaving all of it behind, everything, the pictures, the trinkets, Matt.

"Thank you and I'm sorry. I didn't mean to hurt you. I swear! I know I did, but please, believe me, I didn't mean to. You deserve better than me."

She turned toward the kitchen, but he grabbed her hand and pulled her into his arms.

"Whatever it is... we can work it out... I promise... to be a better husband. I'll postpone everything... whatever. Please, Emma." Matt's words tumbled out between the breaths he sucked in.

She stood still in his embrace for a few seconds, then pushed free. "This is going to sound awful, but I don't want to work it out. I want out."

Turning, she ran to her car, tears pouring out of her eyes. She could barely see enough to drive. Pulling over at the corner, she tried to catch her breath. Searching through her tears for something to dry her eyes and wipe her nose, she found some napkins under her seat. Her head fell to the steering wheel as she sobbed. She'd left her husband. She'd left her life as she knew it. Everything was going to change.

Flipping down the visor, she stared at her reflection. Her face was red with tear trails, her messy bun even messier, her eyes red as a fire engine.

"This is it, Emma, this is what you wanted. Your freedom to be with Jack. Go to him, be with him, don't ever look back. Go get Jack," Emma said to her reflection in the mirror.

Wiping her face with the used napkin, she turned the AC on high to dry her reddened face and eyes. Taking deep long breaths, she found her inner strength and drove off.

Her future with Jack would be exactly as she had dreamed. Waking up with him every morning, making love to him every night and anytime in between. She loved him with every cell in her body. It was a love she'd never felt before. "I can't wait," Emma said aloud and heard Jack's velvety voice,

"I'm here, waiting for you, baby."

CHAPTER 40

Arriving at their rendezvous spot right on time, and not seeing Jack's car, gave Emma a tinge of guilt flooding her. Had she made the right decision, ending her thirty-year marriage for a much younger man?

She smacked her face to bring her to where she wanted to be but panic set in as she glanced around the parking lot and didn't see Jack. Breathing quickly, she drove around looking closely at each parked car; hoping she'd just missed his silver sedan. After three circles, she parked where they agreed and waited.

The voice in her head demeaned her for leaving Matt. *He's a good man, just trying to make a better life for you both and this is what he deserved?*

Shaking her head violently as her hair pelted her face, she balled her fists and smacked the seat. She knew he didn't deserve it, but what did she deserve? To be left every time his damn assistant couldn't handle her fucking job. She threw her head back against the car seat and screamed. Her windows were rolled up tight, no one could hear her.

Looking straight forward, willing Jack's car to appear, her heart thumped harder than ever. He'd never stand her up, that wasn't who Jack was. If he couldn't meet her, he'd be a man and call or text her. There's no way he'd leave her in such a lurch.

Emma drove around the parking lot again, trying to pass the time. She glanced at the car radio and realized he was now twenty minutes late. A lump formed in her throat; her breaths caught on it as she tried to remain calm.

Baby, where are you? Oh God, please don't let me down. I couldn't survive another broken promise. Did Jenna try and stop you from coming to me? Jack, please come to me. I love you. Baby, please. Emma bent over and rested her head on the steering wheel. Her eyes were glassy, a sharp pain going through her heart.

Needing a distraction, she thought about what they could do while in New York City. She'd never been. It was on her and Matt's list of places to go when they had time but never went.

Listing the places, she wanted to see most, Central Park, the museums, the 9/11 memorial. Take in a Broadway show, go shopping at Macy's and Bloomingdale's. Walk hand in hand in Times Square. And that brought her back to him.

"Jack," she yelled, "Where the fuck are you?" Emma pinched her eyes shut and breathed deeply until headlights got her attention. She squinted until she realized it was Jack. She blew out her breath and let her head fall back till she hit the headrest. Her eyes still glassy when she saw Jack coming to her. Her heart filled with happiness and joy. It beat rapidly.

She wiped her eyes dry before opening her car door. Emma jumped into Jack's arms. Squeezing him tightly, she laid her head on his shoulder. "I love you." Kissing his earlobe, she trailed her lips along his jawline, to his cheek, and found his soft full lips. She pressed her tongue into his mouth, tasting her favorite flavor, Jack Bryant.

Keeping her legs tight around Jack's body, Emma cupped his face and gazed deeply into his perfect eyes. "You weren't here when I arrived. I panicked and drove around and around searching for your car. I thought you had changed your mind." Her eyes filling with tears once again.

"I love you, Emma. I won't ever hurt you. I should've been here early and I'm sorry I wasn't. I was at the hospital and was called in for an emergency. A young boy broke his arm. I knew I would be late but didn't think this late. The mom was a bit overprotective and needed to see everything I did. She made what should've taken me not more than an hour, three. Baby, I'm sorry. I never had a second thought about us." Jack's hand traveled up her back and rested on the nape of her neck. Drawing her to him, their lips met again as they kissed passionately.

Her heart smiled, her entire body on fire for Jack. Catching her breath, Emma said, "It's all good now, my sweet. Let's go catch the Red Eye and get far away from here."

***

Embracing one another, Jack and Emma stood on the terrace of their hotel suite in the heart of Times Square. The view took her breath away but nothing like her view of Jack did. She gazed deeply into his amazingly soft blue eyes, realizing she'd wake up and see them every morning for the rest of her life. Her insides trembled with the thought of fucking him every day, forever.

Dr. Jackson Bryant, a man she encountered by chance was now hers and she was his. Nestling herself into Jack's tall firm body, she breathed him in, embracing him tighter, feeling his love for her as he caressed her tenderly.

Leaning in, he grazed her neck with his soft lips and whispered, "Are you happy?"

Emma cupped Jack's smooth cheeks and smiled wide. "I'm beyond happy."

He tugged her closer and kissed her softly.

"Are you happy, Jack?" she asked, her heart skipping a beat.

"I've never been happier. This is the beginning of the rest of our life together. I'll never let you down."

CHAPTER 41

Emma awoke to a beautiful sunrise and was sure she had been dreaming. When she opened her eyes, there he lay, Doctor Jackson Bryant, the man she loved.

He surrounded her with his warm arms as she lay curled up facing him. A few minutes passed before his eyes opened and a smile appeared on his face. He drew her even closer to him, his hard shaft pressing against her body.

A jolt went through her. Raising a hand, she feathered her fingers through his soft brown hair as their lips softly touched. Her hand resting on the nape of his neck.

"Good morning, beautiful," he said to her, but before she could respond, he kissed her again. His tongue sliding between her lips, she tasted her favorite flavor; him.

Catching her breath she greeted Jack, "Good morning, gorgeous." Wrapping herself around Jack's firm body, she sensed his stiff cock. Smiling and gazing into his blue eyes, she spoke softly, "Make love to me, baby."

Jack slid his hard rod into her hot center, moving back and forth creating friction between them.

Arching her back as he thrust deeper into her, Emma moaned, "Baby, you're amazing. Oh, God, don't stop." She closed her eyes as she reached an orgasm.

"Open your eyes, look at me. I want to see you come," Jack said, resting on his forearms above her.

She opened her eyes only to be caught by his. She gasped, her chest rose and fell with each thrust of his thick shaft into her. She held his gaze. The intensity of looking into Jack's eyes while making love made her orgasms incredibly sensuous.

Fisting her hair and pumping her body with powerful thrusts, Jack moaned, "Oh baby." Pushing into her as she arched her back, they climaxed together. Reaching their bliss. Jack's lips wisped by her ear, she trembled when his breath blew across her. "I love you, Emma. Forever."

"I love you too."

They laid in silence for a while as they held one another tight.

***

Emma rose from the bed and turned to face Jack. "I'm going to shower, want to join me?" Emma asked playfully as she turned and walked toward the bathroom.

"Yes," Jack said as he came up behind her.

Stepping into the shower, she let the hot water run down her face and soak her hair. Grabbing the shampoo, she squeezed a small amount in her hand and began to rub it into her hair.

Jack rested his hands on top of hers. "Let me," he whispered. His breath sent chills throughout her body.

Dropping her arms, she let him massage the shampoo into her hair.

He touched her shoulders with his soft lips. The left one received extra attention as he kissed the scars from her surgery.

After rinsing her hair, Jack pulled her to him and lifted her onto his stiff shaft. His large hands cupped her ass. Pressing her back against the tiled shower wall, he felt fabulous inside her. The hot water cascaded down their bodies.

While holding her against the tile wall, Jack thrusts upward into Emma.

She reached for the ledge above her as he pumped her over and over. Jack's kisses and nibbles made her scream, "Jesus, Jack!" She squeezed her thighs tight as she climaxed and seconds later, he came.

***

While lying across the bed in the hotel bathrobe, Emma gasped when she saw Jack carrying the largest bouquet of red roses she'd ever seen.

He placed the vase on the dresser as she stood with her hand over her mouth.

"Oh, my God, they're beautiful."

"Not nearly as beautiful as you, love." He wrapped her in his arms and kissed her.

She embraced him tight, he was perfect to her.

Jack pulled out a box from his pocket, holding it in his palms. "Open it," he coaxed her.

Pressing her hands to her cheeks, she peered up and began to speak but he laid his finger on her lips.

Sitting on the end of the bed, Emma lifted the box from Jack's hands, and with a smile on her face, she opened the long thin box. A diamond bracelet sat on a blue velvet cushion, she drew in a breath and cupped her mouth. Her eyes were glassy, her heart racing.

"Turn it over," he said, sitting next to her and flipping his hands.

The date they'd started their new lives was engraved above two intertwined hearts, each of which held their initials.

Jack's confidence was evident by the date he had engraved on her bracelet, which had happened. There were many obstacles in their way, and they overcame them all.

Meeting his gaze and seeing his full smile, his arms open wide for her. Her eyes danced; her body hummed as she happily stepped into his loving embrace.

"Jack, this bracelet is stunning." Emma brushed a tear from her cheek.

"It matches you, love. Everything about you is stunning, especially your blue eyes."

Emma blinked slowly as Jack tenderly kissed her eyelids.

With her heart filled with all of Jack, she laid her arm out. "Will you?"

Taking the bracelet, he clasped it around her tiny wrist. He brought her arm to his soft lips and kissed her wrist. Glancing at Emma, he pushed the robe sleeve higher and slid his lips across her forearm.

She sighed as his lips met the inside of her elbow. Her robe stopped Jack's progress.

He stood and reached for the sash, pulling it loose. Pushing her robe from her body, his lips traveled up her bicep, shoulder, kissing her scars.

Her head tipped back as Jack's lips wisped against her neck sending hot chills all through her body.

"Today is perfect." Emma wrapped her arms around Jack's waist. Squeezing him and pulling him down onto her, she sensed his full erection as hard as he'd ever been. A delightful smile filled her face.

"It's about to get better." He kissed her. His lips tickled her nipples, making them hard. He nibbled softly.

"Jack," she sighed, her pussy aching for his cock again. As he kissed her navel, she moaned again, "My God, Jack."

He slid to his knees, kissed her thighs, and wiggled his head between her legs.

"Oh, baby," she said breathlessly as she took fast short breaths. His hair softly touching her inner thighs.

Jack's tongue slid along her wet folds, tasting her. He took her clit between his soft lips as she gripped the sheets.

She cried out, "Jack, Oh my God, Jack." Her legs kicked out and her heels landed on the edge of the bed, spreading her core wider. Her ass hung on the end of the bed, she bolted upright when Jack's tongue plunged into her. She caressed her hands through his soft brown hair, and moved her pelvis into him, wanting his velvety tongue as deep into her as he could go. Her body writhing in ecstasy, reaching her bliss, she screamed, "Fuck me, baby, fuck me hard."

Jack rose from his knees and slid his arm across his mouth. A devilish grin appeared as he stripped before her.

She reached for him, wriggling her fingers, inviting him to come to her, fuck her.

He crawled into the bed, and over her quivering body.

Opening her legs wider he pushed his hard shaft into her, leaning down and kissing her breasts. His thrusts were hard and fast, sweat dripping from them both. "Emma, baby, Jesus you feel so good."

Their bodies smacked softly together. Emma gripped Jack with her legs as her body reached its climax.

He collapsed onto her with one last plunge and a sigh, "Oh, God, Emma."

Drowning in his blue eyes, she feathered her hands through his deep brown hair over and over. Kissing his cheeks, his lips, his neck, her palms caressed his smooth jawline. She adored this man lying beside her.

He held her heart in his hands, she knew he'd never hurt her, or let her down. She trusted him with every fiber of her being. Finding Jack's hand, she threaded her fingers with his, tightly squeezing him.

"I love you, Jack."

"I love you too, Emma."

EPILOGUE

"Emma, answer the damn door. I know you're in there. Emma!"

Her eyes widened as she grabbed Jack's arm when he stood and headed toward the front door of their condominium.

Whispering, Emma said, "No, don't answer that. Please, Jack. Let me talk to Matt. Go." She pointed to the spare bedroom door and nudged him toward it. Her eyes pleading. "Please."

Dropping his head to his chest, Jack went to the spare bedroom.

Emma waited until she heard the click of the door closing before answering the front door.

"Emma," Matt's voice rose.

"I'm coming," she called out. Drawing in several breaths and taking a gulp of the whiskey she'd been sipping, Emma went to the door, sliding the security chain across before opening it. "What do you want?" Her voice was cold as she looked at Matt through the small opening.

"Can we talk, please, baby?" Matt tried to push the door open, but the chain stopped him. He puffed out a breath. "Really, Em. You're not going to let me in?" Matt took a step back and roughed up his already messy hair.

"We can talk just fine like this." Emma folded her arms across her chest and watched him rocking from one foot to the other.

"You know I would never harm you. Please, Em. We need to talk. Please."

Emma met Matt's gaze and noticed his eyes were bloodshot. She panned his clothes and realized how messy he had dressed. Her heart tightened as she looked at the man she had loved for so long. She blinked rapidly to dry the tears coming.

"I'm sorry, Matt. Not tonight. I'll text you when I'm ready. I need more time," her voice was low.

"How much time do you need? I know where you've been," Matt pushed back.

"What do you mean by that?" Her eyes grew when she realized she hadn't turned off her location app, the one that connected her phone to Matt's.

"You were in New York City. Is he there? Is that why you left?" He leaned on the door as she began to close it.

"Yes, I was in New York, and no. No one was there with me. I went to get away from here. I'll text you soon. I need to go. Goodbye, Matt."

"We're not over, Emma. I'll be back, we need to talk."

Emma slowly closed the door. She went to the picture window behind the sofa. Kneeling on the sofa, she pushed the blinds to watch Matt as he went to his car.

His arms flailed as he kicked the ground with each step.

Emma sucked in a breath when she saw him turn back around. Their eyes met, she slammed closed the blinds and ran to check the locks. Leaning against the door, she blew out that breath and jumped when Matt shook the door, pounding hard and yelling, "Emma, I'm not leaving. Emma, please talk to me. Emma!"

To be continued...

Here's a sneak peek into THE CHOICE

"Emma," Matt's voice cracked as he continued pounding on the door. "Emma, open the door, please."

The door to the spare bedroom creaked. Emma peered toward it and shook her head from side to side. She waved her arm at Jack to go back into the bedroom. Taking a few steps his way, she whispered, "Let me take care of this. We can't let Matt know it's you I left him for. Please, Jack. Let me handle him."

The knocking continued. "Emma," Matt's voice boomed louder.

"I don't care if he knows," Jack quietly replied as he walked to her.

"No, he can't know, ever. I can talk to him. Please. I love you."

"Okay, but if I feel you're in trouble, I'm coming out of the bedroom."

"Fine. Trust me." She turned Jack's body and nudged him back into the bedroom. Her eyes trailed him as he closed the door slowly.

Drawing in a deep breath, she summoned as much courage as possible before ambling over. Unlocking the door, she pulled it open all the way.

Seeing Matt fully in front of her and not just through the tinted window of the condo or the small slit of the door when the chain prevented it from opening completely, her heart sank.

Covering his face with his hands, he wiped himself fiercely. He scratched at his scruffy beard, then dragged his hands through his hair. His eyes appeared dull, his face puffy from crying.

Emma fought the urge to embrace him. And there it was, the love for which she'd been hunting. *Fuck, where the hell was this when I searched my heart for it months ago? Why show up now? To make me feel like a complete cunt.*

"Emma, please, we can work this out. Please, baby, let me in. Talk to me." He pushed past her into the condo.

Her eyes darted around the open area that was the living room, dining room and kitchen of the condo. Finding Jack's backpack, she moved to block Matt's view of it. Watching him pace, she kept moving back toward Jack's things. Bumping them with her foot, she pushed them under the table and back out of sight.

"Emma, we've got over thirty years together. You don't want to throw that away." Matt's voice brought her attention back to him again.

She tried to slink her way to the other side of the condo, where she'd seen Jack's wallet, keys, and phone lying on the small stand.

"Em! Are you even listening to me?" Matt walked toward her.

Her eyes wide as she followed his gaze. She knew he was searching for someone, anyone. Standing in front of the table she needed to keep out of Matt's sight, she said, "I'm sorry. I need space, please." Emma's head fell to her chest as she sucked in a nervous breath. Raising her head, she shook her hands at her sides. "I need time to get my head straight." Her voice trembled as she lied. Her eyes stole a glance at the spare bedroom door.

"You had a week of space in New York… if you were really alone."

"Matt…" Emma huffed out a breath as she crossed her arms and stared angrily at him.

"You can have all the space you need at home. I'll sleep in one of the other rooms. I'll let you have your alone time. Just, come home. I love you; I need you." Matt's shoulders slumped with each word that fell from his mouth.

"I can't. I need to be here. Completely alone. I've never asked you for anything, and I know it's an awful thing to ask, but I need you to go. Leave me. Now." Emma peeked at Matt's bloodshot eyes, as she tightened her fists by her side; but inside she crumbled, her heart shattering into a million pieces.

Taking steps toward the door, Matt hung his head. As he passed her, he ran his hand across her arm.

She kept her eyes to the floor, shivering, knowing if she looked at her husband, tears would fall.

"If that's what you really want. I'll go. I won't give up on us. I won't. Emma…"

"Just go, Matt, go." Her own voice sent ice through her body. Emma knew she hurt him. She broke him.

"I love you, Emma. Only you."

"Please, go," she said, her voice low and monotone. She needed Matt to leave. Swallowing hard as her chin trembled, she pulled in a breath to summon her strength until he left. She tightened her already folded arms across her body and held herself. She hurt so much with him nearby. She listened to Matt's feet shuffling. The click of the door closing caused her to collapse into a lump on the floor, her strength gone; her heart ached for what she'd done to Matt.

What have I done? What the fuck have I done? She couldn't stop shaking, crying. She laid in a ball on the carpeted floor, her body heaving with quiet heavy sobs. She hated herself at that moment.

"Emma." Raising her head to see Jack kneeling beside her, she forced a thin smile. Her hair was disheveled, her face drawn, and tear streaked.

She swiped at her nose and eyes with the back of her hand, then yanked her hair behind her ears. Sitting upright, she leaned into Jack. She clenched his arms as he slipped them around her.

His soft lips brushed her shoulder as he pressed against her and squeezed her softly.

She folded herself into him.

"I've got you; I love you," he breathed against her hair, caressing her, settling her heart.

THANK YOU...

To my husband, Randy, for his never-ending love and support throughout this entire process. I love you.

Gail Saladino for being the best sister-mom. Listening when I needed you to, then giving me motherly advice whether I wanted it or not. You and Joe are my family and I love you both.

To the SPS community, I have learned and grown so much since joining this self-publishing school. Thank you.

Jules Hunter, thanks for listening. And your honest critiques of my work. You've made me a better writer.

ABOUT KC SAVAGE

KC lives in Florida with her husband.

She loves to write and read forbidden, taboo, cheating romances.

When she's not busy creating her latest sizzling novel, KC and her husband spend time with family and planning their next vacation destination.

BOOKS BY KC SAVAGE

Love, Emma
Series:
The Encounter
The Choice
The Decision

A Dual Lie

Escape To Wonderland:
The Club Wonderland Series

Unexpected Love

www.lyladcreations.com

Made in the USA
Columbia, SC
06 June 2024